Sanibel Sisters

A Shellseeker Beach Novel
Book Four

HOPE HOLLOWAY

Hope Holloway

Shellseeker Beach Book 4

Sanibel Sisters

Copyright © 2022 Hope Holloway

Cover designed by Sarah Brown (http://www.sarahdesigns.co/)

Introduction to Shellseeker Beach

Come to Shellseeker Beach and fall in love with a cast of unforgettable characters who face life's challenges with humor, heart, and hope. For lovers of riveting and inspirational sagas about sisters, secrets, romance, mothers, and daughters...and the moments that make life worth living.

For release dates, excerpts, news, and more, sign up to receive Hope Holloway's newsletter! Or visit www.hopeholloway.com and follow Hope on Facebook and BookBub!

Chapter One

Katie

How was this possible? How could Jadyn Parker be standing on the sands of Shellseeker Beach right now? No one knew where Katie Bettencourt had been hiding for five and a half years.

Well, obviously *someone* knew. That someone was a living, breathing wicked stepsister, and the last person Katie ever wanted to see again.

Maybe she could run and hide. It wouldn't be the first time. But Katie wasn't the scared, pregnant teenager who'd run away from home because she refused to give up her baby. Now, she was a strong, capable mother of a beautiful five-year-old, surrounded by people who loved her, and she was much better equipped to face the family she'd left behind.

So she'd better go over there and face Jadyn.

Her stomach clutched at the thought.

She took one more look at the man next to her, feeling a drop of disappointment. Seconds ago, after more than a month of a slow-burn friendship, she and Noah Hutchins had been having one of their first truly personal and honest conversations. As they dipped their toes into the warm water of how they felt about each other, Jadyn showed up.

And where was Harper?

At the thought of her daughter, she looked around frantically, suddenly realizing what Jadyn's arrival could mean for her little girl. Harper didn't even know Katie's estranged family in Massachusetts *existed*. How would she—

"Katie? Katie, is that you?"

With a bit of pressure from Noah's hand on her back, Katie took a few steps forward, squaring her shoulders and lifting her chin. Jadyn reacted by smacking both hands over her mouth to stifle an excited squeal as she shot closer.

That was out of character for Miss Supercool, who, let's face it, had never been exactly thrilled to see Katie. The competition and mutual dislike between the two stepsisters had been fierce, and they'd never done much but argue.

"I found you!" Jadyn lifted both hands as they neared each other, but Katie didn't respond in kind. Had they ever hugged? Only for show.

"Yes, you did." She blinked at the woman in front of her, seeing Jadyn...but not the Jadyn she remembered at all. She always had such lustrous, caramel-colored hair that poured over her shoulders in waves. Now her hair was shorter, poking out from a ballcap with ringlets, darker than Katie remembered.

And had she ever seen Jadyn with no makeup? No lash extensions or perfectly waxed brows? This girl was as pretty as Katie remembered, but so natural only a person who'd seen her step out of the shower would recognize her.

"How?" Katie asked, the question burning in her head. "*How* did you find me?"

Jadyn shook her head with a soft laugh, then looked up at Noah. "It was this guy right here. Noah Hutchins, yes?"

"Noah?" Katie whipped around and looked up at him, sucking in a shocked breath. "You told my stepsister where I was? You know—"

"I did not!" he denied vehemently. "I've never seen or talked to this woman in my life."

"Oh, no, we've never met." She gave up waiting for Katie's hug and slid her outstretched hand toward Noah to shake his. "I'm Jadyn Bettencourt."

"Excuse me?" Katie choked. "Your name is Jadyn Parker."

She shook Noah's hand, but turned to Katie, her hazel eyes softer, probably because she hadn't painted eyeliner along the bottom lids.

"It's Bettencourt," she said. "Just like you. Your father legally adopted me."

Katie stared at her, quite literally speechless. Why would he do that? Dad had married Brianna Parker when Jadyn and Katie were barely teenagers, but there had been no talk of adopting his second wife's daughter. Why would he do it now, when she was a grown woman of twenty-seven?

"And Noah's right," Jadyn continued. "He never

contacted me. I found you by that social media campaign he's been running to drum up interest in...this?" She gave a vague gesture toward the beach party that Katie had forgotten was happening all around them. "Dante's Pop-up Pizzeria? You were in a few of his Instagram pictures, and he tagged you."

Katie still couldn't quite catch her breath.

"Oh, man, Katie. I'm sorry," Noah muttered. "I didn't even think about someone finding you."

"It's okay," she assured him. "I didn't think anyone would recognize the 'FloridaKatieB' name." She narrowed her eyes at Jadyn. "Unless they were looking really hard."

"Guilty," Jadyn admitted. "It took me almost two years, but I found you."

"You looked for two years?" The idea that she even noticed Katie was gone seemed a little hard to comprehend. "I know my dad hired a PI, and I can believe your mother might have a passing interest in finding me. But you? Hardly."

Why lie? Jadyn was the closest thing to a nemesis that Katie had on this Earth.

Except this woman didn't even seem like the Jadyn Parker she knew. This was not the flamboyant, attention-loving party girl Katie remembered, and that just made the whole situation harder to process.

"Why were you looking for me?" Katie asked.

"Because you're my sister," Jadyn said. "And before you argue that, it's true. I carry the adoption papers to prove it, if I have to."

"Convenient for you, I suppose," Katie said, partly under her breath. It was better to be the adopted daughter of a billionaire than his unadopted stepdaughter.

Jadyn's expression changed, her smile wavering. "I guess it's fair that you would think that, Kay."

She flinched at the use of a nickname she hadn't heard in years. Only her dad had called her Kay. For a while, after he married Brianna, he tried to call the stepsisters Kay and Jay, but it hadn't stuck. Mostly because, despite being less than three years apart in age, the girls loathed each other.

"Money isn't why he adopted me," Jadyn said. "But I guess you might think that. The truth is, they thought I was going to die, and he wanted me to die with his name. We're pretty close now."

Katie eased back slowly, certain she hadn't heard that right. Despite the late summer heat, a cold chill crawled over her. "Excuse me?"

Jadyn reached out and took her hand, and this time, Katie didn't reject the physical contact because...they thought Jadyn *was going to die?*

"You've been gone five and a half years," Jadyn said softly. "So much has happened and so much has changed. The most important thing of all is that I am now, legally and in my heart, your sister. And your child's aunt. So, to answer your first question, that is why I'm here. Because we're family and we've been separated for too long."

Was it really? Or had she come—possibly at the request of Katie's father—to make some kind of wild claim on Harper? Katie had had no contact with him except through an intermediary after Dad had launched a private investigation. Miles Anderson, a local PI and now a friend, had found her, but after a long discussion, he'd agreed to not give away her location.

In exchange, she'd allowed Miles to get word to her father that she was safe and healthy. She'd stipulated that she'd reach out to him if there was an emergency and asked that he do the same, through Miles.

That way, if something were to happen to her father, she'd find out. But she hadn't made that stipulation of Jadyn or her mother, Brianna.

"What do you mean they thought you were going to die?" she asked, almost afraid of what she might hear.

Jadyn glanced up at Noah, who'd been quietly taking all this in, his expression guarded as he kept his thoughts to himself.

"Do you mind if I take your girlfriend for a walk?" Jadyn asked.

"Oh, she's not my..."

"It's fine," Katie said, saving him from the explanation, and very much liking the idea of a private conversation before Jadyn left. "Let's go down to the beach and you can fill me in on everything."

Noah put a hand on her shoulder, drawing her closer. "I'll keep an eye on Harper for you."

"Harper?" Jadyn asked. "Is that...you had a girl? I have a niece? She wasn't in any of the pictures."

"Because I was protecting her privacy," Noah said,

offering Katie an apologetic look. "I guess I wasn't careful enough."

"Don't worry." She smiled up at him, aching to go back in time to the conversation they had just been sharing, to the sweet admission that this was more than a friendship. Instead, her life just got flipped upside down. "Yes, please watch her and I'll be back."

Turning to Jadyn, she gestured toward the boardwalk, steeling herself for whatever she might find out as they started to walk. "Let's talk before you leave."

"Leave?" She laughed softly. "I'm not going anywhere. I booked one of these cottages indefinitely."

Katie froze mid-step. "What?"

Jadyn answered by putting her hand on Katie's shoulder. "I'm not the same person, Kay. And it looks like you aren't, either. Will you give me a chance? Please?"

Everything in her wanted to scream *no*.

She knew that Jadyn had to be the center of attention, that she was selfish and snarky and just plain mean. She liked to drink too much, had way too many relationships with the boys and young men who flocked around her, and had never been anything like a sister.

She didn't want this conniving, fake party girl anywhere near her, or Harper.

But there was one thing she couldn't deny—either Jadyn was an Oscar-worthy actress or she really had changed. Guess she was about to find out.

THEY DIDN'T TALK MUCH until they were well away from the gathering, both of them kicking off their sandals when they reached the bottom of the boardwalk.

"You really looked for me for two years?" Katie asked, pretty sure that had to be a classic Jadyn exaggeration.

"Let's see...I was diagnosed three years ago and—"

"Diagnosed with what?" she asked, her heart tightening just at the word.

Jadyn slowed her step a little, then frowned, looking at the sand around her feet. "Is this normal?"

Nothing about this was *normal*.

"There must be ten billion seashells." Jadyn squinted left, then right, her gaze scanning a beach that was always covered by as many shells as sand.

"This is Sanibel Island," Katie said. "It's known for..." She huffed a breath. "Diagnosed with *what*, Jadyn?"

She bent to pick up a shell, her face down as she muttered, "Cervical cancer."

Did she just say—

Jadyn popped up and held out a perfectly shaped clam shell. "So pretty! I'm keeping this. Look at the pink inside. Isn't that the sweetest color?"

"Jadyn." She ground out her stepsister's name, frustration zinging up and down her spine. "What did you just say? Cancer?"

"Yes, I did. The C word. In my case, the double-C word." She tipped the bill of her hat higher and looked into Katie's eyes. "It didn't kill me, Kay. Just my chance of ever having a baby."

"Oh." Katie felt her whole body sink as the words hit,

her heart filling with an ache she'd feel for any woman who'd gotten that news. "That's...wow. Jadyn."

"It's okay. I didn't come here for sympathy." She narrowed her eyes. "Or guilt."

Guilty? Did she feel...oh, yeah. She did. She'd been gone—literally disappeared without a trace—while Jadyn went through *that*.

"I'm so sorry for you. I didn't know, obviously."

"Would you have come home if you did?"

Katie looked down at the shells, and tried to muster up the right answer, like, "Of course I would have!" As much as she'd like to think she'd be a bigger person, she wasn't going to lie.

"I don't know," she confessed. "I left on the worst imaginable terms with you and Brianna and my dad."

"Also *my* dad now."

She flinched, definitely not used to that. Stepfather? Yes, that's what Clive Bettencourt was to Jadyn Parker. Apparently, not anymore.

"I guess I really missed a lot," she finally said, slightly embarrassed by the understatement.

Jadyn merely slid the shell into her pocket, her eyes locked on the sand, searching for another good shell from the thousands available.

"Things got pretty ugly when you left," she finally said, which did nothing to assuage Katie's guilt.

She clenched her teeth to hold back the reminder that Jadyn's mother had wanted her to terminate and Dad had all but arranged a European adoption. Instead, she listened.

"Mom and Dad fought. A lot. Like, whoa. For a time, I wasn't sure they'd make it."

More guilt punched at Katie.

"As you know, they hired the best PI money could buy, who looked for you for more than a year and gave up."

"He found me."

This time, Jadyn stopped. "He did?"

"He hired a network of investigators and one of them found me. In fact..." She glanced over her shoulder in the direction of the party. "We just passed him on the boardwalk."

"Seriously? They were told you couldn't be found."

"Miles—that's the local PI—got to know me and my story, and didn't give away my location, just a message that I was safe."

"I never heard that."

Katie shrugged. "I don't know what Dad did with that info, but no one has ever come after me since. Until you."

Jadyn gave a smug look. "Jadyn Bettencourt, super sleuth. What do you think of that?"

She thought...it was going to take a while to get used to having the same last name. "How about telling me what happened? When did you get sick?"

"Like I said, three years ago. So, two years after you left."

"How did you know you had it?" Katie realized she knew next to nothing about cervical cancer and Jadyn had survived it. This time, guilt tromped up her chest and power-kicked. Yes, her father should have contacted her, but maybe he knew she wouldn't have come home even if she'd known her stepsister had cancer.

"I had some weird bleeding and pain," Jadyn replied to her question. "I went to my gyno and wham! Life changed in one single day. And I mean it *changed*. Ooh, pretty one." She dove for another shell, examined it, and frowned at a chip. "Not perfect but I'll keep it." She put it in her pocket and went back to talking about cancer like it was the weather. "The minute they found it, all hell broke loose."

"Did you have to do chemo and radiation and all that?"

"Yes, yes, and if by 'all that' you mean have a hysterectomy, yes."

"At twenty-four? Is that what you were then?"

"I just made twenty-five."

Twenty-five, the age Katie was right now. How would she feel if she were told she couldn't have another child? Or, as in Jadyn's case, none at all? Not in her wildest dreams could she imagine the sense of loss that must have caused.

"I'm sorry," she said simply. "Did it hurt?"

"Surgery?" She lifted a shoulder. "Nah. Long recovery, but manageable. That kind of cancer wasn't painful, but chemo was a *beast*."

"A hysterectomy," Katie said on a sigh. "That must have been a wretched decision."

"Not much deciding involved. Kind of a do-or-die thing, if you get my drift."

"Oh." Katie closed her eyes, imagining what this did to life in the fifteen-thousand-square-foot mansion in Weston that the Bettencourts called home. One of them, anyway. The others—in Geneva, Aspen, St. Barts, and London—were also possibilities. "How'd your mom handle it?"

"Like you'd expect," Jadyn said, surprisingly wry. "Denial for a while, then she wanted to keep everything hush-hush, like cancer was a dark stain on the family. Then she accepted her fate as the mother of a chemo patient, joined the local board of a cancer research non-profit, and redecorated the entire house, because every single room needed a pop of color to 'bring back the joy.'" She imitated her mother in a surprisingly dead-on match of Brianna Bettencourt's snappy voice. "Now we have chartreuse velvet chairs in the media room. You're welcome."

Katie bit back a laugh. She'd forgotten that even in her worst moments, Jadyn could be funny.

"She had to have been upset."

"She was. Her life was...disrupted."

"Jadyn! You're her daughter and you were extremely sick. I know she's a social climber, but—"

"A social climber? That's like saying that ocean out there is a sweet little pool of water."

"It's the Gulf, not the ocean, but I get the idea. I still believe your mother had to have been wrecked at the idea of her daughter being that ill. I know I would..." Katie caught herself, not wanting to share anything about Harper. At least, not yet. Not until she could trust Jadyn

—and one heart-to-heart walk on the beach was not going to wipe out all those years of hating each other. "I would guess it was very hard for Brianna," she finished.

"What was hard," Jadyn said slowly, "was that her husband never forgave her for losing one daughter."

"Brianna wasn't entirely to blame for my leaving," Katie said.

Although her hateful stepmother had been a huge part of the decision, and Jadyn herself no small part. Dad's indifference and tendency to take Brianna's side in everything had sealed the deal.

"I don't know, Kay, but when Dad thought they'd lose me, too? Well, old Clive became my biggest supporter."

Katie considered that, eyeing Jadyn. "How so?"

"Like I said, he adopted me, that's how so." She bent over for another shell, but tossed it and straightened, looking out toward the water before turning to Katie. "Look, I know you had your reasons—one of which is named Harper and is five years old, which is the sum total of what I know about my niece—but you *did* make a choice that affected a lot of people. You can't forget that, or get all cavalier about it. You left our family. Maybe not the world's greatest gathering of humans, but we are, for better or worse, family."

Katie swallowed, not able to argue that. Her choice to leave the family and cut ties was extreme, but she certainly could, and would, defend it. And if she thought for one minute that she would lose Harper, she'd do the same thing all over again.

"I made the decision I had to make at the time. I

didn't think I mattered that much to anyone up there. Dad was beyond preoccupied with his businesses, and your mother certainly didn't care if I lived or died."

"Katie, she—"

"Don't defend her, Jadyn, or try to change history. Brianna's only concern was how a pregnant college freshman in the family would impact her standing with the Brahmin set, especially if they found out the baby's father worked for our landscaper." Oh, that had sent her stepmother into a tizzy. "And let's be real, Jadyn," she added in a serious voice. "You wanted me to leave. You hated me."

She braced for Jadyn's hard denial of the facts, but instead, her shoulders sank and she dropped her head in shame. "I'm so sorry."

She was?

Clearly fighting for her composure, Jadyn managed to add, "I was so awful to you."

That was true. She'd been beyond awful, with brutal comments and icy stares, all the while gossiping about Katie to anyone who'd listen. Jadyn had been downright victorious that the "good girl" who got straight A's and accepted into Brown University and had never been in trouble for one single minute had gotten herself knocked up by the help.

But all that faded in the late afternoon sun with the sound of Jadyn's broken voice.

Katie's heart shifted and cracked, and she did the only thing she could do—she reached for Jadyn and put her arms around her.

"I'm so sorry," Jadyn repeated, choking on a sob. "I really thought I was going to die at one point, Katie, and that I would go to hell for being so mean to you."

Was *that* why she was here, then? To make up for that?

"And I would have deserved hell." Jadyn eased back, showing a face genuinely ravaged with pain. "I know I wanted you to leave. I wanted to be the only kid in that family, and I was already twenty-two when you left, which is even more shameful."

"It's okay, Jad—"

"It's *not* okay. But it happened." She wiped her face with the back of her hand. "And you're wrong about Dad. He was really upset that you were gone. If he was buried in work, it was because that was how he coped with the fact that your mother died. He's never gotten over that, and I know that because in a weak moment during a chemo treatment, he told me that."

All the air whooshed out of Katie's lungs. Her mother's passing when she was not much older than Harper, and the agonizing years that followed, remained the darkest, saddest, worst time of her life. Katie never talked about it, and didn't want to start now.

"When I got sick," Jadyn continued, "Dad was the one with me all the time, every trip for chemo, every radiation treatment, right next to me when I woke up after surgery. During every difficult day, Clive was praying for me and throwing money at the nurses and getting the legal papers done for an adult adoption."

"Dad *prayed*?" Of all the things Jadyn said, that one really threw her.

"He did then."

"What about your mother?"

She shrugged. "She hates anything she can't control, so just the word 'cancer' sent her into a spiral. At first, she was mad. Then she accepted my fate, threw a big fundraiser that cost more than she raised for the non-profit, and bought me the most gorgeous wigs. She did what she could, but Dad did more."

None of this really sounded like the family she remembered, but a lot of time had passed. "And you?" she asked.

Jadyn closed her eyes. "I got really depressed after the surgery," she admitted. "Facing the fact that I'd never have kids or a family..." She struggled to swallow and visibly fought more tears.

"Did you freeze eggs?"

"We tried, but it didn't work. Very complicated with the cancer."

Katie sighed, wishing that answer had been different.

"But, wow, I wanted to find you," Jadyn said. "It became an obsession. I believed that somewhere, some-day, you would show up on social media and I would find you, and I could meet the child you had, and make my official apology for being the worst possible sister." She managed a smile. "Hello, here I am."

It was still a little difficult to process this news and the change in Jadyn, but Katie could feel her heart soften whether she wanted it to or not.

"Why did it matter that much?"

"Because you're my *sister*. I knew you had a baby and that I was an aunt, which might be the closest I come to motherhood." She reached out and put her hands on Katie's shoulders. "Please let me be Aunt Jadyn. Please let me be your sister. Please let me show you that I've changed, Katie. Please."

How could she possibly say no to that?

Katie responded with another hug, hoping so hard that this was all true and that Jadyn Parker hadn't just thought of yet another way to make Katie's life miserable.

As much as she wanted to, she couldn't possibly trust Jadyn completely. Not yet.

Chapter Two

Eliza

As the crowd thinned down to only a group of their closest friends and some locals, Eliza Whitney squinted into the setting sun, watching Katie hug the stranger on the beach, unable to place the other young woman.

"Do you know who that is with Katie?" Eliza asked Teddy, who sat across from her at one of the tables on the sand.

They'd been sipping tea and chatting with the many friends, neighbors, and guests who'd descended on the beachfront resort they ran.

Teddy followed Eliza's gaze and shook her head. "Maybe a friend from her book club?"

"They hug and cry? Must have been quite a book." Eliza pulled her attention back to the party, watching Claire laughing with DJ as they headed into the hut that used to only serve tea, but today—and maybe for many days in the future, based on the enthusiastic response—they served world-class pizza created by Dante "DJ" Fortunato. It wouldn't be a bad business to add to Shellseeker Beach, that was for sure.

Whatever the outcome of DJ's incredible pizza-making skills, it was clear his real focus was Claire and Noah, the son they'd conceived while still in college and who Claire had given up for adoption. The three of them had just "met" but the family connection was profound and wonderful for all of them.

"Something tells me Claire's unexpected reunion is going to last a long, long time," Eliza mused, watching the interaction between her sister and the handsome, vibrant man. DJ seemed to be in the process of sweeping Claire Sutherland off her feet, twenty-seven years after he'd done the same thing the first time.

"*Something* like the house the three of them just rented?" Teddy brushed back some of her white curls, laughing softly.

"That and the fact that DJ can't wipe that smile off his face."

"Wouldn't you be smiling if you got struck by lightning and survived with nothing but a ringing in your ears which is gone now?"

"He wasn't technically struck," Eliza corrected. "The pizza oven next to him was."

"Close enough to change your life," Teddy said. "Not to mention he has the son he never knew he had at his side, along with the woman I hear him describe daily as 'the girl that got away.'"

"Aww." Eliza gave a little shiver of joy. "I'm so happy for her. For all of them."

Teddy lifted her teacup and pinned her blue eyes on Eliza, nothing but determination in that gaze. "Now it's your turn to be happy."

"Excuse me?" Eliza inched back. "How could I *be* any happier? One, my house in Los Angeles is sold. Two, my daughter has moved from Seattle to live right here on Sanibel Island to open a boutique and seems to be falling in love with Connor Deeley. And three, I'm working side-by-side with the woman who is like a mother and a best friend." She put her hand on Teddy's arm. "That's you, Theodora Blessing, in case you're too humble to realize that."

She laughed. "I know. Finish your happiness list. It lifts my heart."

"Is there more?" Eliza asked lightly. "Oh, of course. My sister is right there, after a lifetime of not knowing her. Let's see, we've just completed some much-needed improvements on Shellseeker Cottages and are ready for the busy season, my first ever. Moreover, I really think this little resort, the shell shop, and now this potential pizza goldmine are going to give this place a record year. Teddy, how could I possibly be any happier?"

Teddy just lifted a shoulder and gave a sly smile.

"What?" Eliza pressed.

"You know what."

She frowned, nodding as she realized what the older woman meant. "Not only have I come to terms with the distant relationship I had with my late father, I can confidently say that the grief over my husband's death lightens every day." She gave Teddy's hand another squeeze. "Take a bow, dear healer. None of that would have happened without you."

"It's been nothing but a pleasure. But Eliza," she pressed. "You're still missing something."

"I'm missing something that could bring me joy?" Now she was confused.

"Some*one* that could bring you joy."

"Oh, please," Eliza scoffed, rolling her eyes. "I should have known you were going in the direction of Miles Anderson."

"Only because that direction is the one I know you want to take."

Want to? Yes. She couldn't deny the pull to spend time with the man who'd had her attention since she arrived on Sanibel Island nearly five months ago. But could she act on that attraction? That was a whole 'nother issue.

"How long are you going to hold him off?" Teddy asked. "The man—and his dog, I might add—are falling harder for you every day. I can see him over your shoulder, you know. Right this very minute."

"Teddy—"

"He's talking to Deeley," she continued, staring past Eliza. "But every five, ten, maybe fifteen seconds, he glances over here, just waiting for me to get up so he can swoop in and invent a reason to talk to you."

"He doesn't have to invent anything. We're friends." Still, while Eliza listened to Teddy's speech, she had to fight that same desire she was describing—the urge to look over her shoulder to check out Miles. She was as guilty of the sneak peeks as he was.

"Friends?" Teddy challenged.

"Yes, friends," she said softly. "It hasn't been a year yet since Ben died. After that...maybe."

"Is there an official amount of time you have to grieve? This isn't the 1800s when widows wore black for one calendar year or some such nonsense."

"I have to be ready, and I'm...terrified."

"Of what? That man would jump off the top of the lighthouse before he hurt you. He's a good guy, with a fine heart, and you know I read people's emotions like others read books."

"Oh, I *know*," Eliza replied with no small amount of dry humor. "So you should know all that I'm feeling every time this subject comes up, which is frequently with you."

"Well, I know you're not feeling terrified, even though that's what you say. I'm getting a different color completely."

She fought a smile, but knew better than to argue with Teddy's colors and vibes. "Forget *me* for a second," Eliza said. "What is Miles feeling?"

"Impatient and ready and quite hopeful ever since you came back from Los Angeles a truly free woman."

Eliza made a face. *Was* she free? "I did feel better after selling the house. It was an amazing week with Olivia and Dane, and a huge step for us as a family to say our last goodbyes to Ben. That's not to say we don't mourn him," she added quickly. "He'll always be their father and my husband, but it was a good way to let go of my old life."

"Then you're ready for a new one?" Teddy asked, relentless on this particular quest.

"A new life? I'm in the middle of a new life." Eliza gestured toward the glorious beach around them. "I'm living here, sharing your beautiful beach house, helping you run this waterfront resort, sinking my toes into the sands of Shellseeker Beach every day."

"Sink deeper."

"Any deeper and I'll...I'll...*fall* flat on my face." She glanced over her shoulder just in time to catch Miles throwing his head back with a hearty laugh over something Deeley had said. Even in profile, he was handsome, a man in the prime of his late fifties, silver haired, in shape, with warm green eyes and an easy smile.

Yep, she could fall all right.

She turned before he caught her looking, although it wouldn't be the first time that happened. And every time it did, their eye contact gave her a neat little thrill that she hadn't felt for many years.

Not that her late husband hadn't thrilled her, but they'd been married for more than thirty years, and the last few had been rough. Ben had been sick more than he'd been healthy, and nursing him to the end of his illness took any thrill out of their relationship. Not the love, never the love. But the butterflies? They'd been dormant for a long time.

"What's stopping you?" Teddy asked, but before Eliza could even open her mouth to answer, the other woman pointed a playful finger at her. "First thought. No filter."

"Guilt." She didn't even have to think about it, because if they were playing "no filter," then that was the unvarnished truth.

She expected Teddy to be surprised, but then she remembered nothing surprised this empathetic healer. "I thought so," Teddy said.

Casting her eyes down, Eliza examined her heart, wanting to elaborate because she trusted Teddy so completely. "The thing is, I took a vow and I honestly feel like I'm cheating on Ben."

"Eliza! Yes, you vowed 'til death do you part.' He's gone, but you're still very much alive, a beautiful, bright, fifty-three-year-old strawberry-blonde angel with so many great years ahead."

Eliza had to smile at that description, one only Teddy could come up with.

"Ben wouldn't want you to be alone," Teddy added.

She lifted a brow and dug for more raw honesty. "He never said that. Not in all those hours of nursing, all the time both of us knowing that while his death wasn't inevitable, it was pretty darn certain. He never said, 'Go forth and fall in love again.'"

"Did you ask?"

"No! I never said a thing that could steal one molecule of his hope. I was careful with every word, always optimistic and encouraging." She gave a wry smile. "But believe me, I rolled into a ball some nights and wept myself to sleep because nursing a dying man was hard and thankless and heartbreaking."

"Oh, trust me, I know." Teddy had kept Dutch

Vanderveen alive for two more years than the doctors had given him to live, and those years had been happy ones for Eliza's father.

"And you've shared enough about Ben's illness that I know you've really been alone for many more months than just the nearly nine since he died," Teddy added. "He was in hospice last year at this time, am I right?"

Eliza nodded, remembering that bleak October. "In and out of consciousness."

Teddy angled her head. "Eliza, you've passed a year."

Not technically. "I guess the problem is not that I don't feel *ready*," Eliza confessed. "It's that it doesn't feel *right*."

"You don't know *how* it feels. Have you kissed Miles? Have you held his hand and walked on the beach under the stars?"

Eliza laughed softly. "Please. I'm almost fifty-four and he's even older. Save that stuff for Olivia and Deeley."

"Pffft." She flicked a hand. "You are not too old, not too widowed, and not too afraid." She leaned closer. "Would you just give him a chance? I know he's dying to ask you out on a proper date."

"Really? What color in his essence told you that?" she teased.

"He told me that himself." Teddy crossed her arms and gave a smile of pure satisfaction at Eliza's surprised look. "That's right. Over a month ago, when you were in L.A., he asked me if I thought you'd be amenable to a date. I told him to give you some time."

"Good advice," Eliza said. "That seems to be exactly what he's doing."

"And then he asked me again this morning."

Eliza's eyes popped at that. "What did you say?"

"I told him that I would grease the skids for him."

"Is that what you're doing now? Greasing skids, whatever that means?"

"I'm telling you..." Teddy inched closer. "He's going to ask you on a proper date, and you should follow your heart. Also any other part of you that's interested in Miles."

All of her was interested in Miles. And that just made her wallow in *more* guilt. Laughing with Miles, sharing meals, talking about their lives and their kids and their jobs...she'd been doing that for a few months. But once it went past that? Once there was something physical?

She shuttered her eyes at the thought, her brain and body going to war. On one level, being with another man was unthinkable. On another? Well, she'd done a fair bit of thinking about it.

She swiveled her head and took one more look at the subject of their discussion. Of *course*, the very second she did, Miles looked at her and gave that sly half-smile that made her toes curl in her sandals.

For one heartbeat, maybe two, neither looked away. As if on cue, Tinkerbell popped up from a nap at Miles's feet, shook off, and stared right at Eliza. Without a nanosecond of hesitation, the adorable little Frenchie-

Boston terrier mix trotted right over to Eliza, who Tink had long ago claimed as hers.

As Eliza reached for the pup's sweet black and white head, she laughed and looked at Miles, who chuckled and shook his head. Tinkerbell's unabashed adoration of Eliza was not just a source of constant humor for them, it was another connection, and they all liked that. Especially Tink.

Turning back to the table, Eliza sneaked a sliver of pepperoni from her plate and slipped it to Tinkerbell with some soft words of love.

"Here he comes," Teddy said, pushing up from the table. "I'll leave you to get rid of your guilt and fear and silly timelines so you can take a chance on something, and someone, amazing."

She didn't really need the encouragement, but Eliza clung to it anyway, and prayed she'd be able to say the right thing when Miles asked.

"That dog," Miles said as he sat down, "always does my dirty work for me."

Eliza smiled and gave Tink a loving rub on her head. "If dirty work is stealing pepperoni from my last slice of pizza, then, yeah. Her work is done."

Tinkerbell dropped onto the ground, positioning herself between them with her snout peeking out from under the table, as though she needed to hear the conversation above her.

"Enjoying the party?" Eliza asked, bracing herself for him to ask her out, now that she knew it was coming.

"The turnout was crazy," he said. "Papa Luigi himself showed up—the king of Sanibel pizza."

"I'm afraid he's about to be dethroned."

"I know." He patted his stomach, which didn't look like the pizza had done any damage to it. "I ate four slices and might go back for more." He glanced toward the hut, the slightest bit of awkwardness hanging between them.

Maybe she was imagining that because of what Teddy had said.

"I'm sure there's still plenty," she said. "And I know I'm not an official owner of this place, but as Teddy's unofficial partner, I'm going to beg DJ and Noah to make this pop-up pizza a weekly thing. Maybe more often as we cruise into the busy season. It could be a great add-on business for Shellseeker Cottages."

He nodded, looking back at her with a smile and an expression she couldn't interpret.

"What?" she asked when the look lasted a beat too long.

"Nothing. I'm just thinking about you and this resort. I'm marveling at how far you've come since you got here and waltzed into my house—"

"I waltzed?" she challenged on a laugh.

His grin grew. "You floated in on a breeze that neither Tinkerbell nor I were expecting."

"Aww. You know, I barely remember that first visit beyond the fact that you were so kind and capable," she said, looking out toward the Gulf for a moment as she recalled just how sad and angry she'd been when she arrived here last June. Locked up, grieving, furious at the mess her late father had left with his property and... wives. "And you were so willing to help me on my mission to find a sister with nothing but a decades-old photograph. Thank you for that."

"It was my pleasure."

She let her gaze move past him to catch a glimpse of her sister. "I can barely imagine life without Claire. And, of course, her mother, who's become such a part of our life here."

"You always thank me for finding Claire and Camille. You forget that you were the one who found that business card from the French attorney, and that's how we found the two of them."

"All that matters is that you helped bring my sister and her mother to Shellseeker Beach and I am forever grateful for your private investigative skills."

He shrugged, as if his superpower of finding people who weren't easy to locate was no big deal. "As I recall, at that time you'd planned to stay, what? A few days on Sanibel?"

She pointed at him. "Now that is the curse of Teddy Blessing."

"The curse of Teddy Blessing. Sounds like a movie, doesn't it?"

"It should be. Or a song. 'You can check out any time you like, but...'"

His eyes flashed and his brows shot up as she sang the familiar melody. "I sure hope that means you're never going to leave, like the song says." There was a note of pure, raw optimism in his voice, and it touched her deeply.

"I'm homeless, remember? I'm literally living with Teddy, rent-free, I might add. I'm also jobless, since I'm not officially on the payroll, no matter how much Teddy wants to put me there. Where else am I going to go?"

"Why would you go anywhere?" he asked. "This is paradise."

"It is," she agreed on a sigh. "So, here I am and here I'll stay."

"We should celebrate that," he said, shifting in his chair as if he were just the tiniest bit nervous again.

"I think DJ stashed some champagne back there." She hiked her thumb toward the tea hut. "But if we bring out a bottle and one of the city council members is in this group, we're doomed. No liquor license, just food."

He laughed. "Never, ever mess with the Sanibel city council. I have a better idea." He moved a fraction of an inch closer and those stomach butterflies she wasn't used to feeling took a dive in formation. "Let's pop the bubbly on the boat later this week, Eliza. We can take a sunset cruise on *Miles Away* to celebrate your decision to stay."

"Oh, that would be..."

Yep. That would be a date and all she had to do was say yes. But the words weren't forming.

"Just the two of us," he added, no doubt sensing her hesitation. "In case that wasn't clear."

Instantly, Tink's head popped up with a question in her brown eyes, giving them comic relief and letting Eliza have one more second to think while he fussed over the dog.

"I meant *three*, Tink." Miles reached down and reassured her with a loving pat. "As if you'd let me take Eliza on a date without you coming along."

She had to smile at the elegant way he slipped that in, clearing up any possible confusion. He'd asked her on a *date*.

"Well, she is my little buddy," Eliza said, stalling some more. "Isn't that right, Tinkerbell?"

"Uh-oh, Tink," Miles said with a rueful smile for the dog. "I think you've been friend-zoned." He waited a beat and looked up to catch Eliza's gaze. "I think we both have."

"Miles..."

His smile faded as seconds ticked by.

"You have not been friend-zoned," she finally said. "I'm just..."

"You think I'm going to sunset cruise you right out of your comfort zone, don't you?"

She laughed softly. "Something like that."

"All you need to do is say yes," he told her. "I'll be the captain of comfort and promise you a great time will be had by all. And by all, I am including your one-dog fan club."

How could she say no to that? And why would she? Miles was a wonderful man, funny and smart and handsome and...not Ben. Plus, she'd been on his boat a dozen times, maybe more.

Yes, there'd always been others around, but half the

time they only talked to each other anyway. They'd laughed a lot, enjoyed the occasional touch of each other's hands, and chosen the anchor spot to toast the glorious Sanibel sunsets. And every time it had been—

"Eliza, it's okay. Don't make yourself—"

"Yes." She cut him off before he talked her out of it. "Yes, I'd love to."

He searched her face. "Should I be waiting for the but?"

"No. There isn't one. I'd love to go out on the boat with just you, Miles." She notched her head toward the dog. "And Tink can chaperone."

He laughed, the same hearty sound from his chest that she'd witnessed a few minutes ago with Deeley, and he looked every bit as handsome. Why would she even *think* about saying no?

"What night's good for you?" he asked.

"Any night this week. We have a few groups checking in, but Teddy and I have it under control. You let me know."

"I certainly will." He smiled at her for a moment, then shook his head. "Like I said, you've come a long way, Eliza Whitney."

But had she come far enough to even think about letting another man into her heart? Guess she'd find out this week.

Just then, Teddy came back, her eyes bright. Immediately, Miles stood to offer her his seat. "She's all yours, Teddy. I want to grab more pizza while DJ is still serving." He gave a lingering look to Eliza, nothing but warmth in his eyes. "I'll call you and we'll pick an evening that works."

"Thanks, Miles."

As he walked away, Teddy's brows shot up. "Can I assume that means you said yes?"

"To a date, not an engagement," she joked. "Settle down, Theodora."

"I can't. I have jaw-dropping gossip." She settled in and clasped her hands together. "Do you remember the reservation we got through a broker last week, the one with no name?"

"Who wanted an open-ended stay and we put them in Slipper Snail?"

"Not them, *her.* Just one person. One very important person..." She dragged out the words for drama. "Katie's sister!"

"What? Her stepsister from the awful family who isn't supposed to know where she is?" Concern rose in Eliza. They were all so fond of Katie, and protective of her privacy, and her little girl, Harper, was like their own personal angel.

"Not stepsister," Teddy told her. "She was adopted by Katie's father and she's a legal sister, come to reconcile."

"Really?" Eliza sat up straighter and looked around for the two young women she'd seen on the beach. "I had a feeling she wasn't just a book club member. Is Katie okay?"

"Hard to say, since we barely had time to talk. She

filled me in quickly, and took off to introduce Jadyn to Harper."

"Wow. Big change."

"Huge. Now tell me about Miles. When are you going out? Where is he taking you? How did he ask?"

Eliza felt a smile pull on her face, not the least bit bothered by Teddy's curiosity. On the contrary, she loved the woman more for it.

"You know, I think when this whole shindig is over in a little while, we need a girls' gathering at the house," Eliza said. "I can answer all your questions and add a few of my own then."

"A grand plan," Teddy agreed. "I'll see who's staying after the party."

The impromptu evening gatherings at Teddy's beach house had become a frequent event, especially since Eliza had moved into Teddy's spacious guest suite.

Claire, Olivia, Camille, Katie, and even Harper, who mostly snoozed or colored while the ladies talked, had all grown even closer during the hours when they'd share problems, offer encouragement, and gossip a bit about the guests and locals.

"I'll whisper to Claire," Eliza said. "And let's plan on it."

"Is Jadyn invited?" Teddy asked.

Eliza considered that and lifted a shoulder. "I guess that's up to Katie."

Teddy took a deep inhale. "This is kind of my worst fear, you know."

"That she'd reconcile with her family?" Eliza guessed.

"Of course. If she does, what's to keep her here? They're billionaires with multiple homes and staff and private planes. Everything Katie could possibly want."

"*Does* Katie want all that?"

Teddy looked miserable. "Doesn't everyone? I couldn't bear to say goodbye to her, or Harper." Her eyes shuttered. "They're like family. No, they *are* family. We can't lose Katie and Harper."

"I doubt we'll have to. This is home to Katie. Also, have you seen the way she and Noah look at each other? I don't think she's going anywhere."

But Teddy still looked worried. "What if sending Jadyn to reconcile is a ploy to get her to move back home?"

"Would it be that awful if she reconciled with them, Teddy? Even if she visited them or didn't need to work here, I don't think she'd ever leave Shellseeker."

"I don't know."

"Just relax." Eliza put a comforting hand on the shoulder of the woman known for comforting others. "We'll talk it all out tonight. No one's leaving Shellseeker Beach." She winked. "Not even me. I have a date this week."

That made Teddy smile.

Chapter Three

Olivia

"It's not exactly the private party you planned, is it, Elizabeth Mary?" Olivia whispered to her mother as they placed some cookies on a tray while Teddy brewed tea in her cozy, coastal kitchen.

Eliza looked out toward the living room where a group of women had gathered. "I know, Livvie. But Katie didn't want to just drop Jadyn in Slipper Snail and forget about her, even though I was hoping we could give her a chance to vent about this new arrival."

"I could hardly turn Jadyn away," Teddy said. "Apparently, that girl almost died from cancer and has had a change of heart and wants a reconciliation."

"Really?" Olivia felt her eyes pop, then taper to distrustful slits. "Do we believe this?"

Her mother laughed softly. "Of course the queen of the skeptics thinks the woman blew into Shellseeker Beach and lied to us."

"Uh, the last time I *wasn't* a skeptic? The guy played me like a Stradivarius. Two words: Baldwin Hotels. What makes us think the developers have backed off from trying to buy this place? Maybe they paid her to come and spy."

"Doubtful, since her family could probably buy and sell Baldwin Hotels a few times over." Teddy lifted the teapot and checked the darkness of her brew in the glass container. "My feeling, for what it's worth—"

"A lot," Olivia and her mother said in perfect unison.

"—is that Jadyn's legit, as you would say, Liv. I think she's here to resolve issues with a sister who ran away five years ago. Her color is rosy and her aura is open. But my fear is that she's also here to take Katie home, and that will break my heart into a thousand pieces."

"So convenient to have a mind-reader in the family," Olivia joked, giving Teddy a teasing elbow nudge.

"Empath," Mom corrected. "And, apparently, a matchmaker."

"How's that?" Olivia asked.

Teddy gave a smug smile, passing them on her way out of the kitchen with a tray of tea. "I got your mother a date."

As she slipped away, Olivia's jaw dropped. "Did she say—"

"It's nothing, Liv. Just a run-of-the-mill boat ride with Miles like I've done a dozen times."

Olivia raised a brow. "Who else will be there?"

"Tinkerbell."

"Mom!" She squeezed her mother's arm. "That's awesome. And about time, if you ask me. Miles has been waiting, and you..." She eyed her mother's uncertain expression, knowing every soft line in her lightly freckled face, and when those gray-blue eyes grew cloudy like they were right now? Olivia worried. "You're not sure?"

"It's complicated. And I'm not ready to talk about it yet. How's Deeley?"

"Not too complicated," Olivia echoed. "And I'm always ready to talk about it."

Her mother grinned, uncertainty replaced by true joy. "Are you in love, my sweet daughter?"

Was she? Olivia wasn't quite there, but, wow, that elusive L word seemed close. She was crazy about Connor Deeley. Would that work?

"Let's stick with 'like' at the moment. But stay tuned. Now that I know where he goes when he falls off the face of the Earth for a day or two? I feel better."

It hadn't been easy for Deeley, but when he realized Olivia was a no-go in the romance department unless he came clean with her, he'd taken her to see the reason he frequently left Sanibel Island and didn't say where he was going.

It turned out he'd been taking care of a woman whose husband had been a friend and fellow SEAL, a man who'd died in a terrible underwater explosion. Although Deeley had been cleared by the Navy after an investigation, he still believed he was responsible for Tommy Royce's death on their last mission before both he and Deeley left the military.

Tommy's wife, Marcella—or Marcie, as she was called—had been pregnant at the time and now had a toddler, Sebastian. She also had a few too many vices, spent money like she had it to blow, and was not ever going to win a Mother of the Year Award. Mired in guilt and a keen sense of responsibility, Deeley did everything he could to help them.

Not only did Olivia now understand where he'd been going, but she understood a lot more about the man's heart. She also knew why he lived like a pauper even though he owned a successful paddleboard, kayak, and beach accessories rental business on Shellseeker Beach. He gave the lion's share of his profits to Marcie, and God only knew what she did with the money.

"Has he taken you back to her place?" Mom asked.

"We went once and babysat little Bash. Oh, my goodness, that kid is cute but does not know the meaning of the word 'no.' And Marcie?" She shuddered. "Also doesn't know the meaning of the word 'no'—at least when it comes to really awful men and...other things."

Other things being booze, Olivia added silently. She didn't want to share too much about the woman her boyfriend considered his personal problem. It wasn't her place.

"It's really a tough situation," Olivia said instead. "I feel sorry for her, but I also want to smack some sense into her. And put the Wild Thing in time-out. Deeley said she's been on her best behavior this past month, so I'm bracing for her to go on a bender. Frankly, the worst place in the world for that woman to work is a bar."

"Why don't you bring the little boy here?"

"She's adamant about him not leaving her house. She claims she worries about him, but I think she's just embarrassed by what a holy terror he is. Probably because his mother is a dumpster fire waiting to happen." She took the tray. "Speaking of dumpster fires, let's go find out what Miss Jadyn is all about."

Olivia walked into the living room where the other women were scattered about the big sectional, on chairs, and even the floor. Definitely more than the usual intimate gathering.

She counted heads and saw seven—no, eight with Harper, who was sitting on Jadyn's lap getting her hair braided.

Well, that was sweet. Teddy was next to them, no doubt her empathy radar antennae in full vibe-finding force. Mom settled next to her sister, Claire, the two of them never too far apart.

And then there was Claire's mother, Camille, stretched out on the chaise end of the sectional, which had somehow become her spot. It suited *la grande dame*, as Olivia had come to think of her business partner, who was French, fabulous, and occasionally flat-out crazy.

Roz, the woman who managed the shell and souvenir shop that Olivia had run earlier in the summer, was snuggled next to her own daughter, Asia. Well, maybe not *snuggled*. More like breathing down her neck to make sure Asia, a new and first-time mother, was holding baby Zane just the right way.

Asia, as always, ignored whatever maternal advice Roz offered, doing what she wanted with her darling baby, which, at the moment, was tucking him under her shirt for a late-night snack.

Roz looked like she might burst, so Olivia could only surmise that this was not the proper time, place, or position for nursing. Thank God her own mother wouldn't be that controlling when Olivia had—

She pushed the thought away. Too soon. Not to mention the fact that she and Deeley had had exactly one casual conversation about kids, which had occurred after a day with the world's most undisciplined child.

No surprise, Deeley's response had been, "Not in this lifetime."

"Sit here, Liv." Claire tapped the empty chair close to the edge of the sofa, where Katie was perched, watching Jadyn braid Harper's hair.

Olivia slid into the chair and scanned the group, zeroing in, like most of them, on the new girl.

"So, Jadyn," Olivia said. "I understand you're staying for a while."

"If that's okay," she said, looking up from the braid.

"Yes! Stay!" Harper reached behind her and practically poked one of Jadyn's eyes out with her fingers.

Jadyn ducked and missed the wayward finger, laughing. "Easy, kiddo."

"She's my auntie!" Harper announced with that mouse voice that went up an octave when she tried to get louder, which only made her more precious.

"I *am* your auntie, Harper," Jadyn said, putting her hands on the little girl's shoulders. "And I'm your braider, too. So be still and we'll do a French braid. I think. I used to know how."

"I know how," Camille chimed in.

"I should hope so," Olivia teased.

"So, you're from France?" Jadyn asked, looking up

from the braid to Camille. "I thought I heard a faint accent."

"I was born in France, lived there much of my life, and in Canada. Now, I'm here." She smiled and tipped an elegant hand toward Olivia. "And, with this brilliant partner, am about to open Sanibel Sisters, the finest women's clothing boutique on the Gulf Coast."

"We hope," Olivia added.

"You hope you'll open it, or you hope it'll be the finest?" Asia joked.

"Both." Camille and Olivia answered together, making everyone laugh.

"When does it open?" Jadyn asked. "I love a good shopping excursion."

"We're having a soft opening in the next couple of days," Olivia said, then pointed to Camille. "And then, as soon as this one stops being a perfectionist who insists on silk-covered guest chairs and beveled mirrors in the dressing rooms, we'll have a grand opening event of some kind."

"Beveled mirrors?" Asia snorted. "And I thought *you* were a control freak, Mama."

Roz ignored the dig. "What's a soft opening?" she asked. "And why haven't I had one at Sanibel Treasures?"

"Because the shell shop has been open since I was a little girl," Teddy said. "I guess a soft opening is like a test, right, Liv?"

She nodded. "Open for business, but still working out the kinks and pricing, figuring out our best merch layout."

"When we do open," Camille said to Jadyn, "there will be gorgeous clothes, if...you'll still be here."

"I'll be here," she said confidently.

Teddy told them the reservation was held "indefinitely," so she must have put down a small fortune to hold it in the busy season.

Even Olivia couldn't stay in one of the cottages indefinitely. She had enjoyed a few months in Sunray Venus during the slow summer months, but recently found a cute two-bedroom rental house just off Rabbit Road. Camille lived in the largest cottage known as Junonia, but she'd been looking at townhouses in Sanibel, so Teddy could offer the best and most profitable bungalow on the property to guests again.

But unlike Olivia and Camille, Jadyn was paying high-season rates, no doubt thanks to her insanely rich father, so Teddy was probably happy to have the booking. But was Katie happy to have her sister here...and how long would she stay?

"Do you work up in Boston, Jadyn?" Olivia asked, going at the question from a different direction.

"I'm finishing my education," she said, keeping it vague. "I'm getting my certification to be a preschool teacher. Someday I'd like to own a daycare center."

They all reacted with various forms of, "Wow," and, "How nice," except for Katie, who could only stare, her eyes wide.

"Excuse me?" she half whispered. "Did you say—"

Jadyn held up her hand to hold off whatever Katie was about to ask. "Don't fall over in shock, Kay. I'm taking online classes and hope to be certified in a matter of months."

Katie visibly worked not to react, but Olivia knew the young woman well enough to see she was trying not to sputter. "That's...*huh*. A preschool teacher? Not really what I remember you wanting to do."

"You remember me partying and staying out all night and..." She caught herself and leaned closer to Harper, playfully covering her ears for a second. "Nothing you will ever do as long as you're alive, my sweet little niece, who is destined for great things and will never attend a party unless it's one like this."

Everyone laughed, but Katie could barely muster a smile. Distrust and uncertainty clouded her eyes, making Olivia want to reach out and just give her a hug of reassurance.

"Anyway, yes, I want to be a preschool teacher," Jadyn continued. "I'd like a room full of little angels just like this one."

Harper turned. "But I'm in kindergarten, Aunt... Jay...Jay."

"Aunt Jay-jay? I love that name!" She tapped Harper's nose. "Can I keep it forever and ever?"

"Yes!" Harper threw her arms around Jadyn's neck. "Auntie Jay-jay! Yay!"

While everyone oohed and awwed over the saccharine moment, Katie lost all ability to keep a smile on her face.

Instead, she stood and reached out for her daughter. "I hate to be the bearer of bad news, little one, but it is way past your bedtime, even for a Saturday night. Aunt Teddy said you could sleep in the spare room, and I'll be in later so we can snuggle like bunnies."

"You stay here?" Jadyn asked. "Not in your own place?"

"We bunk here a lot," Katie admitted, adding a self-conscious laugh. "It's easier when we have one of these nights, and I have to be at work early to start cleaning."

"What does Harper do when you clean?"

"I help!" Harper announced.

"Well, school's started and she's in kindergarten now," Katie said quickly.

"We're all here to watch her, too," Teddy added. "Harper is known and loved by everyone in Shellseeker Beach."

"And it's time for her to go to bed," Katie said, bringing the conversation to a halt.

Harper's lower lip shot straight out, and Jadyn looked just as disappointed.

"Mommy! I want to stay up with Auntie Jay-jay! *Pleeeeeease?*"

For a long, awkward minute, every eye in the room was on Jadyn, who may or may not have realized what a test she was taking.

If she slid to the kid's side? Great aunt, terrible sister. If she supported Katie? Well, that was the right thing to do, but from the bits and pieces Olivia had picked up? This young woman didn't always choose the right thing.

Jadyn shook her head and put her hands on Harper's

little cheeks. "I think you better skedaddle off to that room, Harpdawg."

The nickname made Harper smile.

"And guess what?" Jadyn continued, pulling her closer to stage-whisper in her ear. "I have an idea for something fun tomorrow."

"Fun?" Harper's eyes lit up. "What is it, Auntie Jay-jay?"

Olivia could have sworn Katie shifted impatiently from one leg to the other during the exchange.

"Go to the beach!" Jadyn exclaimed. "I saw a lot of seashells down there."

"It's called Shellseeker Beach," Harper said with hilarious childlike seriousness.

"I heard that! Maybe we can pick shells and glue them on cardboard to make a picture."

"Shell art!" Roz chimed in, leaning forward. "That's my specialty. And we can sell anything you make at Sanibel Treasures."

Jadyn made a big-deal face with an open jaw, hands on her cheeks, all for Harper's benefit. "Did you hear that? We can make something together and sell it in a store? How cool will that be?"

"So cool!" Harper popped up and twirled so fast she almost fell.

"Then off to bed with you, little missy." Jadyn leaned in and planted a kiss on her cheek. "Dream of our seashells!"

Katie swooped in and picked her up, carefully rounding the coffee table. "Say night-night to everyone!"

She waved to a chorus of goodnights, which died down the minute they were gone, leaving everyone staring at Jadyn, who'd obviously passed the test. And got extra credit, to boot. But all she did was grab a cookie from the tray on the table and glance around at the women.

"I know you've only heard bad things about me," she said without taking a bite. "But the truth is, people change. And I hope each and every one of you will give me a chance to prove that is true."

"We don't pass judgment," Roz assured her, getting a side-eye from Asia. "Well, we pass a little judgment," she corrected, laughing. "But only on our own daughters."

"We all love Katie very much," Claire said, leaning forward. "So you can expect us to be protective. But we're happy you're here, and certainly hope this means she can reconcile with her family."

"I hope so too," Jadyn said softly, brushing some cookie crumbs on a napkin. "Because when I leave here, she's coming with me."

And that was met with dead silence around the room.

Chapter Four

Katie

Sundays were always the most challenging day for the housekeeping staff of one at Shellseeker Cottages. And a Sunday when they were almost at full capacity, with five of the seven cottages rented, presented an even bigger problem. Most of the guests were checking out at eleven, and no one wanted her to clean before they left. But the new arrivals would come by three, so that gave her four hours to clean all the cottages.

This Sunday was particularly difficult because... Jadyn Parker—no, *Bettencourt* now—was the guest in Slipper Snail, which Katie would love to clean first. But if Katie knew anything about Jadyn, it was that she was still asleep at nine in the morning.

So, as she sat in Teddy's kitchen after having spent the night in the spare room with Harper, Katie had to make a decision about whether or not to take Harper to work with her. She normally did, since they had a routine and she didn't want to ask Teddy to watch the child when she was busy preparing for the afternoon arrivals.

But something in her wanted to keep Harper away from Jadyn. It wasn't easy to go from remembering years of torment to trusting the other woman, adopted sister or not, with her precious daughter.

"More tea?" Teddy asked, holding the pot aloft in front of Katie. "You look like you could use this spearmint to cheer you up."

"I'm okay," she assured her friend. "No more tea. I'm just trying to figure out my cleaning schedule."

"I'm available to help."

She gave Teddy a look. "Don't even think about it. We have a deal, Theodora."

They'd made it years ago, when Katie started working at Shellseeker Cottages. Teddy didn't clean. She could do anything else, but she didn't clean the cottages. House-keeping was Katie's domain and she loved it, owned it, hired help when she needed it, and took tremendous pride in her contribution to Shellseeker's success.

"I didn't mean help you with the cottages," Teddy said. "I meant help you with the stress, worry, and uncertainty that is so thick in your aura I can barely see through the fog."

Katie laughed. "I should have known."

"Is it Jadyn?" she asked.

"Of course. I'm not sure why she's here. She says she wants to reconcile and...I don't know. I get that she wants to make up for the past now that she's beat cancer and has a second chance, but..."

Teddy gave her a knowing look. "I do think Jadyn's sincere in that. Don't you?"

"I don't know. Sincere and Jadyn aren't two words that usually show up in the same sentence."

"She was very open and honest about wanting to get you back home, even for a visit. She said quite clearly that she isn't leaving Shellseeker Beach without you."

"Then she's staying," Katie replied without hesitation. "Because I am *not* leaving Shellseeker Beach, not for all the money in the world, not for supposed forgiveness from my father, not for anything."

"What if your father came to see you?"

She just curled her lip, already imagining how he'd take one look at Harper and want to scoop her up and whisk her to Boston and turn her into one of them.

"I'm sorry, Teddy. I can't snap my fingers and change the way I feel about how they all acted five years ago. My pregnancy was treated like some kind of ruination of the family crest. I realize it was a dumb mistake with the wrong guy, but I was young and desperately unhappy in that family. A shrink would surely say I was compensating for a father who ignored me."

"And the mother you lost," Teddy said gently.

Katie nodded. "Whatever the reason I got into that situation, the way they handled it was deeply hurtful. There was no support, no love, no sympathy, nothing but, 'Get rid of it, one way or the other.'" She closed her eyes and shuddered. "My little Harper."

"Maybe they know that now," Teddy suggested. "Especially after nearly losing Jadyn. Maybe it is time for forgiveness. Maybe you could go for a visit."

Could she do that? A housekeeper visiting one of the many mansions her parents owned? "I don't even feel like I belong there anymore."

"A visit," Teddy repeated. "It means you'll come home when it's over." She reached out and put a hand over Katie's. "This is your home, dear."

"I know, I know."

"You'll figure it out," Teddy assured her. "For now, just enjoy the fact that your sister is here and Harper seems to adore her."

She rolled her eyes. "Of course she does. *Everyone* adores Jadyn. Harper looks at her like she hung the moon."

"You don't like that?"

"I don't *trust* her. She's always had an agenda to... compete with me. Well, she won, even though I was the good kid and she was the one always getting into trouble. Except..." She bit her lip and looked guilty. "Somehow I was the one who got pregnant by a boy who worked for the landscaper at one of our vacation homes, not Jadyn. So if it was a competition to see who could screw up their life and break more taboos? I won."

Teddy shook her head, her silver curls bouncing around her face. "I don't sense that she's here to compete with you."

Katie stared down at her tea, thinking, then looked up into Teddy's understanding blue eyes. "I'm scared Harper is going to get attached to her, Teddy," she admitted on a rough whisper. "I'm scared she's going to fall in love with her *Auntie Jay-jay*." She made a face and said the name in a mocking voice. "I'm scared Jadyn's going to tell Harper all about her real family and the mansions all over the world and the private plane and the—"

"Knock-knock!"

They both spun around at the sound of Jadyn's voice outside the sliding glass doors, which were still closed, thank goodness. She couldn't have heard Katie's diatribe.

"Hey, there." Katie popped off her counter stool to head to the door and let her in, trying to see the positive. At least she could get Slipper Snail cleaned now. "You're up early."

"I thought I'd help you."

"Help me clean?" She almost laughed. Had Jadyn ever so much as picked up a stray hair from a bathroom sink in her life?

"Well, you said last night that Sundays are a pain, so I thought I'd help you out. I dressed for it." She gestured toward designer khaki shorts and a T-shirt that probably came from the most expensive boutique on Newberry Street.

Okay, Katie had definitely woken up in an alternate universe. "Well, I guess, but it could get...dirty."

"Teach her the ropes on Slipper Snail." Teddy breezed over with welcoming arms open for Jadyn. "I'm sure Katie would love the help on a Sunday." She gave Jadyn a quick hug, then turned to Katie. "Then you could tackle Junonia, because Camille is headed to the boutique today. And the family in Wentletrap said they were taking a tour of Ding Darling before heading home, so they're checking out at ten."

Jadyn gave a laugh. "What language do you all speak

down here on Sanibel Island? Ju...jubee? Wentle...trip? And Darling Ding?"

"Katie will teach you all the local places and the cottages, which are all named for seashells," Teddy told her.

Katie fought the urge to give Teddy a stern look. She didn't want to drag her sister around to see what she did, so Jadyn could judge and roll her eyes and text her dad that Katie was a maid. She didn't want to bring her into this special world and share it with her. She didn't want—

"Auntie Jay-jay!" Harper came zooming out from the back, arms outstretched, her *Frozen* nightgown fluttering around her ankles. "You're still here!"

She literally jumped into Jadyn's arms, and got swung around with a hoot of joy. "Of course I'm here, sweet little niece of mine."

"We can play while Mommy's cleaning!" Harper said. "We can get the shells!"

"Oh, but I told your mother I'd help her." Still holding Harper possessively, she turned to Katie. "Or would my taking Harper for a few hours at the beach be a bigger help? Whatever works best for you, Kay."

Talk about being in a no-win situation. Except they were trying to help her win and not accepting the assistance was just dumb.

"Babysitting Harper would be a big help, but even more than that? Harper would love a morning of shellseeking with you."

Harper squeezed Jadyn's neck, her little face set in

her most serious expression. "It's called Shellseeker Beach, you know."

Jadyn threw her head back and let out a belly laugh. "Yes, you told me in that same voice last night. You are the funniest kid on Earth!" she exclaimed. "Let's go shellseeking, Harpdawg!"

"Yay! Bye, Mommy!"

"Whoa, wait a second. Breakfast, teeth, clothes. Are you ready?"

"I'll help you," Jadyn offered. "I'm good at a morning routine. Then we can go shelling."

Harper dragged her back toward the spare room with no more than a cursory wave goodbye for her mother.

Katie stood there, hating that she felt defeated, then turned to Teddy, who was wearing a big old smile.

"That was the right thing to do," she said simply. "And sometimes the right thing is also difficult and doesn't feel so great."

Katie rolled her eyes. "I know, I know." She blew Teddy a kiss and headed out to clean.

JADYN REALLY HAD HELPED her by taking Harper, since housekeeping took a wee bit longer when a five-year-old was tagging along. Once the guests checked out, she could concentrate on a deep clean of each cottage, adding all the personal touches she liked to offer new arrivals.

That included placing a selection of clean, perfect

seashells here and there in each cottage, a job she frequently trusted Harper to handle.

She stepped out of Bay Scallop, ready to search the beach for Jadyn and Harper just as she spotted the two of them making their way up the boardwalk from the sand. Harper was riding piggyback on Jadyn's shoulders, her giggles audible even from a hundred feet away.

Jadyn lumbered a little, probably not used to carrying around forty squirming, screaming, laughing pounds, but Katie had to give her props. She wore a big smile and even lugged a plastic bucket that was no doubt over-flowing with shells.

Katie studied the two of them, the turquoise water and bright blue Florida sky as a backdrop, sun beaming down to cover them in a golden glow. Harper's giddy laughter floated on the air like music and no mother, no matter how jealous or resentful and distrustful she was, didn't enjoy seeing her child soak up a moment in life like that.

Harper deserved some contact with her family, Katie thought begrudgingly. Even if Jadyn wasn't blood, she was truly her sister now. Like it or not. Mostly, she didn't, but—

"Mommy! Mommy! We got you the best shells for the cottages!"

Katie waved. "Perfect timing!" she called back cheerfully.

"I'll show Auntie Jay-jay how to clean them! Wait for us!"

After rinsing their treasures at a spigot near the

boardwalk, the two of them came scampering toward her, sharing the weight of the plastic toy bucket, which looked like it could crack open any second.

"I hear you need some of these for the cottages," Jadyn said, brushing back some of the hair that had fallen out of the baseball cap she wore. "We are here to deliver."

"Mommy, it was so much fun!" Harper tore to her, forgetting the bucket, which Jadyn almost dropped but managed to save.

"Did you have a good time?"

She popped into Katie's arms, vibrating with joy, the smell of salt and sunscreen and Sanibel all over her. Katie hugged extra hard and so did Harper, but that was probably because she'd just had more fun than her little body could handle.

"It was wonderful," she cooed. "We got a bazillion million shells!"

"And I'm carrying all of them," Jadyn called. "Hello? Where did my partner go?"

Harper dropped her head back, her legs still clamped around Katie's waist, looking at Jadyn upside down. "I right here, Auntie Jay-jay!"

Jadyn came close enough to bend over and plant a kiss on Harper's forehead as she set the bucket down. "I right here, too, Harpdawg."

Harper giggled and straightened. "That's what we say," she said in her solemn "explanation" voice, a serious expression to match. "'I right here.' It's like a secret code between us. Not *I'm,* but *I.*"

Katie had to laugh. "Not so secret if I know it, huh?"

She eased Harper to the ground and eyed Jadyn, who looked as if she had just as good a time as the little girl. "How'd you like our beach?"

"It's amazing, Kay. I can see why you love it here. Are you done now? Can we all go hang out? I'd love to rent a paddleboard and get out there on the water."

"I just have to do the shells in all the cottages with check-ins."

"I'll do it, Mommy! I know what you like!" She scooped up a handful of freshly rinsed seashells. "Cantharus first?"

"Canwhatis?" Jadyn asked.

"Cantharus," Katie explained. "It's a snail shell, but quite beautiful. You probably have a bunch of them in there. Go on, then, Harper. I'll be right behind you to get Wentletrap."

"Can she do that alone?" Jadyn asked as Harper took off.

"I follow her and keep her in sight, but it's her one little job and she loves it." Katie wiped some perspiration from the back of her neck and then reached for the bucket.

"I'll help you." Jadyn scooped it up. "Take me to Wentletrap. Is it that little darling green cottage with the yellow deck?"

"That's it."

They walked together, quiet for a moment as they both watched Harper ahead of them.

"I honestly have no recollection of you being this, uh,

industrious," Katie admitted as they reached the cottage. "In fact—"

"I was a lazy sloth," Jadyn finished for her. "I know, I know. But when I got sick, I had so much time to think and read. I started with novels, but I didn't have the concentration. Somehow I stumbled into the motivational, self-help black hole, and fifty-eight lists of true empowerment later, I'm not lazy." She gestured toward a deck chair. "You chill here and keep an eye on Harper. I'll go in and plant the shells like I noticed them in my cottage. One on each table, any shelves, and one on the pillows. Right?"

"That's exactly right," she said, trying to imagine Jadyn Parker, party girl extraordinaire, taking notice of such small things.

While she went inside, Katie dropped onto one of the Adirondack chairs, able to see Harper walk into the next cottage and still rest her achy back. She'd cleaned hard and some days it felt like everything hurt.

"Your little girl is quite taken with Noah," Jadyn called from inside, instantly making Katie forget her back pain. "And she told me you are, too."

"She told you...what?" Katie asked, squishing her face with the question. Jadyn was already infiltrating her life, and she didn't want her all over her friendship with Noah.

"Just that you two are always together."

"You were interrogating a five-year-old?"

Jadyn stepped out, laughing. "I was conversing with my niece. I asked her if you had many friends down here, and she gave me a litany of names, but mentioned Noah at least three times. For a minute, I thought there was more than one guy in your life named Noah."

"There's no 'guy in my life,' Jadyn. Noah's...here. He's Claire's son, given up for adoption when he was a baby, and now they're reunited. His father came, too. Through all of that, Noah and I became friends," Katie finished, and clamped her mouth shut, already mad at herself for saying so much.

"When I showed up, I could have sworn you two were...more than friends."

Katie shook her head, closed her eyes, and purposely didn't answer.

"Okay, you don't have to get mad. I'm just trying to see how deeply entrenched you are in this place."

"Deeply." Her eyes popped open so she could underscore that with a harsh look. "So very deeply," she added. "This is my home, Jadyn. That litany of names, as you call it, are essentially my family, and Harper and I are really, really content here. We have an apartment. I have a job. I'm in a book club. She's in a great school. *Why are you here?*"

Jadyn startled at the last question, clearly not expecting it at the end of Katie's list. "I told you, Kay, I want to—"

"But are you telling me the truth?" Katie demanded. "Do you have some kind of ulterior motive or plan with Dad or secret agenda or otherwise nefarious reason that will upset my happy, happy apple cart?"

Jadyn stared at her, silent for a long, long time. She

finally shuttered her eyes, enough to dampen her lashes. Then she crouched down in front of Katie's chair, looking as vulnerable and honest as Harper.

"No," she said on a simple whisper. "No motive, plan, or agenda—nefarious or otherwise. I just stared death in the face and made a decision to change my life. You, and a child whose name I didn't even know, were change number one. And two."

Katie sighed, wanting so much to believe that. "Why did you tell my friends that you weren't leaving here without me?"

"Because I want to bring you home. I want to bring Harper into our family. I'm not going to lie about that; it's what I want. But if you don't want to go, then I'm going to stay for a while, because, like it or not..." She reached out and took Katie's hand, which had to be a first in the entire time they'd known each other. "I'm your sister."

Katie looked down at their joined hands and sighed. A sister. She didn't want to like it, but sometimes, she did.

"All done!" Harper called, skipping and dancing toward them.

"She never just walks, does she?" Jadyn mused, giving Katie's hand a squeeze.

"Why walk when you can pirouette?"

Beaming at Harper, Jadyn let go and stood up. "I love her already."

With that, she scooped up the bucket and met Harper on the path. "Let's do all the rest together and let your Mommy just sit there and relax, okay?"

"Okay! Bye, Mommy!"

Off they went, skipping and hopping as well as they could with the bucket between them, leaving a wake of laughter and a few fallen shells.

Katie watched them disappear into the next cottage, then looked down at the hand that Jadyn had held, still warm from her sister's touch.

This sure was going to take some getting used to.

Chapter Five

Deeley

He'd been dreading this afternoon for longer than he cared to admit. This should be a normal Sunday in October for Connor Deeley—hot as blazes, but with a big old line out the door of the cabana full of people who wanted to throw money at him for the joy of renting one of his paddleboards or kayaks.

And if he got his way with the city council and got a license to rent motorized vehicles? He'd be renting out that Jet Ski he had his eye on for a great way to expand his business. Contrary to what the outside world thought, Deeley wasn't satisfied with the status quo. He did want more than a life as a beach bum handing out toys to the tourists. He wanted to grow the business, maybe find another location on Sanibel and open a second rental business, and add bikes or scooters.

He wanted to make more money, but making money took investment. At the moment, the lion's share of his profits · went to Marcella Royce and what he wryly thought of as the Guilt Fund.

That woman, no matter how bad her choices frequently were, was alone in this world without a husband because of a mistake that Deeley had made. The

Navy might not think so, but Deeley couldn't shake that guilt.

If not for the explosive that Deeley set, Tommy Royce would have left the Navy the same month Deeley did, proud of the work he did as a SEAL, part of the brotherhood for life. And Tommy would have come here, to Fort Myers, Florida, where his then-pregnant wife waited for him, and Marcie and Bash would have been Tommy's problem.

Deeley would have gone back to North Carolina, taken over Pop's farm, and followed his dream to turn it into a fancy mountain winery like his brother-in-law ran. He even had a name for the place and the wine— Carolina Seal—to play on his background in the Navy and the wax seal he'd put on each bottle.

Instead, Tommy Royce came home in a box, and Deeley assumed the responsibility of taking care of Marcie and her baby. It had taken one trip to meet her and offer his condolences to know this somewhat unstable woman wasn't going to do the job on her own.

The day he met her, he'd fought the knowledge of what he had to do for her. Wallowing in self-loathing, he'd gone from Marcie's house due west, hoping to just drive and drive and drive until the Gulf of Mexico swallowed him whole.

But he'd stumbled into a cottage on the beach, met a healer named Teddy, and, slowly, he took ownership of his responsibilities. This was his fault, so Marcie's problems were his problems.

Another dollar in the Guilt Fund, son.

So, not the Sunday he wanted. Instead, he was going on a mission of mercy for the umpteenth time, paying a teenager to run the cabana so he could take care of the devil child and fix whatever leak, hole, broken appliance, or similar problem had cropped up at Marcie's tear-down of a house.

At least this time, he wasn't doing it alone.

That made him smile as he turned his truck onto the street where Olivia Whitney now resided in a far nicer house than he could ever afford. She was the one consolation in all this. Now that she knew his secret, Livvie understood why he lived paycheck-to-paycheck at thirty-three. Even though that had to be the polar opposite of any go-getter she would normally date, it had been a huge breakthrough for them.

She accepted, even embraced, the ugly truth, letting him finally take down the wall he'd put up to keep them apart.

Not only was Livvie understanding of his situation, she wanted to help. She wanted to *fix*, which he'd learned was a hallmark of her personality. She was definitely a roll-up-your-sleeves and work to solve the problem kind of girl, which was probably why she excelled at her business.

He loved that about her, and really loved that she didn't flinch at the hellacious situation surrounding Marcie and little Sebastian.

On the contrary, she'd offered to join him today and help watch Bash while he checked off the handyman list.

He pulled into the driveway and saw the Mazda in

the carport, getting a kick from the car she'd bought after arranging to sell the one she owned in Seattle. Yep, she was a get-things-done woman.

A few weeks ago, she'd gone back to Seattle and over the course of three days, she'd quit her job, sublet her apartment, packed up what she wanted, and arranged to ship the rest. She was here now, partnering with Camille to own a boutique and...being with him.

He couldn't put a name on what they were yet—dating? Boyfriend and girlfriend?—but he liked it. He liked her. A *lot*.

"Hey, handsome." Livvie pushed open the screen door and stepped out, tucking her fingers into the pockets of her Daisy Duke cutoffs. With her dark hair pulled up in a ponytail, blue eyes bright without a speck of makeup that he could see, and white sneakers that accentuated long, tanned legs, she looked like a fresh-faced teenager, not the almost-thirty, shrewd corporate player he knew her to be.

"You look cheery after a late night of binge-gossip with the girls," he said, stopping a foot in front of her so he could extend the anticipation of their kiss.

"With Teddy? All you get is a tea hangover," she joked, reaching for him. "C'mere."

He obliged, about the same height with her on the raised concrete step. Before he kissed her, he stood still, his mouth inches from hers, savoring the smell of citrus and sunshine all over her.

"You ready for this?" she asked.

"For this?" He brushed her lips. "Yeah." He didn't let

her answer, but deepened the kiss, lost for just a minute in the sweet softness of her lips.

"Mmm." She inched back. "I meant this afternoon."

"What? A few hours with the demon child and at least nine projects at the hell house where he lives?"

"Deeley."

He backed off, holding up his hands. "Just callin' it like it is, Liv. Wouldn't you rather be at the beach today? Or absolutely anywhere else at all on Earth? Having a root canal and a colonoscopy at the same time would be preferable to this."

She laughed and poked him. "Nah. It'll be fun. Look at the bright side—at least Marcie's not going to the bar tonight for work. She got a daytime job, and that's huge progress."

"If the babysitter works out," he said, already certain that Marcie's new job as a cashier at a store in the outlet mall would be a problem. Like today, the first Sunday she worked, her already undependable sitter had bailed.

"The babysitter will work out," Livvie assured him. "This was just a weird thing and I'm happy I can help. Let me get my purse and we can go."

He followed her into the tidy rental house he'd helped her find a few weeks ago when she decided to stay on Sanibel. It was still sparsely furnished, but once the truck arrived with the stuff from her apartment in Seattle, she'd be settled in for good.

He still couldn't believe it. Livvie wasn't leaving.

The only problem with that? He couldn't give this woman the life she deserved, the family she longed for, the big house with a yard and a fancy car and all the stuff he knew she grew up with and expected in her life.

She scooped up her bag and then hauled a backpack from the kitchen counter, flinching a little at the weight before he snagged it from her.

"Here, I got that—whoa. What's in here?"

"I grabbed some toys and a bunch of children's books from the room where Harper stays in Teddy's house. A little girlie, so sorry, Navy SEAL. But Bash has such a paltry selection of toys and books, so..." She patted the stuffed backpack. "Harper donated to the cause. I just hope the little guy is okay with the movie *Frozen*, because it appears to be stamped on everything. That girl is *obsessed*. What? Why are you looking at me like that?"

How was he looking at her? Like she was a literal angel who'd fallen from heaven and landed on Sanibel Island? Like she might be the sweetest, prettiest, most thoughtful human on the face of the Earth? Like he could throw his arms around her and tell her that his heart just melted?

"Nothing," he said, digging up his finest air of nonchalance. "It's just, you know, thoughtful."

"I'm nothing if not that," she quipped, tugging him to the door. "Let's go. Marcie's shift starts at noon and we don't want her to be late."

"No, *we* don't." He slid her a look when she went by, not lingering on her incredible body or shiny hair or lovely face. No, all he could see was her heart and...and... yeah. He had it bad for this woman.

"Seriously, Deeley, come on. If she gets fired, she's

back at the bar. Working nights, picking up losers, and coming home reeking of cheap booze and cigarettes," she called.

If she came home at all, he mentally added.

"Let's roll, Connor!"

But he took one more second to linger and stare and catch so many feels they were heavier than her pack full of books and toys.

THEY ARRIVED AT CHEZ NIGHTMARE, it turned out, too late. Not because of the wretched traffic, thanks to the snowbirds starting to descend on the Gulf Coast of Florida in October, but because Marcie *had already been fired*.

"What?" He stabbed his hand into his hair and stared at her, the Florida sun beating down on her brown hair, making it look a little greasy and messy. She wore her usual uniform of once-had-been-white shorts, a ratty T-shirt, and flipflops that showed toenails with little bits of chipped green polish.

"The manager was a total bas—" She glanced to her left, seeing that Bash was busy dragging books out of Livvie's magic backpack of fun and squealing in joy. "Oh. Did she bring him toys?"

"Just something to play with. Marcie, you seriously got fired already? You didn't work there for two weeks."

"Two terrible weeks. I didn't even get a discount on clothes, so what's the use of working in an Old Navy store? It's fine, I'll find something else. How long can you stay?"

He blinked at her. "You're not working, so—"

"I'm still going out!" she barked at him. "It's Sunday and I need a break from being a single mom. Oh, and I got a honey-do list, but then, you ain't my honey. You're hers." She grinned toward Livvie, proud of her joke. "There's a ton of things you could do while you're hanging with Bash."

Hanging with Bash? They were babysitting, spending their precious Sunday making sure the kid was bathed, fed, and happy. And being used by an ingrate.

Swallowing all that for the sake of one Thomas Royce, he asked, "What do you need?"

"The bathroom sink is leaking again. There's water all over the inside of the cabinet." She made a face. "I put towels down there, so they'll need to get washed."

Great. "Okay. I'll fix it. Anything else?"

"You know, don't mind the mess."

In other words, clean the kitchen, pick up the toys, and maybe find the vacuum and put it to use. He just nodded.

"Oh, and the internet isn't working." She rolled her eyes. "God knows I can't fix that, but I'm sure you can."

"I'll do my best. When will you be back?"

"I don't know, Deeley," she shot back, her voice rising even above Bash's. "I have to find another job, right? I can't keep working nights, I can't get a sitter, I'm out of money, and I can't help it if the manager was awful to me." Her voice cracked, as it so often did when she got worked up. "It's hard, Deeley. It's hard to live my life!"

Cha-*ching* went the Guilt Fund. "Okay, I get it, you can—"

"Mama! Lookie!" Bash stole her attention and they both turned to see Livvie with Bash on her hip, waving a cardboard book dangerously close to her face.

But she just eased his arm and the book down with one capable hand and hushed him as she came closer. "I'm sorry to hear about your job, Marcie," she said.

"I'm sorry, too," she shot back, not acknowledging Livvie's kind comment with any courtesy, not to mention the fact that she'd just given her kid a backpack full of stuff. The two women had only met about three times, and each time Livvie was nicer and Marcie was just...not nice at all.

"I'll find something," she said, flipping her hand. "I heard they might be hiring at the mini-mart where I get my gas. Still might be nights and—"

"That's not a safe place to work," Deeley said.

"I can't worry about safe, pal. I need cashola. And they pay—"

"Did you like working in retail?" Livvie asked.

Marcie shrugged. "It was Old Navy, you know? I liked being on the floor and talking to people, but mostly they wanted me to run that cash register and it might as well have been a supercomputer." She looked from one to the other. "Anyway, really glad you're here. My sitter quit on Friday and—"

"She quit?" Deeley choked.

"I can't say I blame her," Marcie said defensively, pointing a not-so-playful finger at the toddler. "'Cause somebody was a very bad boy and had a few temper tantrums."

Livvie, instinctively it seemed, put a soothing hand on Bash's blond curls, stroking them. "Oh, I'm sure he just needed a nap or was hungry."

Marcie started to respond with a hoot of laughter, but seemed to catch herself.

"Yeah, probably. He's always hungry. Kid's had two breakfasts already and trust me, he'll be looking for his Pop-Tarts in a minute, won't you, buddy?" She reached out toward Bash and lifted her hand, then kind of dropped it, as if she had no idea how to be affectionate with her own kid. "Yeah, I better get going then. Those applications aren't going to put themselves in. See you in a few hours. Or so."

With that, she took off, hustling to a beater that looked like the engine could fall out at any minute.

Swearing under his breath, Deeley turned and tamped down all the frustration and fury this woman brought out in him. What did Tommy ever see in her, anyway, he wondered. Of course, Tommy had issues of his own and a few battles with the old bottle.

He tried not to think about it, but marched into the house, which was dark, dingy, and smelled like burnt bacon.

"Hey." Livvie caught up with him in a second, holding the book in one hand, Bash still perched on her hip. "I feel your anger," she said softly. "Just take care of the sink and the internet. I'll watch Bash and, uh, pick up a little bit."

His shoulders sank on a sigh and the weight of all he was thinking, but instead of saying a word, he just smiled at her. In a rare moment of cooperation, Bash dropped his head on Livvie's shoulder and stuck his thumb in his mouth.

"Nice soft place to fall, eh, kid?"

His long, long lashes fluttered like a nap was the next thing on his agenda.

"It's going to be okay," Livvie said.

He wasn't sure if she was talking to him or Bash, but they both needed the comfort. He looked from the kid to Livvie, searching her face, drinking in every color of silver and blue in her eyes, which were always such a stark and beautiful contrast to her dark hair.

"It is now, Liv," he said. "Thanks for being here."

About an hour later, the leak was fixed, the internet was working—once he called the provider and gave his credit card number to cover the bill and the next three months in advance. Livvie had the washer running, and the house spotless. Bash was currently sleeping in his playpen in the living room. He could practically hear the angels sing.

And on the couch, Livvie sat calmly texting. Speaking of angels.

"Wow, how'd you do that?" he asked, staring at the sleeping child, who was downright adorable when he wasn't tearing through the house shrieking.

"Not by giving him a Pop-Tart, that's for sure." She

looked up from her phone. "I have a plan. I think I know how to help her."

He didn't know whether to laugh or cry, so he just sat down next to her and wrapped her in a grateful hug. "I can't drag you into the Marcie problem."

She drew back, shaking her head. "Marcie's problem is that she doesn't have any help."

"Other than a free handyman who babysits when he has to and pays more than half her bills?"

"That's not what she needs, Deeley." She drew even further back to make her point. "She needs a woman—"

"Like a cleaning lady? I don't think she can afford—"

"No! She needs a mentor, a person who can guide her into the workforce and help her navigate her way. You said her mother died, but where's the rest of her family? Aunts or cousins or sisters or friends?"

"I have no idea if she has any of them. She moved in here when Tommy went into the Navy and lived with her mother, but, yeah, she died right after Bash was born. Really rough on Marcie, but she did get the house. But, it's kind of a dump and something is always, always broken." He pushed up to get some water. "You want anything?"

"Just...permission."

He shot her a dubious look as he stepped into the kitchen, found a clean glass, and filled it from the tap. "Permission for what? Or should I be afraid to ask?"

"Permission to step in and be her mentor."

He closed his eyes as he flipped the faucet off, not sure he wanted to hear this. "Her mentor?"

"I actually did this in Seattle, through a program that Promenade Department Stores ran. It's a very cool thing, so hear me out."

He returned with his glass of water, intrigued, scared, and one more baby step closer to love.

"It was a great empowerment and mentoring concept and I loved doing it," she said. "They offer this program to young women who are struggling, especially single mothers, who need a break and a chance to work in a field with a little more career potential than fast food."

He studied her, thinking. "What do they do for them?"

"We hire them to work at Promenade Department Stores all over the country, but they aren't in it alone. A person from the management team—and I did this about six times—mentors them. We help them put together a work wardrobe that Promenade gets from inventory that's going to go on clearance, and teach them the tricks of the retail trade on the shop floor. And the store offers childcare for them."

"That's awesome, Liv. A great corporate program, but there aren't any Promenade stores in Florida. Do you think some other department store would do that?'"

"No, it was exclusive to Promenade and we got tons of great publicity from it. There isn't a Promenade, but there's Sanibel Sisters."

He gave her a look of sheer incredulity, putting what she was saying in context, even though nothing quite fit. "You want to hire Marcie to work at your new store?"

"Yes, because here's what I learned from working in

the PEW program." At his look, she explained, "Promenade Empowers Women. I learned that most women in Marcie's situation really, really, *really* want to do it on their own. They don't want someone to pay their bills for them, they want to do it themselves. But figuring out *how* is the hardest part. They can't afford the work clothes, and even if they could, they don't have experience to put on a resume. And childcare is so expensive. But if we take that out of the mix, and offer real career guidance? It's a game-changer for single mothers and women who want a better life."

"Like the whole 'hand up, not a handout' thing?" he guessed.

"Exactly. Why couldn't we have a program like that at Sanibel Sisters and have Marcie as our first empowered woman?"

"You could, I guess, if Camille could be persuaded."

She tapped her phone. "Done. Not exactly with enthusiasm, but she trusts my judgment."

"Oh, wow." He dropped back on the sofa, still not sure it could work. "What about Bash?"

"That's my only issue. I want to find a place on Sanibel offering childcare, so I texted Katie, because if anyone knows, she would. We'd cover the cost as part of Marcie's salary."

"A brand-new startup store? You can't—"

She held a hand up. "Trust me. This is not only a huge write-off, it's a PR dream. Part of her job would be to participate in interviews, and if we can get some local press on the program, Sanibel Sisters will be the real beneficiary. That will help us launch, and generate tremendous local goodwill. Once Marcie moves on to bigger and better things, we can bring in another young woman."

"Livvie," he breathed the name with nothing but admiration in his voice. "I can't believe you'd do that for her."

"And for you." She tucked in closer. "I can't let you think I'm purely altruistic, although I deeply believe in the program. This whole situation is really hard on you. I want to help you as much as her."

He just stared at her, truly at a loss for words. "What did I do?"

"What did you do?" She laughed at the question. "For what? To earn some help from me?"

"To deserve you," he said softly, putting a hand on her cheek. "I believe that the universe works on some kind of balancing system. Karma, or whatever. You do good, you get good. I—"

"Feel responsible for your teammate's death," she finished. "And you take on all of his problems as yours."

"Something like that."

"I don't think it works that way, babe," she told him. "You deserve this help from me, because I really, really care about you."

He closed his eyes and leaned in for a kiss, way too overcome with emotion to say anything. She responded by wrapping her fingers around his neck and pulling him closer, intensifying the connection with a soft whimper of pleasure.

"Wibbie! Wibbieeeee!"

They broke apart at the sound of Bash's scream, turning to see him gripping the side of the cloth playpen and shaking it so hard, Deeley thought the thing might break in the bruiser's hands.

Livvie was up in a flash, reaching for him. "I'm right here, Bash." She gave Deeley a guilty look. "I taught him my name and can't bear to correct him from Wibbie."

Deeley smiled. "Wibbie."

"Come on, Bash," she said, wrapping him in her competent arms. "Let's check that diaper and read the pretty book about Anna and Elsa, okay?"

"I hungry, Wibbie," he groaned, nestling into her.

"Okey-doke. Diaper first, lunch second."

"Cookie!" he cried as they walked toward the bedroom.

"Oh, I don't know about that. I think we can do better."

As she carried the toddler away, Deeley fell back against the sofa. For the first time in more than two years, he truly, truly felt there was a little tendril of peace in his heart. Wrapped up in hope, and covered in relief.

He had no idea what he'd done to deserve Olivia Whitney, but he'd move heaven and Earth to keep...*Wibbie.*

Chapter Six

Eliza

"Life changes out here, doesn't it?" Miles leaned back on the white leather banquette after he anchored the sport fishing boat off the coast of Captiva as the sun dipped low. "I just forget the world."

"What world?" Eliza smiled and lifted the wine glass he'd just filled with a crisp sauvignon blanc. Her other hand was planted firmly on Tinkerbell's head, which had been attached to Eliza's thigh since she sat down. "We're...miles away."

He chuckled, looking out at the gleaming deck of the thirty-plus-foot vessel that he clearly took tremendous pride in maintaining and pleasure in using. "It's a great name for a boat, isn't it? I love a good double entendre."

"Did you come up with *Miles Away* by yourself?"

"Actually, it was Janie's idea. My daughter is the creative one in the family." He stretched his arm along the seat. "She's also the best looking, the brightest, and the apple of my eye."

"I'd love to meet her. Does she ever come down to Sanibel?"

"All the time in January and February, along with the rest of the free world. At least it seems like it when you're trying to drive one mile on Periwinkle during the winter months." He frowned, thinking. "Although, I don't know if she's coming this year. I guess it depends on..."

She waited, looking at him, spinning through what she knew about his daughter. She was married, in her thirties, lived in Virginia, and they were close. He never mentioned her without breaking into a huge smile.

"It depends on her job?" Eliza guessed when Miles didn't finish, remembering that she was a professional photographer but ran a small framing store in Charlottesville.

He shook his head.

"Her husband?"

"Her, um, cycle. Ovulation." He made an uncomfortable face. "Things a father doesn't talk about too much, but I do know she's trying very, very hard to conceive."

"Oh. I hope that happens for her."

"I do, too. She's become a little obsessed. I keep telling her to relax and it'll happen, or they can adopt. Whatever, she's trying too hard, if you ask me. Which she doesn't, because there are things I guess it is better that she talk to her mother about."

She searched his face, thinking of how rarely he mentioned his ex-wife. Eliza didn't even know her name.

"Are they close?" she asked. "Janie and...her mother? I forget her name, I'm sorry."

He gave a wry smile. "Slick, Eliza. You don't know her name because I don't say it. It's a deliberate choice."

She picked up her wine and took a sip, giving him time to elaborate. He didn't.

"Oookay," she finally said. "Is that a closed door I shouldn't even knock on, or are you opening it up to questions like 'why' and 'what happened' and 'will you tell me anything about it'?"

He laughed softly, but didn't answer, which made Eliza sit up a little straighter.

"Wow. I had no idea you had such...issues."

"On our first date, Eliza? This is the subject you want to talk about?" He was joking, but there was just enough truth in his words that she sensed the answer to her question was: don't knock on that door.

"So, it's official then." She took a teasing tone to keep it light. "First date? I certainly didn't think that would ever happen to me again." She picked up the glass and clinked his. "But I'm happy it has, and I'm sorry if I overstepped my bounds."

"Not in the least. It's my kryptonite."

She looked at him over the rim of her glass before sipping. "You know you're just intriguing me even more with statements like that."

He took a drink, swallowed, sighed, and repositioned himself on the leather bench. Quiet for a good ten seconds, he looked toward the sunset. During that time, Eliza studied him, his strong features, the crinkles around his green eyes from sun and laughter, the tiniest little vein pulsing in his neck.

"Her name is Diane," he finally said. "Diane...Manning."

Eliza nodded, filing that. "I take it she remarried?"

"Instantly. Pretty sure the ink wasn't dry on the

divorce decree when she and Martin hit the old Justice of the Peace."

"Oh." She put a hand on his arm and tipped her head to the lovely charcuterie board he'd prepared for her. "Grab cheese and a cracker, Miles. It'll get the taste of bitterness out of your mouth."

He laughed and put his hand over hers. "Sorry. And of course you know exactly what to say. I'd really rather talk about how amazing you are, Eliza. Can we?"

"You're the captain of this ship, and we can talk about anything you like. But I'm a boring subject."

He looked at her, his eyes warm and bright. "You are anything but. Talk about intrigued. From the moment you walked into my house, Tink and I were smitten."

She laughed and bent over to kiss the dog's head. "Tink did adore me from the get-go. Why do you think?"

"Because you're a gorgeous strawberry blonde with a warm smile, a good heart, and a sharp mind. Oh, wait— that's me. Tink just sensed a pushover for treats."

Smiling, she realized he still had his hand over hers, so she flipped her palm and threaded their fingers. "You were both very kind to me. I was still...you know."

"Grieving. And don't think I just assume that's over, Eliza. I know you loved your husband." He sighed. "I'm jealous, to be honest. You had a great love and not many people can say that."

She gave his hand a squeeze. "I take it you did not."

"Not going to let it go, are you?"

She thought about it for a minute, biting back a smile, then shook her head. "First dates—real, official ones—are the time to share your story. You know mine, mostly, by default and the fact that I've talked non-stop about Ben."

"Not non-stop," he corrected. "Not at all. But when you do speak of him, I can hear the love and respect in your voice. So I'm guessing he never cheated on you."

She wrinkled her nose. "Did Diane?"

"How do you think I broke into the PI business? I was a lawyer, Eliza. A judge advocate general in the Navy. But, out of necessity, I learned how to dig for information, whether I wanted to know the answers or not. Once I figured out how to track a cheating spouse, I realized I could charge—a lot—for the misery of others."

"You caught her, I take it?"

He nodded, his gaze distant again. "Walked right in on her in a hotel room," he said. "It was classic, out-of-the-movies stuff."

"Oh, Miles. I'm so sorry. How could anyone cheat on you?"

"See?" he asked on a laugh. "That's why I like you. Not the details of what happened, but how could that happen to *me*."

"I'm serious."

"So am I."

"You're such a fine man. So smart and warm and good. And as far as the details, I'm sure it was heartbreaking."

He pushed up to get the bottle of wine on ice and refill glasses that didn't really need it, but she sensed he wanted to move.

"Not that heartbreaking," he said after he topped off

their wine, checked the anchor, and scanned the horizon all the way to Captiva. "By then it was a matter of making sure she couldn't take everything I had. I knew she was involved—deeply—with a guy at her job. I knew the first time I saw them talk at a company Christmas party, trying to act like they weren't..." He shook his head. "This is boring."

"This is your pain," she corrected. "I don't mean to sound like a shrink or something, but I think you need to talk about it before you can let it go." She waited a beat before adding, "And let someone else in."

His lips lifted in a slow smile. "Does that mean I have a shot?"

"I'm here, aren't I? Still in that first year of being a widow and I'm out with you." She cringed. "God, I hope he's not watching from heaven."

He lifted his brows. "Sounds like someone else needs to let go of their pain—or guilt—before she lets me in."

For a long time, neither spoke, only looked at each other. Eliza let herself slip a little deeper into his emerald eyes, as intoxicating as the wine and the warm Gulf breeze.

"You go first, Miles," she said. "Tell me anything you need to about Diane or your marriage or what that's done to your life."

He nodded, reaching to the charcuterie board to pop a grape in his mouth. After he chewed it and thought for a moment, he said, "What it's done is keep me single and alone because I don't trust anyone. Being a PI who makes a good part of his living tracking down cheating spouses hasn't done a thing to quell that cynicism and distrust."

"What's different about me?" she asked.

"Besides everything?" he shot back, laughing. "I don't know. You're worth the risk?"

"How do you know that?"

He leaned closer, narrowing his eyes, then putting both hands on his dog's head. "Tink knows quality when she falls for it."

Tinkerbell startled at the show of affection and gazed at them with big, curious brown eyes, making them both chuckle. She rose up on her hind legs at the attention, her snout close to Eliza's face.

"Look at that. She even has the nerve to kiss you."

She let her nose touch Tink's and laughed at the quick swipe of the tongue she got in response.

"You're a good girl, Tinkerbell," Eliza said, wrapping her hands around the dog's neck and burying her face in Tink's fur because she wasn't quite sure how to respond to the kiss comment. Then she looked up and into Miles's eyes, both of them quiet for a second.

"You don't need nerve, Miles. Just the right time."

"Will you let me know?"

Her smile faded as she studied him and thought about kissing him. Really thought about it, imagining the way it would feel, how he would taste...what Ben would think. Oh, goodness. Was she really—

"Eliza?"

She snapped out of the thought. "What?"

"I lost you." He dipped his head and looked closely. "Tough subject?"

"No, I just..." How could she tell him that Ben was there, all the time, in her heart, and she would feel so utterly guilty if she kissed Miles? She was on a date, for crying out loud. What did she *think* was going to happen?

"You see why I think I need nerve."

"You don't need nerve. I do."

He nodded. "You'll know when you're ready."

"You'll be the first person I tell," she promised.

"That's all I can ask."

"Now. Diane?"

He rolled his eyes. "Let's talk about our kids instead. They're better. I told Janie I had a date tonight and I swear she almost flew down here to check you out."

While the sun set into the Gulf, he shared more stories about his daughter, and his son, his father's pride in them reminding her of Ben, which relaxed her as much as the wine and made the rest of the night sweet, perfect, and right in her comfort zone.

When Eliza returned from her outing with Miles, she was pleasantly surprised to find that Teddy was not only still awake, but Claire, Olivia, and Camille were in the beach house living room, chatting. Or...waiting up for her. That was actually more likely.

Teddy, curled in her favorite chair with a cup of tea

in one hand and a quartz crystal in the other, beamed at her. "Hello, my darling."

"Hello." She glanced from one woman to the next. "I see the post-date discussion committee has gathered," she joked as she dropped a kiss on Olivia's head, and blew one to Claire and Camille.

"We are not here to discuss your date," Olivia said.

"We're not? Speak for yourself." Claire popped up and ushered Eliza toward the kitchen to chat. "I need a soda. Want one?"

She suspected that was sister code for, "Let's talk privately," so Eliza followed, dropping her bag on the table and rounding the counter into the kitchen where they were alone.

"So?" Claire reached for her. "Was it fun? Do you like him? Did you kiss him?"

Eliza just laughed. "Do I ask you all that about DJ?"

"Well, you know all that about DJ. Yes, he's always fun. Yes, I like him. And, yes, I've kissed him."

"But that's all, right?"

Claire blinked and her golden-brown eyes popped. "He wanted more than that? Miles? The nicest guy on Earth? In front of Tink on the boat? I can't—"

"Stop!" Eliza snorted a laugh. "You're crazy, you know that? Of course he didn't even suggest anything except a sideways comment about maybe a kiss...sometime."

"Okay, well, that makes more sense. So, do you like him?" She searched Eliza's face. "Was it a good time?"

"A very good time," she assured her, but added a sad smile. "It isn't going to be easy."

"Dating Miles? What could be difficult about it? He's such a great guy."

"Oh, he is. A fantastic man. Easy to talk to, funny and entertaining, worldly, wonderful, considerate, great-looking. He kept the evening completely...comfortable."

"So..."

Eliza tipped her head and added a look that surely her sister could interpret.

"You're still not ready to date?" Claire guessed.

"I'm not ready for...what goes along with dating." She shuddered a little. "Claire, I haven't kissed a man who wasn't Ben Whitney since I was twenty-two. I'm fifty-three. Do the math."

"The math says you're a little rusty." Claire shrugged. "I know you've struggled with guilt thinking that Ben is somehow watching in judgment or that you're breaking your sacred bonds of marriage, but you told me you'd let a lot of that go when you sold your house."

"I did," Eliza insisted. "But honestly, it's not the guilt. I thought it was, but tonight, I didn't really feel guilty. Only a little. I said I did, and that kept him from giving me a kiss, but by the time I got home I realized that I'm scared out of my mind. Maybe I can kiss, maybe a little more, but..." She made a cringy face. "I think I'm closed for business down south, if you get my drift."

Claire bit back a laugh. "Oh, I get your drift."

"You think you get it, but you're eight years behind

me, little sis. Wait until the only thing 'hot' on you is the flashes."

"When you feel it, Eliza, it'll be different, I'm sure. You'll be ready, not scared."

"I'm *petrified*, Claire. I honestly don't think I remember how, not to mention, you know. How things look down there."

"I'm sure they look fine and as far as remembering how—"

"If you say it's like riding a bike—"

"Camille! How can you say that?" Olivia's voice, strained and high, cut their conversation short.

"Whoa." Eliza turned toward the living room. "What's going on?"

"Those two are at each other's throats," Claire said. "Camille did not like the potential new employee."

"Deeley's friend? Marcie?" Eliza wrinkled her nose. "I haven't met her but from what Livvie told me, well, I can see that she wouldn't be up to your mother's very high standards."

"You're being ridiculous!" Olivia exclaimed.

"Oh, boy." Eliza tugged Claire out of the kitchen. "They need a referee."

Together, they headed into the other room, where tension was thick between Camille and Olivia while Teddy tried to surreptitiously push a quartz crystal closer to them.

"Put that thing away, Teddy," Camille barked. "It isn't going to solve a disagreement between business partners."

"It cleanses the air."

Camille shot her a withering look as Claire and Eliza settled on the sectional.

"So I take it Marcie came in to Sanibel Sisters?" Eliza asked.

"Blew into my store for a job interview wearing *shorts.*" Camille said it like Marcie had shown up covered in mud.

"*Our* store," Olivia said softly, the comment making Camille angle her head in concession. "And it was eighty degrees out. Shorts are appropriate."

"Not *those* shorts."

Olivia rolled her eyes, but didn't argue the point. "We'll provide her with the right clothing. That's part of the program," she insisted.

"You cannot provide her with qualifications, a lovely personality or...polish."

"Nail or the other kind?" Eliza asked.

"Both," Camille muttered.

"I disagree," Olivia said vehemently. "She can be trained and she can learn. She'll dress the part, and learn the language of sales, and she won't be running after Bash."

"Bash." Camille practically spat the child's name. "Which was exactly what he did to one of my dressing room walls."

Eliza's eyes grew wide. "She brought her son? Was he as bad as you said?"

Olivia's face told her all she needed to know.

"What's her plan for babysitting when she takes the job?" Eliza asked.

"*If* we offer her the job," Camille shot back.

"Look." Olivia glared at Camille. "I will work the schedule so that you are not in the store when she is."

"I'm always going to want to be there."

"At four in the afternoon?" Olivia challenged. "I'm pretty sure that's your nap time."

Camille couldn't argue with that. "I do need my beauty sleep, but if I'm not there, she might—"

"Wildly succeed," Olivia finished. "We agreed I'm going to handle afternoons, and now let's agree I'm going to handle Marcie Royce."

"And the Basher?"

Olivia looked toward the ceiling with a frustrated sigh. "I'll figure out how to get him in daycare for a few hours."

Eliza leaned forward, anxious to end the argument. "Honey, I think what you're doing for her is amazing. It's altruistic, genuine, and could be life-changing for this young woman."

"Yeah," Olivia shrugged. "I hope so. I also hope it helps Deeley get out from under the weight of this burden."

Camille shot her a dark-eyed glare. "I *knew* you were letting your hormones make business decisions, and I don't like that."

Olivia's jaw dropped. "Excuse me?"

"I'm just speaking the truth," Camille said. "You

want to impress him while we are supposed to be making money, not giving it away on charity cases."

With a low growl of frustration, Olivia pushed up to a stand. "You're telling *me* about making money? I was the one who introduced you to the concept of a gross profit margin spreadsheet and SKU limits to increase revenue. Remember that retail lesson?"

"Some of it. Not the numbers part. But Oliv—"

"Secondly, community goodwill drives publicity, which increases traffic and the urge to splurge. Which, by the way, is what we are asking from women who lay down two hundred smackeroos for a French-labeled dress when they could get something similar in Ross or Marshalls for forty-nine ninety-nine."

Camille curled her lip. "Shopping in a warehouse is—"

"And, last," Olivia continued, riled into high gear now. "I'm not thinking with my hormones. I'm thinking with my far-more-experienced-than-yours business brain and my much-softer-than-yours heart. Not for Deeley, for Marcie. How about bringing some goodness to someone who needs it?"

"I'm all about goodness, but—"

"You said we were fifty-fifty partners, Camille," Olivia reminded her. "This hire is coming out of my fifty. I'm bringing her in for training before the soft open, and I will personally fund her wardrobe and daycare or a sitter."

"Don't forget a haircut and maybe a lesson on how to properly wear eyeliner," Camille added, making the others either groan, gasp, or just look at her in disbelief. "What?" She flicked her fingers. "Sanibel Sisters has an image to maintain, and our staff needs to look like someone the clientele can relate to."

Olivia blew out a breath as she looked around, spied her bag, and grabbed it. "I'm going home. 'Night, all."

Once again, all eyes were on Camille, and none too loving, either.

Without thinking, Eliza popped up. "I'll be right back," she said, darting to the door to catch Olivia as she bolted down the stairs and rushed to her car parked behind the house.

"Hold up there, Liv," she called.

"It's fine, Mom." She waved her hand over her shoulder. "I need to cool down."

"Then you shouldn't drive," Eliza responded, like any mother would. "Just talk to me for a minute."

Olivia slowed her step with another noisy exhale, looked down, and finally turned. "Sometimes she makes me want to tear my hair out."

"You knew she wasn't the easiest person in the world when you joined forces with her," Eliza said. "But for what it's worth, you are on the side of the angels here."

"Am I?" All the swagger from her speech inside disappeared, replaced by raw uncertainty. "What if she's right? What if this is a huge mistake that I made because...because I'm trying to impress a guy? That is so not like me, a rather brilliant businesswoman, as I just announced to the world."

Eliza put her hands on her daughter's shoulders,

using a calming technique she'd perfected when Livvie was five and vibrating with her need to bend an inflexible world to her will.

"You are not trying to impress a guy. I know you better than that. If you didn't think this was the right thing to do, you'd find another way to help Deeley. Because, yes," she added when Olivia opened her mouth to argue. "You *do* want to help him. You help the people you care about. An act of service is your love language."

Olivia snorted. "Wow, you've been spending too much time with Teddy."

"Never too much," Eliza retorted in her dear friend's defense. "But I'm right. You are doing this to help him, but also because it's right on every level. Don't let Camille get under your skin."

"I won't," she said on one more sigh, this one much calmer. "After all those years at Promenade, my skin is thick. But everything's on the line with this store and I think we're both really stressed out." She looked up at the house. "Should I apologize to Marie Antoinette?"

Eliza gave a soft laugh at the nickname. "Not after the way she just talked to you, no. But don't second-guess anything, Liv, and trust your instincts. They are impeccable."

"Thanks, Mom." She melted into a hug and squeezed extra hard, then inched back. "But I was so busy fighting with her that I didn't get any deets on your date. Did you have fun?"

"I did."

"You left the guilt on the dock like you promised you would?"

"Mostly," she said, keeping it purposely vague. "Now, you get home safely and take a hot bath and sleep tight. You have a big week ahead."

"Thanks. Love you, Mom."

"I love you, too." Eliza stayed where she was, watching Livvie slip through the shadows to the car, waiting until she'd pulled out and headed home, satisfied she'd really helped her daughter.

Sometimes, she mused, being a mother came so much more naturally to her than being a...woman.

Chapter Seven

Olivia

"That woman hates me," Marcie hissed from inside the dressing room when Camille called out her goodbye and locked Sanibel Sisters front door behind her.

"No, no," Olivia assured her as she folded brightly colored T-shirts outside the dressing room and waited for Marcie to come out in one of the outfits she'd picked for her. "She's just...French." Also judgmental, small-minded, and determined to have the last word, which had nothing to do with her nationality, but Olivia was being squeezed from both sides.

"She's a witch," Marcie murmured.

"She's not as warm as...as one might like." A pathetic excuse, but what else could she say? "Anyway, you won't be working with her, Marcie. You can work afternoons until we close at seven, and I'll be here."

"So, one to seven?" she asked as the curtain fluttered and a zipper closed. "No more than that?"

"Did you want more than that?" Olivia asked. "I figured you wouldn't want to be away from Bash that long."

"Are you kidding?" She flipped back the drape noisily. "The more time away, the better."

Olivia spun around from the table with a soft gasp of shock. Was she serious?

"I guess that means you like it," Marcie said, completely misinterpreting Olivia's response. Which meant she *was* serious with that comment. Gosh, the kid wasn't *that* bad.

"Oh, yes," she said, covering for her reaction. "That skirt fits like a dream."

"If my dream is to be a nun." She hiked it up to mid-thigh. "Could you hem it?"

"No, that's the style. And we're going for understated here, and elegant. I think you look very nice. You don't have to tuck the sweater in, though."

"But my waist is one of my nicest features. I love to show it off."

In a bar maybe, Olivia thought, taking a few steps closer.

"Let me show you." She reached to pull out the top from the skirt and let it drape. "There. Much more comfortable, too."

Marcie turned to the mirror and curled a lip. "I seriously look like my grandmother. I'm only thirty, you know."

Wow, they were the same age? Olivia felt like she lived on a different planet than this woman. But she refused to let her own experience cloud this relationship, and she wouldn't be as judgmental as her business partner.

"This is totally age appropriate," Olivia said simply. "You can repeat the skirt with a few different tops, then wear those white jeans with a few more, keeping it light, beachy, and upscale casual. That's really all you'll need for the hours we had planned."

"Shorts would be beachy."

"Elegant beach," Olivia corrected, ignoring the fact that Marcie hadn't even whispered a thank you.

"But since this place isn't open yet, can I change back into what I wore? You just want me to fold stuff and hang and crap like that, right?"

Crap like that?

Olivia turned back to the clothing table and decided to let it go. Yes, mentoring was part of the process and gentle corrections on language and presentation were to be expected, but this woman hadn't signed up for mentoring and manners. She wanted a job. The other stuff would come, Olivia hoped.

"That's all we're doing, so sure. Save the work wardrobe and get comfortable."

A few minutes later, Marcie stepped out of the dressing room in her shorts and a T-shirt, and dropped all the new clothes in a pile on the table.

"Maybe you could fold and bag those," Olivia said gently. "And leave them in the back office so you can take them when you leave."

"Sure. And the bags are..."

"Under the cash register table." *Like I showed you,* she added mentally, gritting her teeth. God, she didn't want this to be a disaster.

"Okay, here they are. Fancy bags." She pulled out one of the large logo-embossed shopping totes that Camille had splurged on, stuffing all the clothes into it without folding them. "These are nicer than my freakin' suitcases."

Swinging the bag, she took it to the back, and Olivia had about ten tops folded by the time she finally came out.

"Had to pee," she said.

"Oh, feel free to *use the bathroom* anytime," Olivia said, praying Marcie would learn the classier lingo by example. "Now, you can take this pile of T-shirts and affix the price tags by adding them to the existing product tag. Each one has a price marked with a small sticker, which you'll remove. I'll—"

A man tapped on the glass door.

"Answer the door," Olivia finished, frowning at the new arrival.

"I can get it. 'Cause he's kinda cute."

Olivia shot her an "are you kidding" look.

"Well, you have a boyfriend," Marcie fired back.

Before she could answer—not that she knew what to say to that—the man tapped again. "I'm here to do the sign," he called.

"Oh, yes!" Olivia exclaimed as she hustled to the door. "The Sanibel Sisters sign is going up. I'm sorry Camille didn't stay for this."

"I'm not," Marcie mumbled but not very quietly.

Oh, please, someone give me strength, Olivia silently begged as she unlocked the door and greeted the man who had their beautiful wooden, gold sign with the inter-connected S's of the logo they'd had designed.

She chatted with him, discussed the placement over the door, and grabbed her phone to take some memorial-izing pictures...and Marcie still hadn't finished the pricing when she was done.

"Okay," Olivia said brightly when that was all finished. "Let's pick up the pace here and I'll help you. We still have that entire rack of dresses and the new knit beach coverups. I think those will double spectacularly as something that can be thrown over a sundress for an evening out in an air-conditioned restaurant. Remember, that's the kind of suggestion you want to make to our customers."

"These things?" Marcie lifted a white three-quarter-length coverup that Olivia had already snagged for herself from the Jazzberry line she loved. "There's nothing to them. You can stick a finger through the knit-ting and..." She flipped the tag. "Ninety bucks? What the—"

"Marcie," she said through gritted teeth. "We are catering to a wealthy clientele, and your job is to find the value, not question the price."

"But, geez, what's the markup on this thing?"

Olivia eyed her, somehow doubting she was asking as her first tutorial in basic retail management. "Enough for us to make a profit. If you're interested, I'm happy to go over some simple retail concepts."

"Why would I want that?"

Olivia sighed. "So that you can learn? Grow? Maybe buy that coverup someday?"

"What's the employee discount?"

"Marcie," she said softly, tempering her frustration. "I don't want you to think of this job as the same as what you did for Old Navy."

"No kidding," she scoffed. "That thing at Old Navy would be twenty bucks and maybe a BOGO. Do you ever run those?"

"I'm serious."

"So am I," she fired back.

"I want you to think of this as an opportunity to learn and expand your professional horizons."

Marcie just stared at her, obviously trying not to laugh.

"You can do that in a job like this," Olivia continued. "I'm happy to teach you, to help you, guide you into management, even."

Marcie appeared to consider that, looking hard at Olivia, who hoped she'd finally touched a chord.

"Would that be more hours?" Marcie asked.

"Do you want more hours?"

"Well, sweetie," she said. "As long as you're footin' the bill for daycare, I'll work morning to night. Did you find a place to take Beastie Boy yet or are you just gonna keep covering a sitter like today?"

Irritation tapped all over Olivia's chest. "Not yet, and I know Bash is a handful, but I think he'll benefit from some..." She didn't want to say *discipline* and risk offending the other woman. "Some structure," she said instead. "I'm not a mother, so I can't say for sure, but I think you'll see some real change in him after he's been in daycare."

Marcie rolled her eyes and picked up the next Jazzberry coverup, uncharacteristically quiet as she slapped a price sticker on the tag. Crooked, which was probably how she was used to seeing them in the places she shopped.

Olivia gently took the item and lifted the tag. "If you can try to—"

"No, you're not a mother," she ground out. "So you don't know diddly about structure or daycare or what a bad, bad kid is really like."

Olivia blinked at her. "He's not bad."

"What the heck would you call it?"

"He needs..." Oh, why not be real? "Discipline. Boundaries. And attention."

She narrowed her eyes, nothing but disgust in them. "He needs a *daddy*!"

Oh, God. She'd walked right into that one.

"I'm sorry, Marcie," she whispered. "I really wasn't thinking. You have a very difficult job as a working, single mother and I was completely out of line."

The apology cooled the other woman off a little, and her shoulders sank. "It basically sucks."

"Oh, but you have a beautiful son and...and memories, I assume, of Tommy."

She threw a sideways look at Olivia. "Memories? Of Tommy? He was gone more than he was around."

"I can imagine he was deployed a lot."

"Yeah." She gave her head a quick shake, as if she didn't want to talk about it, so Olivia took a breath and started to gather up some clothes to make room for the next batch, purposely not asking any more questions.

For a good long minute, they worked in silence, until Marcie finally tossed up her hands.

"He was no stinking hero, you know," she announced. "I mean, I fell for the whole hot Navy SEAL thing when we met. I married him because he asked, 'cause he was leaving for God knows how long, and... and...anyway, he had problems, you know?"

"I don't know," Olivia said. "And to be perfectly honest, I don't want to. The man is dead, he died in service, and that's all I need to know about his heroics. I can only imagine how your heart broke when you heard the news, so there's no need to relive it."

"Mmm." She smoothed out some linen trousers with a slightly rough touch, but Olivia had corrected and reprimanded her enough for one day, so she let it go. "Bash has always been this way, a pain in the butt since the minute I found out I was pregnant."

Olivia looked up from the top she was folding, the note of true agony in Marcie's voice catching her attention.

"And it wasn't an easy pregnancy," she added. "And the stress of worrying about Tommy was so hard on me, I thought I might lose Bash 'cause I had to be on bedrest. The government paid for the doctors, but then my mother died. All the while he'd send me these emails and texts and he was...struggling. We both were." A tear threatened to spill from her eye, but she wiped it with the back of her hand, smearing her thick eyeliner. "You're right. Let's not talk about Tommy. Ever. It's better that way."

"I'm very sorry you've had such a rough time," Olivia said, her heart sliding around in her chest.

"Sorry enough to let me go early?" she asked.

Oh, man. Was she being played or what? "If you need to, but—"

"I mean, if we're done here."

"You want to get home early to see Bash?"

"I want to..." She made a pretend guilty face. "I've been seeing a guy."

Olivia inched back, not expecting that. "Oh...really?"

"Yeah, he's in construction and just texted me that he's getting off early tonight, too, and since I had a sitter already..."

A sitter that Olivia was paying for. "Marcie, I think—"

"I'll pay the extra time," she said quickly. "But this guy is awesome and I want to see him."

Olivia dug for a reason to say no, but that felt small and spiteful. They weren't open. There were no customers. "Of course."

"Great. Then what's the plan? Do I get hours posted somewhere?"

"I'll text you for the soft opening hours, which is when we have the doors open and we're taking customers, but we won't announce it."

"And the daycare?" she pressed. "I seriously cannot afford that sitter."

"Let me take a few more days to figure out the child-care situation, Marcie. I'll find something."

"Cool." She darted to the back room, grabbed her bag of clothes, and waited while Olivia unlocked the front door. "Oh, the sign looks nice," she added just before she pulled a ringing phone out of her bag. "Hey, Eddie. Great news! I'm on my way."

While Olivia tagged the rest of the inventory, she hoped to God Camille wasn't right about this woman.

Chapter Eight

Katie

Dang it all, she was late. Again.

Katie made a face at her phone when she saw the time, then scooped up her bucket and mop, charging down the path toward the storage room under Teddy's house, already imagining the look Blanche Ellison would give her for arriving late the second time this week.

This problem was only going to get worse as the season wore on, even if she hired another housekeeper, which she usually did after Thanksgiving when they were slammed. Still a lot of weeks between now and then.

"Hey, where ya goin', sis?"

She spun around at the sight of Jadyn stepping out of her cottage, wearing a T-shirt over her bathing suit, her hair in a ballcap as usual, a can of Diet Coke in her hand. Katie didn't flinch at "sis" but an ancient wave of sibling rivalry washed over her, taking her back to the years when Katie was studying to get A's in school and Jadyn was off to another party.

It always seemed Jadyn had life so much easier.

"I'm late," she said, lifting the bucket, as if that

explained anything. "I can't talk until later. We can have dinner, like I promised."

Undaunted, Jadyn hopped off the wooden deck and snagged a pair of flipflops that were left on the armrest of the Adirondack chair. "Late for what? Another cottage to clean? I'll help you."

Katie slid her a look, almost tempted to call her bluff and hand her the bucket and mop. But Jadyn didn't know what to do with those tools any more than...than Katie had when she arrived. The only difference? Katie was motivated to work. She sincerely doubted Jadyn wanted to learn the subtleties of being a top-notch housekeeper.

"I'm late to pick up Harper at her after-school care. And the warden's gonna let me have it, so..." She notched her chin forward. "I gotta run."

"I'll go with you." Jadyn dropped the flipflops, stuck her feet in them, and jogged to catch up with Katie. "Why do you call her a warden?"

It wasn't worth taking the time to try and talk Jadyn out of this. She could come, as long as she didn't slow things down. "Because she treats those kids like they're in jail."

"A kindergarten teacher?" She choked softly. "I'd find another school."

"It's not actually a school, and she's not the kindergarten teacher. I love Ms. McAllister, her teacher. She's a doll, but kindergarten is over at two and the kids who can't get picked up get in a van, which I absolutely hate, and get taken to an after-school place run by a woman who really should be in a different job. She's never met a kid she actually likes."

"Oh, that's awful!"

It really was, but Katie didn't have another option. They reached the storage facility and Katie set her cleaning supplies on the ground and dug into her pocket for the key. As she unlocked the door, Jadyn grabbed the bucket and mop without even being asked.

"Thanks," Katie murmured, getting a little kick of guilt because maybe she really didn't give Jadyn enough credit for having changed.

Jadyn didn't answer, still shaking her head. "See? I want to be a preschool teacher because I love kids."

Since when? But Katie kept the question to herself as she put the last of her tools in place, tossed the dirty rags in the washer and started it up, knowing Teddy or Eliza would come down and throw them in the dryer for her.

"Why don't you find another after-school place?" Jadyn asked while Katie locked up and motioned toward the parking lot.

"On Sanibel Island? They are few and far between, crazy expensive, and all have waiting lists a mile long. Olivia was asking me for one the other day and I honestly couldn't find anything for her."

At the car, she unlocked her door, let Jadyn in, and peeled out of the lot. But the minute they got off Roosevelt Road, she hit the brakes with a groan.

"Looks like the snowbirds are arriving more and more each day."

"I can see why. This place is awesome," Jadyn said. "I

took my rental car up to Captiva today and saw a bunch of amazing houses. Dad should buy a place down here."

Oh, yeah. Just what she needed. "Doesn't he have enough houses?"

"But he could be close to you and Harper."

She hit the gas a little too hard and slid into an opening in the traffic on Periwinkle.

"It's just a thought," Jadyn said. "I haven't even told him I'm with you."

"Where does he think you are?"

"In Mexico, on vacation."

"Why'd you lie?"

"Because he'd be down here in a heartbeat to see you."

Katie had a hard time believing that, remembering nothing but ice in the air at their home. Homes, plural. Still, the idea of her father wanting to see her enough that he'd be here "in a heartbeat" did something to soften her own heart, whether she liked that or not. What if it was true? What if Jadyn's illness had changed *all* of them?

"So how is he?" she asked. "Still making billions?"

"Yeah, but he's pulled back a lot. Sold a few of his companies, and focuses a lot on the hedge funds that make him the most. He's really got an impressive portfolio."

Katie checked the time and ran the yellow light. "I'm surprised you don't want to go into business with him," she said. "Since you two are so close and all."

Jadyn chuckled softly. "I don't have your brains, in

case you forgot. Math is my personal nightmare and if there's one thing Dad does a lot of, it's math."

"Brains? Me?" Katie scoffed. "A single mother who works at a resort cleaning other people's toilets? Yeah, I'm a genius."

"First of all, do you forget you were at Brown University when you got pregnant?"

Actually, she'd been in the boathouse of their Marblehead mansion on Christmas break of her freshman year, and never finished the spring semester.

"Last time I checked, that's an Ivy League school," Jadyn reminded her.

"It is, but it doesn't change the fact that I'm a maid."

"You're not a maid," Jadyn said. "I never saw any housekeeper in my life—and God knows my mother went through them like water—who took as much pride as you do in your work."

"Thanks," she said under her breath, more than a little surprised Jadyn would even notice that.

"You're like a partner with Teddy and Eliza, one of the key pieces that keeps that resort running."

Katie smiled, turning onto a side street to get to the daycare. "You gunnin' for a job for real?" she joked.

"Nope. I told you what I want to do."

"Preschool teacher. Do you really want to do that, Jadyn?"

"More than anything. And I know it might seem out of character for the girl you think you know, but..."

"That girl has changed."

"That girl is never going to have a child of her own,"

Jadyn said quietly. "And it wasn't until that was taken away from me that I realized how much..." Her voice cracked. "How much I wanted it."

"Oh, Jadyn. I'm so sorry."

"It's okay. I figured out a solution. I am going to do something with kids, and I am going to be the world's most amazing aunt for Harper and any others you have."

The passion and sincerity in her voice cut right through Katie, making her reach out one hand as she parked in front of the facility. And by facility, she meant a motor home that had been transformed into Miss Blanche's Sunshine After School.

"You are the most amazing aunt," she assured her. "And I'm sure you'll be fantastic at whatever you do."

"I don't know about fantastic, but I should be fun," Jadyn said, trying to lighten the moment and turning to see where they were. "*Oof*. A trailer park?"

"No park, just a trailer. It's what we parents are told to call 'a portable.'"

"Eesh." Jadyn slowly unlatched her seatbelt. "Sorry. I know you're working your butt off and I really am proud of you, whether you believe it or not. It's just putting Harper in this..."

"Dump," Katie agreed. "I didn't realize there wasn't after-care at the school when I registered her for kinder-garten, and I was lucky to get this place. She's only had to come here a few days a week since school started last month, when Teddy's super busy and I don't want to impose on anyone. I'll figure something out. Come on, let's go face the wrath of Blanche Ellison."

"Blanche? She sounds like the mean governess in a gothic novel."

"Nailed it," Katie joked, thinking of the matron with a helmet of gray hair and a penchant for too much green eye shadow.

Of course, Harper was standing in the doorway, book bag in hand, ponytail halfway out, an expression of pure dejection on her pretty face.

It disappeared when she saw Katie, and turned into pure sunshine when she saw Jadyn.

"Auntie Jay-jay!" She whizzed past Katie without so much as a kiss in the wind, arms out to be scooped up by her new favorite aunt.

Smiling at that, Katie watched the two of them greet each other with an airspin, a squeeze, and a squeal of each other's nicknames. She'd have to have a heart made of pure concrete not to enjoy seeing her little girl that happy.

"You're late again."

Katie closed her eyes at the sound of Blanche the Gothic Governess's voice. Tomorrow she would definitely beg Teddy to pick her up after school. It was just that everyone was so busy these days and—

"And you know I'm going to bill you for a full hour."

Katie turned, ready to deliver her apology and beg for forgiveness and not to be charged, but Jadyn came forward, with Harper still wrapped around her waist.

"All my fault, ma'am," she said. "I'm her aunt. Favorite one, right, Harpdawg?"

"Auntie Jay-jay!" She threw both hands in the air, but Jadyn had her tight in her arms.

"I don't care if you're the Queen of England," Blanche said with a scowl firmly in place. "We have rules we expect the children to follow, and we have rules for the adults."

Very slowly, Jadyn lowered Harper to the ground, pushing up the bill of her ballcap, presumably so she could give Blanche the death stare.

"Well, we have rules, too, for daycare providers."

Blanche drew back, her drawn-on brows lifting. "And who do you think you are?"

"I'm this child's aunt, as you just heard, but I'm also an inspector with child services."

What? Katie did everything in her power not to gasp or let her chin hit the ground.

"Excuse me?" Blanche asked.

"Could I have a tour of your premises?"

"Who do you think you are?" Blanche demanded again.

"I don't think, I am Jadyn Bettencourt, certified state inspector for the...Department of Children and Families. In Tallahassee. Do you need to call my county supervisor? I'm sure he'll be able to meet me here in a few—"

"Of course not."

"Then you won't mind an unscheduled inspection, which are supposed to take place at least once every two school years."

Blanche glared at her, then tipped her head. "Right this way, Miss." She made a sweeping gesture into the small structure that Katie knew smelled faintly of markers and popcorn. And bug spray.

"You go first," Jadyn said. As the woman walked in, she turned to Katie and made a face and mouthed, "Play along," before hustling in.

She was really doing this? As a joke? As a threat? Katie had no idea, but the last thing she wanted was for her sister to closely inspect this place. Or for Harper to get kicked out.

She was stuck for childcare a few days a week. It wasn't so bad when a few other kids were here. Harper was so easy to please and was sick of following Katie around at work. And she really would—

"Ms. Ellison!"

Katie startled at the sharp tone in Jadyn's voice, then took Harper's hand and headed in.

"Is there a problem?" Blanche asked.

"These window blind cords should not be accessible to children," Jadyn said, flicking her fingers over the blinds. "That is a breach of the Internal Premises Safety protocol, statute fourteen, line 7A. All window treatments must be secure and bolted, with no cords, ties, loose shutters, or exposed nail heads."

Blanche stared at her.

"Ms. Ellison, every child and daycare facility in the state must follow the safety protocols, which I'm sure you agreed to when you signed your state license. Which, by the way, should be posted. Am I missing it?"

"Um, no. I have it..." She went to her desk. "I just don't...I have it, though."

It was the most flustered Katie had ever seen Blanche, and the most "in charge" she'd ever seen Jadyn. Still holding Harper's hand, she watched in awe as her sister stepped over toys, ran her finger over the air-conditioning vents, and tested the windows.

"Here it is." Blanche pulled out a piece of paper and waved it victoriously. "I'm fully licensed."

"But, Ms. Ellison." Jadyn pushed her cap back even more, revealing a very serious expression as she stood by the sink and lifted the bottle of liquid soap. "This is empty. Are the children—and you—not properly washing hands?" She shook her head. "That's a severe violation of the state board of daycare and childcare health standards. I believe it is regulation 1901, but..." She pulled out her phone. "Let me call the headquarters and confirm."

"No, no, that's not necessary," Blanche said quickly. "We just finished that soap after playtime." She rushed over to flip open the cabinet under the sink. "And I have a refill ready to go..." Bending over, she stuck her head in deeper and while she looked, Jadyn turned to Katie and winked.

Just old enough to understand she was in on a secret something, Harper squeezed Katie's hand and gave a little shudder of excitement that they were playing some kind of game on her least favorite caretaker of all time.

"Well, it *was* in here," Blanche said as she straightened. "I have some in storage and I'm not closed, just cleaning and preparing for tomorrow." She took a breath and planted a fake smile on her face. "I'd appreciate it if you'd give me a little leeway."

"Of course," Jadyn said, then lifted her brows. "And when did you have your last fire alarm and carbon monoxide check?"

"Oh! Yes. I have that paperwork."

Carbon monoxide check? It was all Katie could do to keep from reacting to this. Was Jadyn a complete fake? An actress of true skill? Or...did she know this stuff?

"Here you go." Blanche whipped out another paper. "We're all up to date."

"Excellent." Jadyn read it—or at least appeared to—then gave it back. "That is definitely sufficient."

"Thank you." It seemed like Blanche's whole being relaxed as she turned and looked down at Harper. "And will I see you tomorrow, princess?"

"No," Jadyn answered for her, breezing across the room and taking Harper's other hand. "She'll be with her Auntie Jay-jay tomorrow. As soon as I finish my other inspections. Bye!"

"Bye!" Harper called as the two adults whisked her out so fast, her little feet came off the ground, making her giggle.

They all were giggling, in fact, and it didn't stop until they were in the car.

"Jadyn!" Katie stared at her. "What was that all about?"

Her eyes glinted with victory. "I told you I'm taking online classes to get my preschool teaching certificate. I wasn't kidding, Kay. The last course I took was on child-care facility inspection preparation."

Katie's jaw loosened. "So all that was...real?"

"Oh, the part about my supervisor and child services? Nah. I was winging it. And, dang, I remembered Tallahassee was the capital of Florida. That wasn't in my class but, miracle of miracles, I learned something in high school. As far as the childcare inspection test? I got an A, so I knew exactly what an inspector would look for."

"Miz Ellison is scared of you, Auntie Jay-jay," Harper chimed in from her car seat in the back.

"Not really, but I bet she cleans that place up a bit," Jadyn replied, turning to her. "Do you like her, Harper?"

She shook her little head. "Sometimes she's mean."

Katie's heart dropped with a thud. "I'm going to fix it," she promised. "I'm trying to help Olivia find care for her new employee's little boy, and between the two of us, we can find another day—"

"You found one."

Katie frowned. "Blanche the Governess?"

"Jadyn the Sister." She leaned in and fluttered her lashes. "Let me watch her after school or during your work hours or whatever, and the kid for Olivia, too. I'll set something up in my cottage."

"Can you do that?"

"Will Teddy let me? I mean, I'm just babysitting. I'm not going to call it official daycare. But it would be amazing experience for me, and I would love it. Please?"

"Are you sure you want to?"

She pointed over her shoulder. "Do I want to watch her? She's a gem and we'd have a blast."

Katie thought about it, realizing what a huge help it would be. "Oh, but Livvie said that her employee's son, who's just a toddler, is, uh, not a gem. Apparently, he would benefit greatly from Miss Blanche's School of Overhanded Discipline."

Jadyn swept her hand like no one in the world deserved Blanche. "I can handle it. And Harper can help me. Right, Harpdawg? You'll be my teaching assistant."

"Yay!"

Jadyn lifted her brow at Katie. "I have one vote of confidence."

"I'm thrilled to let you watch Harper, especially since you'll be right at Shellseeker and, yeah. That's easy. The other one? I don't know. I'll text Olivia and see what she thinks."

"Sounds good. Now, where are we going to get ice cream?"

"Ice cream?" Katie and Harper asked the question together, only in two very different tones.

"After-school ice cream should be a thing," Jadyn announced.

For a long moment, Katie just stared at her, feeling something stir in her heart. A memory. An old pain that she rarely let touch her heart.

Her mother used to take her for ice cream after school, when she was very, very little. It wasn't much more than a wisp of a memory, the taste of chocolate and happiness. Did Jadyn know that? She couldn't. Katie certainly never told her.

Jadyn gave a wry smile. "Come on, Kay. After two hours with Nurse Ratched? The kid deserves some ice cream."

"Please, Mommy, please?"

Katie reached for the key in the ignition and twisted it. "Ice cream it is. Gonna ruin dinner, but we're celebrating."

"What are we celebrating?" Harper asked.

Katie threw Jadyn a look. "My sister, who constantly surprises me."

They smiled at each other and took off for an after-school ice cream and a trip to the store to buy supplies for what Jadyn announced would be known as Auntie Jay-jay's Most Fun Ever After-School Care.

Chapter Nine

Deeley

The scream was so loud, Deeley thought it would blow the thatched roofing off the cabana.

"Whoa, buddy." The customer looked up from the credit card slip he was signing, trying to see past Deeley into the back. "Your kid is not happy."

"He's not mine," Deeley said. "I'm babysitting for a friend."

Bash let out another ear-splitting scream and now the man paying for his paddleboard rental looked truly concerned, and his wife stuck her head in, too.

"Is he okay?"

"He's fine," Deeley said over Bash's noise. "Just...exuberant."

"We can wait for the boards," the man said. "You should take care of that kid."

No, he should be up-selling them towels and umbrellas, the way his retail goddess taught him. But Livvie was running her own store today, having the soft opening that was so important to Sanibel Sisters. She'd asked Marcie to come in for the afternoon, but there was no sitter or daycare yet, so...

He glanced behind him at Bash in his portable

playpen, threatening to break down the walls Jericho-style, by simply yelling those suckers into oblivion. The toys Marcie had packed were strewn all over the cabana, tossed out of the playpen in fits of rage and boredom. There was a bottle on the floor, a pacifier covered in sand, and—

"Deeeeeleeeeeey! Lemme out!" He jumped up and down, now threatening to break the floor of his little jail.

"One second, bud," he called, then held up a hand to the very understanding customers. "You can just snag those boards at the end of the rack, and the paddles. I also have—"

"We're good," the guy said, backing away as if Bash just might escape and attack.

Taking a calming breath, Deeley closed his eyes and tried to remember everything Livvie said to do. Not Marcie. When he'd offered to take Bash, she basically handed him over with a sigh of relief and a muttered, "Good luck."

Livvie had taken the time to show him where the diapers were, suggest what Bash might eat, and make sure he put the bottles—shouldn't the kid be off them by now? —in his mini-fridge. Right next to the beer, which, right this minute, was sounding pretty good.

Maybe he just needed to get out, Deeley thought, turning to meet his little nemesis with a big smile. "How about we take a walk and find shells, Bashie?"

The toddler clamped his hands on the playpen and opened his mouth, taking that one second of air that

Deeley already knew would come out as a shriek that could be heard up and down Shellseeker Beach.

Scooping him up, Deeley headed out, looking left and right and not seeing any waiting customers. "Come on—"

"Water!" Bash wriggled and kicked, pointing at the paddleboarders. "Me! Me!"

"You can't paddle, little dude, and I can't—"

"Water, Deeley!" He punctuated that with a swift kick to Deeley's gut and a sticky smack to his face.

"Okay, okay. Hang on a second." Still holding Bash, he marched to grab the last board, lowering him to the sand. "Don't run away, now. I'm going to take you out there."

"Me on water!"

"I'll stand next to the board and you'll do exactly as I say, okay?"

He nodded and even cooperated when Deeley slipped the smallest life vest he had on him and carried him to the edge of the shore, dragging the board behind him while Bash made noise and demands and wriggled in his arms.

"Here we go." Deeley hoisted him up and attached the security leash to Bash's leg.

In a few minutes, he easily got them past the low break in the waves, holding Bash high and steady until the board floated waist high.

Suddenly, Bash was quiet. Beautifully, blissfully quiet and still.

"You happy, kid?" he asked.

He nodded, literally speechless. His eyes were wide as saucers, his little mouth open in an O of wonder and baby teeth, his hands splayed out like he simply couldn't express his bone-deep joy.

"Water," he said again, this time on a sigh of pure contentment.

"You like that, huh? Just like your daddy." He got a jolt in the gut at the thought of Tommy, and how much he'd deserved a moment like this with his son, but he let it float away on the next wave.

"Daddy," he repeated, adding a grin and reaching one of those hands to Deeley. "Daddy."

"No, no. *Deeley*," he corrected. "Daddy is...not here."

"Daddy!" His voice rose, the way it did when he got fixated on something.

"Look, here comes a wave, Bash." It was small but he rocked the board gently, eliciting a squeal of delight. "Daddy! Daddy!"

Oh, *man*.

"I'm not your daddy," he said, a little frustration rising in him. He wasn't sure why, except that maybe Tommy would be furious. And he felt like an imposter.

"Daddy!" This time Bash tried to get up and Deeley grabbed him, keeping him on the board. As he got hold of him, he glanced toward the cabana, spotting three customers milling around the open window. He couldn't afford to lose three customers.

"Daddy! Happy!"

He grunted in frustration. "Party's over, Bash-man." He waved to the people by the cabana. "Be right there!"

he called, carefully guiding the board back to shallow water. A slight wave brought them in, and he freed the leash and scooped Bash up. With the other hand, he tossed the board to the sand and then jogged toward the cabana.

"No!" Bash screamed, starting to kick and slap. "More water, Daddy!"

"Hang on a sec," he called to the customers, who watched with a mix of impatience and amusement while he ducked into the cabana and placed Bash in the playpen.

Somehow, he managed to sign up the rentals despite the epic screeching and screaming behind him.

When they left, he turned to Bash, who was covered in tears and snot and red-faced as he fell on his back, slapping the bottom of the playpen, screaming, "Mommy!"

Well, so much for "Daddy."

"How about a drink, little man?" He went to the fridge where one bottle was left.

"Mommy!"

Looking left and right, he snagged one of Harper's *Frozen* books. "The story about the cold chicks?"

"Mommmmmmy!"

Deeley stared at him, beads of sweat forming on his forehead, his stomach in knots. What could he do with this kid? Back to the water?

"Mom—"

"Yes!" he barked back, bringing Bash to silence. The kid obviously needed a parent. "We'll go see your mommy," he added in a much less harsh tone.

Bash lifted his head, staring at Deeley like he didn't believe it. Had he faked the whole tantrum? Was Deeley being conned by a toddler?

Didn't matter. They were going. He had an hour before that first renter came back, and he'd give up any new business he'd get between now and then just for five minutes of help. It was late in the day, and maybe things had slowed at Sanibel Sisters. Maybe Marcie could take him.

Pulling down the shutters that covered the service window, he slid the "Be back soon!" sign on the door. Stuffing some of Bash's things in the bag, he snagged the kid—who was no longer crying, it had to be noted—with one arm and made the split-second decision to leave the playpen.

He'd buy Marcie a new one. Heck, he'd build her one, but he had to get Bash in the car seat in his truck and down the street to Livvie's store.

"Mommy?" Bash asked as he slapped his chubby little hands around Deeley's neck and hung on for the ride. "See Mommy now?"

"Yep, you're gonna see your dear, sweet mother." He ground out the words, trying really hard to hide his sarcasm from the kid, who might be a little too smart for his own good.

Tommy had been the same way, he thought, as the hot sand and shells dug into his bare feet, flipflops forgotten in the cabana. A relentless bruiser who might look like he didn't have much upstairs, but the guy was a flipping genius. Too smart for his own good sometimes.

And he'd have loved this kid.

With that splash of guilt that always threatened to drown him, Deeley slowed his step, lifted Bash higher in his arms, and took a second to get them both comfortable. The boy was fine now. Tears and snot had been dried on Deeley's bare shoulder and Bash sat up, thumb in mouth, eyes wide, looking around like he'd just got out of solitary.

Bash's inquisitive gaze finally settled on Deeley's face, and his little lips opened into a smile around that thumb.

"Deeley," he said on a sigh, dropping his head, and pulling out all the cute stops now.

Okay, the "Daddy" thing was over. Thank God. "Oh, sure, you're just downright precious when you get what you want, eh, bud?"

"I wuv you." He snuggled closer and Deeley marched across the sand, trying to ignore what the words did to him. That was only Mother Nature, making sure he didn't toss this little beanbag onto the sand.

"There's the truck. Mommy isn't far now, Basho."

But he snuggled his little body even closer, squeezing Deeley with fat legs and greedy arms. "Deeley."

He laughed, because what else could he do?

The rare sweet mood lasted while he buckled the little body into the car seat in the back of the truck's cab and drove out of Shellseeker to the heart of the island.

Realizing Bash was oddly quiet, he looked over his shoulder and Bash was bright red, squishy-faced, and...intent.

"Oh, man." Did he even have a spare diaper?

Didn't matter. He spotted the strip mall and the new beautiful Sanibel Sisters sign. "The end is near, buddy."

But Bash made a face, looked down at his diaper, then back up at Deeley. "Stinker!"

"Yeah." He sniffed and groaned. "I got that."

He whipped into the closest spot to the store, getting Bash out before the inside of his truck smelled like a gas station restroom.

"Oooh, buddy, you're a—"

"Stinker!"

Deeley threw his head back, laughing as he reached the door, which popped wide open, nearly hitting them both in the face.

"Oh, Deeley." Marcie was standing in the doorway, looking surprised. "You're such a natural with—"

"Mommy!" Bash kicked and squirmed and almost threw himself out of Deeley's grip to get to her.

Marcie jerked back, arms in the air. "Don't mess up these fancy clothes."

For a second, Deeley just stared at her. Was she serious? Her clothes?

"You're early." Olivia floated up behind Marcie, beaming at him as she stepped outside where he stood with Bash. "Come on in, it's slow now. You missed the rush."

Unlike Marcie, Livvie came right out to him, putting a hand on Bash's back. "Have you been a good boy?"

He stopped squirming and stuck his thumb back in his mouth, the picture of perfection. A stinking angel, literally.

"Oh, Bash!" Livvie cooed, leaning in closer, then she leaned back, waving her hand under her nose. "Whoa. Is that why you brought him here?"

He laughed. "No, that happened in the truck. I brought him because he missed his mother so much, he was inconsolable." He looked over at Marcie, who just had her arms crossed, watching the exchange with an unreadable expression. "Do you want to change him?" he asked.

"In these clothes?" She swiped her hand over what had to be the most conservative thing he'd ever seen her wear, from buttoned-up blouse to knee-length skirt. "Not on your life, buddy."

"Well, I'm not sure I can—"

"I can change him." Olivia reached out and took Bash. "We have a little changing table in the employee bathroom. Bag?"

Deeley handed her the backpack, sighing in relief. "Liv, you are the best."

"Come on in," she said. "We had an amazing first day with, what would you say, Marcie? Maybe forty customers all day?"

"At least. And, whoa, can those women spend money."

"Cha-ching!" Livvie tapped Bash's nose, making him giggle. "Come on, big boy. Let's get you cleaned up."

And off she went with a kid and a bag and a smile and...where the heck did she even come from?

"She's really good with him," Marcie mused, leaning back on the door so he could come in.

"Yeah, she's..." He looked down at his bare, sandy feet, the only clothes on his body some old board shorts. "I gotta get back to work, so—"

"You're leaving him here?" Her voice rose in clear panic.

"He's miserable, Marcie. He's in actual pain without you."

"Without *me*?" she scoffed. "He doesn't even like me."

He just shook his head, not willing to have this argument. "I'll get his car seat. Hang on." Without waiting for her to reply, he went back to the truck, unlatched the seat and grabbed some miscellaneous stuff that had fallen out of the bag.

She'd gone back inside when he returned, so he was forced to open the door, impressed by the very smell of the place. Of course, *anything* smelled better than his truck at the moment.

He'd been over here a lot in the last few weeks, helping Livvie build some shelves and change out a fluorescent light to a crystal chandelier, but there'd always been a low grade of chaos with piles of clothes and boxes of inventory.

Somehow, Livvie and Camille had managed to create an oasis of calm and peace. With spacious racks of clothing, neatly folded items on glass tables, an inviting sitting area outside of silk-curtained dressing rooms, he could see the appeal to women in a heartbeat.

"I have amazing news!" Livvie called out from her back office, appearing in the doorway with a very contented-looking Bash in one arm, her phone in her other hand.

"Mommy!" Bash called.

Deeley looked hard at Marcie, waiting for her to go to her son. But she just smiled at him, making a show of folding an article of clothing he suspected did not need to be refolded.

"Make it fast, Liv," he said, maybe a little more gruffly than necessary but he was standing in this pristine paradise covered in sand and wearing nothing but a bathing suit. And he was just flat-out furious at Marcie's behavior.

Why didn't she take her kid?

"Short version: we have a daycare solution. Go." She gestured him to the door. "Finish up your day and come over to my house for dinner." She got on her tiptoes and gave him a peck on the lips. "We got this, babe."

He just smiled at her and barely gave a nod to Marcie. "Thanks," he whispered. "I'll cook."

"And I'll love every minute of it."

Bash reached for him, all smiles now. "Daddy!"

Livvie's eyes popped, and behind her, Marcie gasped.

"Kid's confused," he muttered, patting Bash on the head as he opened the door to leave. "But he had his first paddleboard ride, so there is that."

Hours later, the world looked different as Deeley gazed over Livvie's dining table, the one that had arrived on a truck the other day, and watched her finish off the filet mignon he'd bought and cooked.

"You didn't have to do all this for me, Deeley," Livvie said, picking up her almost-empty second glass of wine. "But, wow, am I grateful."

"Are you kidding? I'm the one who's grateful."

"Don't gush anymore," she said after taking a sip. "It's only going to get better, and we had a good first day. She did really well."

He lifted a brow. "She overcharged, undercharged, insulted a customer, spilled coffee on a hundred-dollar hand-painted T-shirt, and drove Camille out of the store."

"She made a few calculation errors, which I fixed," Livvie said quickly. "And it wasn't an insult. She's just learning how to be diplomatic when an outfit looks awful on a customer."

"She called the clothes 'brutal,' Liv."

Biting back a laugh, she shook her head. "Yeah, bad word choice. And I bumped into her with my coffee, which was why it spilled, and Camille was desperate for an excuse, because her feet hurt in stilettos." She angled her head. "Man, I hope I can still wear stilettos in my seventies."

"You are defending her again, and changing the subject."

She sighed, visibly more relaxed than when she got home and had been vibrating with adrenaline from her first day of being a store owner.

"I want her to work out, Deeley. For so many reasons, I want to help her and see her through to a better life."

"She has to want to get there, Liv. And she has to..." His voice faded out, unwilling to say what he was thinking.

"Come on." She tapped his knuckles with the base of her wine glass. "Spill."

"She has to be a better mother to Bash," he said. "It's like she can't stand that kid."

A shadow crossed Livvie's face, but she just looked down, not defending Marcie for once.

"So you agree?"

She shifted in her chair and gave a little shrug. "She's not...comfortable in her mother skin, no, but I don't think you can judge someone until you've walked in her shoes. And he's not easy, as you know."

He looked at the ceiling and grunted. "Understatement."

"He just needs better discipline, and Jadyn, Katie's sister, seems to be up for the task. I talked to them both while I was driving home and they've already got one of the cottages set up for a little daycare, with all the safety precautions. It could be the best thing in the world for Bash, and Marcie, and...you."

He snorted. "What do I have to do with it?"

"Daddy?"

He glared at her. "Don't."

Her eyes flickered and she picked up the wine again. "Look, the sooner she's steady on her feet—financially and as a mother—the sooner you'll be free of your guilt and responsibility."

Would that ever happen? "I guess," he said, pushing

up to start cleaning off the table. "All I know is you're amazing."

"Oh!" She stood, a hand to her chest. "Where did that compliment come from?"

"My heart."

She gave a low chuckle and came up behind him at the sink, wrapping her arms around him and resting her cheek on his back. "You were so good with Bash, you know."

"If by that you mean I didn't hand him off to a stranger and run, then, yeah, I survived. And so did Bash. Barely. He does like the water, so, in that way, he takes after his father."

He felt her stiffen ever so slightly.

"It's okay, Liv. I can talk about him."

"I know you can. Is that why you seemed upset when Bash called you Daddy?"

"No, I was just..." He turned off the faucet and looked straight ahead, out the dark window. "I don't like that name."

"Why?"

"Let's put it this way: I don't like being *called* that name."

She inched away, coming to his side. "Well, you will be someday, right? Unless you want your kids to call you Pops or..." Her voice faded. "You do want kids, right, Deeley?"

"No, I don't," he said without hesitation. "I wasn't kidding when I told you that the other night."

"Boy, Bash did wreck you today."

"I decided that long before Bash. He just iced my decision cake."

She stepped away, her coolness palpable. As he suspected, this wasn't going to be a fun talk. She was obviously great with kids and no doubt wanted a few, but it wouldn't be with him.

"Why not?" she finally asked, going back to the table to get the rest of the dishes.

"I've seen too much crap in the world," he replied. "It's not a place to bring a child."

She gave a dry laugh. "Then the species would die out."

"It won't. But I'm afraid the Deeley line dies with Connor."

"Why?"

There was enough force in her voice to make him turn and look at her. "Because I don't want kids, Livvie. That's just it."

She stared at him, processing that, a frown tugging. "For absolute certain?"

"For absolute certain."

Nodding slowly, she reached for the empty wine glasses, silent as she brought them to the sink.

"Deal-breaker?" he asked, surprised at how hard his heart was pounding.

"You want the truth?"

Did he? Because he was half in love with her already, and didn't want to break any deals. "Yeah."

"Yes. It's a deal-breaker," she said quietly, putting the glasses in the sink. "But who knows?" she added with a forced laugh. "A few more months hanging around Bash and I may agree with you."

In other words, she'd already given up her dreams of marrying some super successful Type A business mogul who'd give her the kind of life she had growing up. And as far as kids? Maybe she'd give up *everything* for him.

He couldn't let that happen. Deeley wasn't worthy of her. He knew it, and she would eventually, too.

Chapter Ten

Eliza

"Thank you, Noah." Eliza lifted her cup of cold hibiscus tea, dropping cash in the tip bin that rested on the tea hut counter.

"It's cool, Eliza," he said. "You're the owner. You don't need to tip."

"Technically, Teddy's the owner, and it's my pleasure. You've turned this beachfront hut into a money-maker for us. You and your dad are planning to hold another pizza pop-up in a few days, right?"

"Oh, yeah. The last one was so successful, how can we not?" He dragged a cleaning rag over an already spotless counter. "This time Papa Luigi is going to make a few pies. Like two pizza titans coming together."

"He and your dad are getting to be good friends, aren't they?"

"They really are," he said, his expression intent while he set up new glasses and refilled the tea.

She studied him as he worked, waiting for the perfect time to tell him what she'd come down here to say. But she took a moment to marvel at how much this young man had changed since he'd arrived with a chip on his shoulder and distrust in his eyes.

He'd relaxed into life on Sanibel Island, and he'd forgiven Claire for her decision to give him up for adoption to parents he'd lost in 9/11. His father's arrival had sealed Noah's new attitude. Now, as Claire, DJ, and Noah formed a family bond in a house they'd decided to rent for the next few months, he seemed downright happy.

And anxious to find someone else to talk to, based on the number of times he glanced past Eliza.

"Not sure who you might be looking for, but if it's Katie, we're having our weekly Shellseeker Cottages staff meeting in a few minutes, right there." She pointed to one of the rattan tables he'd taken to setting up on the sand in the mornings to encourage coffee and tea sales. "Barring an unforeseen housekeeping or Harper emergency, she'll be here."

"Thanks for the info." He gave her an easy smile, one that drew attention to his handsome face and cleft chin. "Or a Jadyn emergency," he added. "Haven't seen as much of Katie since her sister arrived."

"Hey, I know the feeling," Eliza said on a laugh. "Haven't seen much of my sister since you and DJ arrived."

He tipped his head in concession.

"'Sokay," she added. "I'm glad the three of you are having such a great time finally getting to know each other. It's a happy story."

"Thanks, Eliza. We're having fun."

"Good. We want you to stay. And to that end..." She drew out the last few words to make sure she had his attention. "I'd very much like it if you'd come to the staff meeting that's about to start."

He lifted his brows, a little skeptical. "Is it really a meeting? I usually hear more laughter than, you know, business discussion."

"What can I say? We have fun at work. Teddy asked me what I could do to help her improve the whole business a few months ago, and one of the things I initiated was an informal, but informative, weekly meeting. Roz and George fill us in on what's going on at the shell shop, Katie is our person who is in and out of the cottages, and Teddy and I report on reservations and vacancies." She waited a beat and leaned in. "And we would very much like you to come in and report on things at Shellseeker Tea and...Pizza?"

He chuckled at that. "I know you call this place the tea hut, but we can't exactly call it a pizza hut," he joked, but his smile faded. "Why do you want me at the meeting? I'm not on the payroll here, not officially. Although I appreciate the under-the-table cash more than you know."

"That's why I stopped by before the meeting. I would like to change your status at Shellseeker Cottages."

"Oh, really? I guess you could get busted for some tax infraction any minute. Okay." He shrugged, that fake careless one he used to drag out a lot when he first arrived. Like he didn't care, like he expected rejection. She and Claire had just talked about how rarely they saw that shrug these days.

"It's not just about a tax infraction," Eliza said.

"Oh?" His frown deepened. "Okay, well I think I can find a good local bar." At her look, he laughed. "To work at, Eliza. Tend bar. My dad took me to get the rest of my stuff and my car in Miami, and, man, gas is expensive. I don't want to freeload off my parents..." His voice faded as he shook his head. "Still can't believe I'm saying that. My parents."

"Then let me add to your happiness and make myself clear. I'm not asking you to leave, Noah. We'd like to officially hire you as the tea hut manager."

His eyes flickered in surprise. "You would?"

"I think we can agree on a salary that will make you comfortable, and you're welcome to bring your ideas for building up this part of the business. I mean, look what you've already done."

"Oh, just added cold-brew coffee and some stuff," he said, trying to sound humble, but his excitement was evident. "You really want...wait. Did you say manager?"

"Yes, I did. Look, you're here every morning to put out beach tables, and back late in the day to put them away in storage. We love that dedication. The pizza pop-up is definitely going to be part of the business going forward, and since it was your idea in the first place, you deserve a slice of the action." She winked. "Slice. See what I did there?"

Laughing, he came out from behind the small counter to give her a hug. "Eliza! I'm stoked!"

She gave his broad shoulders a squeeze, so pleased with this decision.

He drew back, trying to hide his emotions. "Seriously, I'm really grateful."

"I hope you don't work so much you don't have time to work on that novel."

"I already started it," he said. "And I can write at night."

"Awesome. We can finalize salary and benefits after the meeting, which starts in fifteen minutes, right there in the world's prettiest conference room." She turned to point at the sand and spotted a familiar figure. "Oh, Livvie! I wasn't expecting her this morning."

Her daughter gave a wave, and it was...not as enthusiastic as usual.

"I heard you were down here harassing the help," she joked when she reached them, but even that quip sounded like something was wrong.

"Hey, you." Eliza reached out to give her a hug. "I feel like it's been so long since we talked."

Olivia inched back and threw an "is she crazy" look to Noah. "You were in my store yesterday, Mom. You bought a seriously cute pair of oatmeal jeans and an off-the-shoulder top and denied that it was for a date with Miles."

Eliza narrowed her eyes, then threw a look at Noah. "You didn't hear that."

He held up his washrag. "A bartender—er, *manager*—never talks."

"Manager? So you said yes?" Olivia asked, her eyes bright.

At his surprised look, Eliza answered for him. "He did, and sorry, Noah. We don't keep secrets around here."

"Secrets are overrated," he joked. "Can I get you some iced tea, Livvie?"

"Yes, please," she answered on a sigh that most people might not even hear, but the sadness in the sound instantly alerted Eliza.

"And we have just enough time for a chat," she said, putting her arm around Olivia's shoulders. "Come and tell me about how it went at the store yesterday after I left."

They meandered through Teddy's gardens, inhaling the scents of basil, rosemary, and her beloved hibiscus flowers that went into her signature tea. After a minute, they settled on one of their favorite stone benches to share their tea and a view of the Gulf.

"So, big success on the soft opening of Sanibel Sisters?" Eliza asked.

"Yeah, yeah, it was great."

Nope, that didn't sound quite as high energy as what Eliza would expect from a woman who'd longed to own a clothing store since she was a child. And not nearly as excited as she'd seemed to be yesterday when Eliza and Claire stopped in to visit. Maybe she was just tired from the stress of the whole thing.

"You had a ton of customers when I was there," Eliza said.

"There were lots of regulars coming back in to see what we've done with Sarah Beth's store—oh, and she sent roses. Wasn't that sweet?—and, yes, it went well."

"That's good, honey. Marcie only seemed a little overwhelmed." Eliza searched her daughter's face for clues, knowing sometimes that it was better to wait than pepper her with questions. She'd get to the heart of the matter, in her own time, generally with a subtle dig or a sarcastic crack.

"Marcie was fine until Deeley showed up with Bash," she said dryly. "Then she got so angry and out of sorts, she had to leave."

"Angry? Was Bash his usual, um, adorable self?"

"Actually, he was pretty mellow, but there's only so much you can do with a two-year-old in a clothing boutique. Oh! Did you hear the news?"

"That we're running a teenie-tiny daycare in Slipper Snail?" Eliza asked.

"That's right. You did just tell Noah there are no secrets on Shellseeker Beach."

"None," Eliza agreed. "Yes, we heard all about it, and Teddy and I gave our approval. No more than two kids, though. Then all Jadyn is doing is babysitting. We can't run a childcare center on this property, or we'll have the city council breathing fire down our necks, not to mention child services."

"I totally get that," Olivia said. "But it's a huge help and a great solution. Because God knows Deeley doesn't want to step in and help, even if I'm doing this *all* for *his* friend's widow."

Was *that* the giveaway comment? Strange. Helping Marcie had been Olivia's idea, not Deeley's.

"I thought he took Bash yesterday afternoon and had him down at the cabana," Eliza said.

"Until Bash threw a fit and then he brought him back. It was late enough in the day, so that was okay."

That was okay. Eliza heard the emphasis, and the subtext that said something else *wasn't* okay.

"And then he made me an amazing steak dinner, with good red wine and a salad."

And *that* should have been okay, too. Eliza waited one more beat.

"And then he announced that he never wants kids."

Eliza flinched. "Oh, boy."

"Or girl, apparently." She curled her lip. "Yeah, like it's not happening. Ever. He didn't really say why except some vague, 'The world's a bad place and I've seen it all, Livvie,' that sounded like weak sauce to me."

"You think it's Bash? He's a challenging child—not that it's Bash's fault— but that could sour a less-than-experienced potential father on the whole thing."

"Maybe." She took a deep drink of her tea and stared out at the water. "He asked me if it was a deal-breaker and I told him the truth."

Eliza knew her daughter well enough to know what that truth was. "That you definitely want kids."

"Mom, I've seen so many forty-something go-getters who thought they were too busy or too important or too fulfilled. My old boss's boss, Nadia? Perfect example. Empty hole where a family should be." She shook her head. "I won't be one of them. I'm only thirty, but I don't want to give up this dream."

"I don't blame you," she said, putting an arm around Olivia. "You know, it's early days with Deeley."

"I know, but..." She gave a tight smile, not wanting to say what she was obviously feeling.

"You really care about him, don't you?"

She nodded, her eyes brimming. "But I will either have to uncare, or give up a dream. I don't know what to do."

"Hang on, let me check this text," Eliza said, reaching to her pocket when her phone vibrated. "This could be that reservation from—" She let out a soft squeal of surprise. "Oh! Nick Frye. Wasn't expecting him."

Olivia chuckled. "I never got used to you hearing from celebrities."

"Celebrity," she corrected as she read his message. "Nick was really my only truly famous client when I was a talent agent. And he's a great friend. And..." She lowered the phone and beamed at Olivia. "He and Savannah are coming here to visit! And they're bringing the baby, of course. And the suitcase I left in their guest house when I thought I was only coming to Sanibel Island for a day or two."

Olivia's shoulders sank. "Even he, a god among men, rich, famous, and perfect, wanted a baby."

"Don't make the world about you," Eliza chided softly, leaning into her. "You know Dylan was the result of a one-night stand between strangers. It could have ended up so differently."

"But they're happy and in love and living in a beach-front mansion in the Keys."

Eliza angled her head, not able to argue with those facts. Nick had given up his high-profile Hollywood career and moved to Florida, married Savannah in a televised ceremony on the beach, and was basically the happiest, most stable and together man who ever held a Screen Actors Guild card. "I always said he cracked the code."

Olivia slid her a look. "This is supposed to make me feel better?"

"Actually, Nick might make you feel better."

"He's *taken*, Mom."

"No, that's not what I meant. But if Deeley sees how Nick Frye is with little French Frye—"

"They don't really call him that, do they?"

"Dylan," she amended. "But that's kind of his unofficial nickname. And Nick is a great father, one who might help Deeley see fatherhood differently."

"Unlikely, but I like your optimism, Elizabeth Mary. When do they get here?"

"Tomorrow night. They're driving up from Coconut Key. I'll put them in Bay Scallop. It's one bedroom, but spacious and the guests who were staying there just told me they have to check out two days early." She popped up, seeing Teddy, Roz, George, and Katie on their way to the staff meeting on the beach. "I have to tell everyone."

Olivia looked up at her and held her hand up, obviously not done yet. "Am I overreacting, Mom?"

"No, but you might be prematurely worried about something that won't matter. Deeley is crazy about you. He could change his mind."

"But I'm thirty. Tick-tock."

"Deep breaths, Livvie Bug," she said, leaning down to kiss her daughter on the head. "These things have a way of working out."

Olivia curled her lips, but then brightened. "Oh! Can Nick Frye do an appearance at Sanibel Sisters? Like, just a meet-and-greet? Sign some flyers? That would bring oodles of women to the store! With the baby and Savannah." She gave a clap, already bouncing back to her go-getter self. "Imagine the press coverage!"

Eliza wanted to say no. Nick was incredibly private. But it felt so good to see Olivia joyous again, she just crossed her fingers.

"I'll ask him, I promise. Something tells me that Teddy's going to want to have a party, Roz is going to want to have him do the same kind of appearance at Sanibel Treasures, and Katie's going to go nuts getting their cottage ready."

"Noah and DJ will probably name a pizza after him, and Jadyn will recruit their little boy for her daycare," Olivia laughed. "Then Deeley will want to hang a signed picture on the cabana wall to entice customers."

"Oh, Deeley's going to spend time with Nick, for sure," Eliza said. "We'll make sure of it."

"Like I said, Mom, nice optimism. But I doubt a little 'joys of fatherhood' lecture from a man who made his living as an *actor* is going to change Deeley's mind. The truth is, I'm going to either have to pull back and stop falling in love, or give up on the dream of motherhood."

Eliza just stared at her, sensing both those things

were impossible. But she *was* an optimist, and refused to change.

"Come on, Liv," she said. "Let's go share the Nick Frye news with the team."

Chapter Eleven

Katie

I t felt like all of Shellseeker Beach was vibrating with
the news that a celebrity of Nick Frye's magnitude
was coming to stay. Well, everyone but Jadyn was
excited. She was entirely focused on dragging furniture
around Slipper Snail, triple-checking that plastic covers
were over all the outlets, and setting up two separate play
areas for Harper and Bash.

"You know what I need?" she mused, tapping her
chin as she surveyed her tiny kingdom. "An area of stimu-
lation, and an area of peace."

"From what I hear about Bash, he's not going to be a
regular in Area Two." Katie put a hand on Jadyn's shoulder, still not used to a lot of physicality with her sister,
even though it seemed more natural with each passing
day. "Relax, Jadyn."

"I'll calm him down," she said confidently, ignoring
the advice. "One of my classes last semester was about
the relationship between oral language development and
behavior. From what I can guess, with that mother of his?
Bash isn't learning to communicate clearly, and that's
why he's acting out. I can help him."

She stared at Jadyn for a moment, truly stunned. Was

this the same girl who used to cut class, day drink, and once filled in "extreme shopping" as her sport of choice on a college application?

"What?" Jadyn demanded when that look lasted too long. "I know you have to call this 'babysitting' for official reasons, but I'm not going to sit here on my phone while those kids chew blocks and color. I'm going to help them be better humans."

"Better humans?'"

"Yes, Harper is an A-plus human already," Jadyn said quickly. "She'll help me with the wild one. But I don't want her to be bored. I'm adding music to the curriculum and will ask Eliza to come by as a guest speaker. She was on Broadway, did you know? Harper loves to sing and dance."

Katie just laughed and shook her head. "You do what you want to do, Auntie Jay-jay. The kids will love it. And they'll love you."

Jadyn's smile grew tentative and her whole expression softened, as if she was waiting for Katie to say something like, "And I love you, too."

No, Katie wasn't there. Not yet. Maybe not ever.

"Hey, I gotta work," Katie said quickly, covering the awkward beat of silence. "But I'll stop by later and check in on your progress."

"Great. Oh, a call. Hope Marcie's not backing out." She reached into her pocket and pulled out her cell, then her eyes widened and she snagged Katie's arm. "It's Dad."

Katie stared at her.

"Do you want to talk to him?"

"You said he doesn't know you're with me."

"But we could tell him."

"You tell him whatever you want, except where I am, Jadyn. I'm not ready. Not for...any of this." She stepped toward the door, heat burning her cheeks. She wasn't lying—this was all too much for her. Getting close to Jadyn, talking to her dad. Where could that even go?

Only one place. To Massachusetts. She was not going to give in and drag Harper into that world. This one was too nice.

"Just stay and hear his voice, Kay," she said as she touched the screen. "See how it makes you feel."

Katie let out a noisy exhale, frozen in place as the screen lit up.

"Hey, Daddy."

Daddy? Since when did she call Katie's father Daddy?

"There's my girl." Her father's familiar voice boomed, even from the small phone mic. "Haven't heard from you in a few days. How's Mexico?"

"It's..." She searched Katie's face, their gazes locked. "It was really nice, but now I'm in Florida."

"Florida? What are you doing there?"

She didn't answer for a long time, still staring at Katie with a plea in her eyes.

"Jadyn?" he asked when too much time passed. "You still there?"

"Yes, I'm here, Dad." She moved the phone away and

mouthed, "Please let me tell him. You can listen. You can hear everything. He's worried about you, too."

She just slowly shook her head.

"Sorry, Dad. I got distracted. And, yes, I'm great, but I don't have much time." She glanced around the room. "I'm working on the final project for my Early Childhood Development class."

"That's terrific, Jadyn. You keep your nose to the grindstone and stay safe. Where are you, anyway? Miami? Palm Beach? One of my clients has a place in Naples if you want to stay there."

"I'm in..." She lifted her brows, asking for permission not to lie.

Katie gave a nod, though it was one of the toughest nods she'd ever given. Life had been good without her family, and she just wasn't ready to give up the independence—or share her daughter.

"Sanibel Island," Jadyn said.

"Oh, nice place. The Carlsons have a beautiful house on Captiva that they only use at Christmas. Right on the water, too. Nice place with a boat in the back. I'm sure they'd love for you to stay there and I know they keep a staff there year round."

"That's okay, I'm good. Staying safe and focused on getting that teaching certificate."

"I am so proud of you, Jadyn. And so is your mother."

Really? Katie almost rolled her eyes. Brianna wasn't dying of the indignity of her daughter working as a teacher?

"Thanks, Dad. I gotta go. I'll do a better job of keeping in touch, I promise. Love to Mom!" She tapped the phone to disconnect the call and gave Katie an intentional look. "I wish you'd let me tell him I'm with you, Kay."

"Not yet. Let me think about it some more."

"Okay, but you heard him. We could go have a fun getaway at the Carlsons' Captiva house," Jadyn said, brightening. "Want to? We could bring Harper and let her swim in what I'm sure is a dream pool."

"And let her think it's normal to live like that and pay for a staff to run a house you go to once a year for a week?" She heard the bitterness in her voice and hated it, but she didn't want that life to encroach on this one. She'd done such a good job of keeping them apart.

"She doesn't have to know that," Jadyn said with remarkable gentleness. "I just thought it would be fun. And you can hear that Dad's not a monster."

She notched a brow up. "He was when he wanted to send me to Europe and give up my child for adoption. I can't forgive him for that."

"Maybe you can," Jadyn said. "Just like maybe you can forgive me, and even my mother."

She let out a soft groan, the weight of what Jadyn was asking her to do just too much right then. "I have to clean. I'll zip out when school gets out, pick up Harper, and bring her here. Olivia said she'll bring Bash around the same time."

"I can get Harper at school," she said. "All you have to do is put my name on the pick-up list and—"

"No, no. It's fine." She backed toward the door. "I'll see you later."

As she hustled to the storage unit for her cleaning supplies, the echo of Katie's father's familiar voice haunted her every step.

Jadyn was trying to open a door. And Katie? She could feel her whole body ache with the effort of clinging to the knob, digging her heels in, and refusing to let that door swing open. How long could she hold out?

Hours later, the question still nagged at Katie, but all the stress and exhaustion and worry faded away when she saw Noah leaning on her car in the parking lot as she hustled toward it on her break.

Except for the staff meeting this morning, when all the excitement was around his announcement as the newest hire—and the pending celebrity visit—she'd barely seen Noah since Jadyn arrived. Even though she was late, she slowed her step to just drink in the sight of him, from broad shoulders in a thin white T-shirt to board shorts showing off tanned legs and beat-up Wayfarers on his feet. His thick dark hair was messy, with sunglasses stuck on his head.

But the best part of Noah Hutchins—and there were many good parts—was that blinding smile that led her right to him.

"What are you doing here?" she asked easily as she approached, grinning back at him.

"Some might call it stalking," he said. "Others might say I'm just a boy determined to see a girl I know has to leave at one thirty-eight to get in that car line. Can I come with you?"

She laughed as she reached him, fighting the urge to just wrap her arms around him and pull his warm body into hers. They just weren't quite there yet, however. Close, though. They'd been so close to that point.

But then Jadyn arrived and everything between them seemed to slip back to the easy friendship they'd developed since he showed up in Shellseeker Beach.

"You want to sit in the car line in eighty-five degrees and get scowled at by the vice-principal because kindergarten parents are never supposed to be late?"

"More than anything." He broke the barrier and put a hand on her shoulder, his touch warm and gentle and so, so welcome. "I'm an official employee now, which means I get legit breaks, and I'm taking mine now, with you. If you don't mind."

"I'd love it," she said, clicking the lock with her key fob.

"Want me to drive?" he asked, notching his head toward the steering wheel. "I'm not scared of vice principals. I was on a first-name basis with all twenty-two of them."

She smiled, loving that he could joke about his rough upbringing. She'd always liked that when she got under his gruff exterior, she found a man with humor and heart. That had only increased since he'd gotten so close to his birth parents.

"Yes, please." She handed him the keys and darted around to the passenger side, climbing in with a sigh of relief. "That car line alone is hot and boring and..." She smiled at him and decided to break down the invisible wall a little more. "I've really missed you."

He paused in the act of turning the key in the ignition, sliding her a slow look with a heart-stopping smile. "What's that music to my ears I hear? Katie admitting she missed me?"

She laughed and gave him a playful punch in the arm. "Nothing to admit. Just the truth."

He held her gaze for a minute and finally turned on the car. "I get that you're spending time with Jadyn. How's that going?"

She gave a very noisy, slightly dramatic sigh. "It's...going."

"What does that mean?" he asked, reminding her that Noah wasn't like other guys—not that she had much experience with them. But he listened and cared, two traits she found so very attractive.

"She's changed, I'll give her that. She's much nicer, easy to hang out with, and really seems to have her act together. Honestly? She's like a different person and I like her."

"So what's the problem?" He turned the car onto the main road and threw her a glance. "Other than the fact that she's keeping us apart," he added with a wink.

"I feel bad ditching her at night and leaving her to hang out alone in her cottage. But you're right, that's not the problem."

"Spill." He snapped his fingers. "I love to help other people solve their problems."

Chuckling at that and how sweet he could be, she settled deeper into the seat. "She hasn't told my dad where I am, but I think it's just a matter of time. Now he knows she's on Sanibel Island. How long until he puts two and two together and comes up with Katie?"

"And that's really a problem for you." It wasn't a question, because she'd told Noah everything.

"I listened to her have a conversation with my father today," she told him. "It was the first time I'd heard his voice in five and a half years."

He flicked his eyebrows at that, but stayed silent while she put her thoughts in order, another thing she appreciated about him.

"It wasn't easy," she finally confessed—as much to herself as to him. "It was a little scary, to be honest, and it felt weird."

"Did it make you realize how much you missed him?"

"Not really. It made me realize how scared I am to lose Harper to their world. I know you see Jadyn and she seems perfectly normal, but, Noah, you can't imagine what that kind of money does to people."

"I imagine it gives them a ton of freedom, nice things, and less stress."

And it makes them selfish and entitled, she thought, but didn't want to sound small by saying that out loud. "It's a strange way to grow up," she said instead. "All those maids and cooks and multiple homes. It's not what I want for Harper."

"They're not trying to take her and raise her, are they? Have they said that? I mean, you're a twenty-five-year-old independent woman. They can't do that." He glanced at her. "Can they?"

"Not legally, of course not. But they can lure her."

"Nah." He flipped his hand. "That little thing is un-lurable. She won't stray far from the Mommy Legs she loves to hide behind."

Katie laughed, knowing that was a little bit true. "Turn here. The school's down on the left," she said, eyeing him as she realized how good it felt to talk to someone about this. "What do you think I should do, Noah?"

"I think you should..." He flinched like he wasn't sure he should speak freely. "I don't think you want my advice."

"I do! I just asked for it. I totally respect and trust your opinion."

"Thanks. Well, you have to take my opinion with the caveat that I was raised without a family. It was, as you know, the one thing I wanted more than my next breath most days. So, I don't think having one that wants you is a bad thing, No matter the size of their bank account or mistakes they may have made in the past that they now regret, family is...important, and it's better to have one than not. Or at least," he added quickly, "a relationship with them, if not a day-to-day living situation." He waited a beat, then asked, "Did that make sense?"

Silent, she stared straight ahead, her throat so tight she didn't tell him where to turn, but he figured it out by the trail of minivans and SUVs backed up in the right lane. As he got in the end of the line, he reached his hand over.

"But I wouldn't blame you if you didn't listen to any of that, Katie."

She took his hand in both of hers, pressing it for the warmth and strength she got from him. "I'm afraid you're right, and I'm scared."

"Don't be scared." He ran his thumb over her knuckles, the tender gesture folding her heart in half.

"Thank you," she said softly. They stared at each other for a long moment, a few heartbeats passing in silence. The longer they looked, the tighter her chest got, and the more she wanted to lean across the console and just kiss him right then and—

A horn blared and made them both jump.

"Whoa," he muttered, looking ahead and seeing there were about seven car lengths between him and the car in front of him. "Whoops. Breach of car line protocol. No doubt I'll get called into the principal's office."

She laughed, letting the adrenaline rush of the moment pass. "When you get to that next turn, right after the flagpole, go right. The kindergartners will be over there."

He followed the instructions, quiet, and she looked down at her hands, wishing she were still holding his. Everything in her wanted that, and longed for the connection she'd just felt. She needed it so much.

"Noah," she said softly.

"Yeah? This is the turn, right?"

"Oh, yes, this is it. Get in that other line and we'll see her in a minute." She swallowed some nerves and forced herself to finish the thought. "I want to ask you something."

"Anything. I apologize in advance if you don't like the answer."

"I think I'll like the answer."

He looked at her, curiosity in his dark eyes.

"I just wanted to say that I don't think that Jadyn being here should be a deterrent to our...seeing each other," she finished shakily.

"Of course not," he said. "And now that I'm fully on Shellseeker staff, we'll see each other a lot."

But that wasn't what she meant. "In fact, Jadyn could babysit Harper for me some night," she powered on, undeterred. "And then we could go out."

He tapped the brakes to avoid hitting the car in front of them, a slow, sly smile pulling at his gorgeous mouth. "Are you asking me out, Katie Bettencourt?"

She laughed, a little nervous. "I've never done that before, but...yeah. I'm asking if you'd like to go out with me."

"Just so I'm clear, you mean on a date?"

She bit her lip, knowing deep in her heart that was what he wanted, but was he teasing or was he going to turn her down?

"That is what I mean, Noah."

He dropped his head back and blew out a long and noisy breath. "It's official."

"What is?"

"I have gone from being the unluckiest guy in the universe to...a date with Katie Bettencourt. How does that even happen?"

"Stop it." She jabbed his arm, but he snagged her hand and squeezed.

He looked her right in the eyes and pulled her hand to his lips to press a kiss on her knuckles. "Yes."

Just then, someone tapped the hood of the car, stealing their attention and making them both laugh.

"Keep it moving, please!" a man barked.

"And you have met Vice Principal Bartram."

Still holding Katie's hand, he waved with the other one and inched the car up the line. As soon as he stopped, the vice principal opened the back door. Harper hopped in and Katie slipped out her own door to help her with the car seat buckle.

"Noah!" Harper froze, a huge smile of surprise and happiness lighting up her little face.

"Package deal today, Doodlebug," he said, turning to her. "Good day at school?"

"A perfect day!" She climbed into her seat, looking at Katie like something amazing and Earth-shatteringly wonderful was happening. "And now I get to go to Auntie Jay-jay's special daycare!"

"Yes, you do." Katie gave her a forehead kiss and latched the belt in one easy move, out of the back and into her seat in less than five seconds flat. "Move it, or Bartram will bite."

Laughing, he eased the car ahead, gave a playful salute to Vice Principal Bartram and got them back into traffic while Harper chattered on endlessly about all the fun she had that day.

As they listened, Noah sneaked his hand back over the console and held Katie's, giving her a secret smile, and somehow making her feel like all was right in the world.

At that moment, it kind of was.

Chapter Twelve

Olivia

"He'll say yes," Camille insisted as she reorganized the jewelry into a new display, showing a slight improvement in her merchandising skills. "Why would Nick Frye not want a store full of women fawning over him?"

"Shh." Olivia pointed to the dressing room where a customer was currently trying on clothes. "I haven't been given permission to say his name. Mom says he's insanely private, especially now that he has a baby."

"Well, he won't bring the baby to a grand opening." Camille pooled the necklaces over some silk tank tops. "Unless you think that would help drive sales."

Olivia bit her lip, looking at the less-than-artful necklace arrangement, which would *not* help drive sales.

She fought the urge to correct Camille, and offer up a lecture about using jewelry judiciously to highlight clothes, and show smart accessorizing, and not confuse the buyer. But her business partner did not like to be told how to do things, Olivia had realized, and she wasn't Marcie, allegedly learning the trade. Anyway, she was a quick study.

She'd be leaving soon, and Olivia would rearrange

the necklaces the way she wanted. More than likely, Camille would come in the next morning, mentally catalog the change, and then never make the same mistake again.

Either way, Olivia got what she wanted—displays that sold merchandise. So she watched in mild horror as Camille pooled four, no, five fine gold filagree necklaces into tiny messes on the silk tops. Not only were they ripe for being stolen, they looked atrocious.

"Actually, I think it would be great if he brought the baby, and his wife," Olivia said, pushing off the side of the counter when she heard the drape of the dressing room rustle. "They have an amazing love story. I just don't know if he'd be willing to tell it to our customers."

"I'll convince him," Camille said confidently, moving to the standing rack to straighten the hangers. "We'll get him all loose and relaxed at Teddy's welcoming soirée tonight and he won't be able to say no."

"I'd let my mother handle the asking, since they're so close," Olivia said, surreptitiously checking the time. Marcie should be in at any moment, and she wanted Camille gone. The two of them were oil and water, and the less contact they had, the better. "You've been here since we opened, Camille. Those heels must be killing you."

Camille lifted a brow. "I was a stewardess—excuse the term, but it was what we were called—in the heyday of Pan Am. I flew from JFK to Heathrow in three-inch spikes and perfect lipstick. I can handle a few hours on the shop floor."

Olivia smiled at that, just as the woman came out of the dressing room, holding a few items over her arm. "Did you fly for Pan Am, really?" the woman asked. "My cousin was a flight attendant for TWA back then and her stories are amazing!"

Camille brightened. "Oh, the Trans World girls were our biggest competition," she crooned. "If your cousin is as pretty as you are, I bet she got the best flights." She held up a hand to stop any response to that. "Yes, that was the way it was, like it or not. I happened to love it," she added, making the other woman laugh.

She might not be the best at merchandising, but Camille could turn on the sparkle and customers loved her. Olivia had no doubt her charm would bring locals and tourists back over and over again, and she knew that was worth every bit as much in retail as a good display.

As they chatted about the designer uniforms and the dashing pilots, Olivia rang up a lovely three-figure sale, which she sensed she could increase by asking the lady, all softened and feeling good from the conversation, if she would like to see the new gold necklaces.

But Camille beat her to it, picking one up from the tank tops and dangling it in front of her new friend.

"Just feel the weight of this," she said. "It would be amazing with that sage V-neck you just bought."

"Ooh!" The woman's eyes flashed as she took it from Camille. "I love the filigree on that. And, yes, that's heavy." So was the price, but the lady didn't even look at the tag as she admired the necklace. "I'll take it, and when I see my cousin at the wedding next week in

Atlanta, I'll tell her it was sold to me by a fellow stew-ardess. And, yes, that's what she calls herself, too."

As they laughed about that, the door opened, and Olivia caught sight of Marcie, dressed in...shorts and a T-shirt? Seriously?

Wanting to head off a discussion over why Marcie wasn't ready for work, Olivia stepped to the side and leaned closer to Camille. "Can you close this sale?"

"Of course," Camille said, too cheery with her new friend to even give a side-eye to Marcie, who slinked into the store.

Olivia met her halfway, giving her a look she couldn't misinterpret when Marcie opened her mouth to pour out whatever excuse she had. She shut it just as fast and hustled to the back with Olivia, at least having the good grace to be aware that there was a customer in the store.

"Bash spilled milk on the skirt and the white jeans were still in the dryer and—"

Olivia held up both hands to quiet her. "It's fine," she said. "I have something you can borrow for today, but couldn't you have found something suitable to wear just in case I didn't?"

"This is a clothing store. I knew I could get something more suitable, whatever that means, right here."

Olivia just stared at her, biting down the fact that it was a clothing store, not a free-for-all.

"Anyway, you didn't want me showing up in my Old Navy cotton T-shirt dress. It's the best I got."

Shaking her head, Olivia headed back into the store. "Hang on, I'll find something for you."

As she passed cubbies, she grabbed Camille's bag, formulating a plan. The two women were close to the front door now, because Camille often walked guests out like they'd come to visit her home. It was a quaint and delightful gesture that customers seemed to like.

Olivia went to the front, timing it so the lady had just left, and she could hand Camille her bag.

"Off with you, my dearest partner."

"Do you think I don't know what you're doing?" One dark brow arched north with amused disdain.

"I know you know what I'm doing—avoiding an argument with you and our only staff member. Please? Let me handle her."

"With pleasure. Especially because you were so nice and didn't correct me when I attempted to try some fancy merchandising with the necklaces. Don't think I didn't notice the distaste register in your eyes."

Olivia chuckled. "I am transparent, aren't I?"

"And kind." Camille put her hand on Olivia's cheek. "You're a tough woman, but you've got a gooey center. Don't let her eat you up and spit you out." She patted her cheek. "*Mon Dieu*, to have skin this smooth again. I'm going home to soak in expensive moisturizer and dream of when I was your age so I look fabulous for the movie star tonight."

"Even at my age, I couldn't be as charming as you are after almost six hours on high heels," Olivia said, moved to return the compliment. "Go home and I'll see you at Teddy's tonight."

Camille blew a kiss and headed off, not even wobbling on those stilettos.

One problem down, Olivia pivoted back to Marcie, snagging a pair of cotton pants and a simple T-shirt on the way and eyeing the necklace mess she'd fix once the *other* mess on her hands was straightened out.

"You can wear these," she said, handing Marcie the clothes. "Please do your laundry earlier in the day so this doesn't happen again."

She let out a raspy laugh. "Easy for you to say. You don't have Bash running around like a diaper-wearing lunatic."

Olivia ignored the comment and went back to the floor, because two customers had just come in and were looking at the new offerings in the front.

"Is Sarah Beth here?" one of the women asked.

"She's moved to Amelia Island to marry her high school sweetheart," Olivia told them, "and we bought the store from her. Welcome to Sanibel Sisters, ladies. Are you looking for anything in particular?"

"Well, Sarah Beth," one said, looking dismayed. "We're snowbirds and only see her in the winter, so we didn't know her happy news."

"I have an email address for her if you want to drop her a note of congratulations."

"We'd love to."

"I'll get it. You have a look around. It's a very different store now."

"I can see that," the other woman said. "Allison, look at this maxi dress. It's divine."

"Oh, it's pretty. How much?"

Olivia didn't hear the answer, but she knew the price of that dress wasn't for the faint of heart. As they continued to shop, she went to the back to log onto her computer and get the email address just as Marcie stepped out from the bathroom.

"Oh, that looks nice," Olivia said.

Marcie looked toward the ceiling. "You do love nun clothes."

"Conservative and clean, simple and elegant," she said in a sing-song voice to lighten the familiar awkwardness with this woman. "We have two customers out front who know the former owner. Will you make sure they have whatever they need? I have to get them something from my laptop."

"Sure."

She slipped out and Olivia opened her computer, fighting the desire to run out there and make sure Marcie didn't drive away some regulars forever. Should she be making the first new impression on these snowbirds, who obviously came in often enough to be on a first-name basis with the former owner?

Probably not, but Olivia had to let that little bird fly sometime, right?

Tapping the keyboard, she got Sarah Beth's email and the name of her new store on Amelia Island, wrote it on a piece of paper, and walked back out...to an almost empty store.

Marcie stood in front of one of the racks, and turned, a slight flush on her face.

"They're gone?" Olivia asked.

"I don't think they liked the prices," she said.

What had she said to them? Once again, Olivia bit back the reprimand.

"Well, we are a bit higher than Sarah Beth was," Olivia said instead, stepping to the silk tops and necklaces, channeling all she'd learned in the empowerment training classes. "But the quality of our inventory is better across the board, and that's what we need to gently remind our clientele."

"I guess, but how can anyone tell? I mean, is a hundred-and-twenty-dollar dress *that* much better than one I got at Ross?"

"Yes," she said, looking down at the necklaces as the front door opened again. "And it's your job to show them that."

"Got it, boss. Hello, ma'am. Welcome to Sanibel Sisters. Are you looking for something in particular?"

As Olivia listened to her recite the standard greeting, she could swear there was some sarcasm in the tone, maybe a little—

Hey. *Wait a second.*

She stared at the tank tops with the necklaces. She'd watched Camille lay them out, hadn't she? There had been five, she was certain of it. Five gold necklaces, one on each of these piles.

Now there were three. One was sold to the lady going to a wedding who bought the sage silk top.

So where was the fourth? She lifted the tops, looking underneath, then checked the floor, the surrounding area, and all around the cash register. Could Camille have picked up two to show the woman and set the other one down? She hadn't been anywhere but here and the door.

A low hum buzzed in her chest as she searched and found nothing. It got louder when Marcie came back after the customer went into the dressing room.

"Have you seen one of these gold filigree necklaces?" Olivia asked. "We're missing one."

"No," she replied, sounding overly shocked. "What are they doing on that table?"

At least she knew they didn't belong there, but was the surprise in her voice a cover or was she truly wondering about the table?

Olivia took a quick assessment of Marcie's face, then made a show of looking again, hating that her first thought—her *very* first one—was to consider the possibility that Marcie took one of the necklaces. She'd barely had time to, but where the heck was it?

Camille had to have it.

If she asked Camille, and she didn't have it or know where it was, then her shrewd partner, who already disliked and distrusted Marcie, would have the same first thought. A terrible possibility that Camille would have no qualms voicing.

She wouldn't be wrong. They *couldn't* have a thief in the store.

On a sigh, she rearranged the tank tops and put the remaining three necklaces in a glass display. Not locked—they never locked anything here. But maybe they'd have to start.

Chapter Thirteen

Eliza

"Why do I feel like we're all prepared for a royal visit?" Miles crossed his arms and leaned against the kitchen counter with a wry smile on his handsome face.

"Not royalty," Eliza assured him as she laid out more of the appetizers and checked the time on the large wall clock behind him. "But a dear friend."

"Should I be jealous?" he teased. "After all, this guy is famously a chick magnet."

"Chick magnet?" From the dining area, Noah gave a noisy snort. "You can drop that from your vocab, Miles."

"Really?" Miles looked surprised. "My son once dressed as a chick magnet for a high school Halloween party, and he pinned Barbie dolls to his T-shirt. I thought it was clever."

Noah zipped by, carrying a large metal bucket full of ice and cold drinks, his only response an exaggerated roll of his eyes. He disappeared to the patio where DJ was starting up the barbeque grill, determined to show that his culinary skills extended beyond pizza.

Teddy was out there, too, with Claire and Deeley and Olivia, setting up some chairs in conversation circles.

Roz, George, and Asia were taking some trays of food to the living room. Camille was already settled on her "throne," and Katie was on her way with Harper, having stopped to get Jadyn.

"I think we're all ready," Teddy said as she breezed in, her color high and her silver curls bouncing around her face. "Probably the biggest celebrity we've entertained on Shellseeker Beach since..."

"Teddy Roosevelt?" Eliza suggested.

"Actually, Christie Brinkley stayed here."

"Now that I'd like to see," George joked as he came into the kitchen.

"And Denzel Washington," Teddy continued.

"No!" Asia exclaimed, giving a squeeze to little Zane, who was sleeping in a wraparound sling against her chest. "My celebrity crush!"

"And you should see him in person," Eliza told her. "He came into the agency where I used to work once and he's..." She fanned herself.

Miles lifted a brow. "You're killing me, E."

She smiled up at him, the simple nickname taking her by surprise. Had he ever called her that before? Had anyone? Ben sometimes called her Liza for short, but not E. She liked it. And she was still smiling. And staring, she realized, suddenly looking away.

A little commotion erupted outside when Harper danced up the stairs to the deck, twirling in a brand-new pink tutu, her tiny voice barely audible even through the wide-open sliding doors.

A few of them headed out to greet Katie and her

sister, but before Eliza could go, Miles slipped his hand around her arm and tugged her closer.

"Hang on a second," he whispered, sending yet another set of chills down her spine. "I have a feeling I'm about to lose you for the night."

"I'm not going anywhere."

"You're the de facto hostess who knows the famous guests. I'm just the schmuck who's here as your...what am I here as?"

"Whatever you like." Her voice rose just a little flirtatiously and she was glad they were alone. She loved teasing and flirting with Miles, but wasn't quite ready for all of her friends and family to see that yet.

Not that they didn't already know about this budding romance, but it was still a secret. In her heart, anyway.

"I'm whatever you want me to be. Your friend, your personal private investigator, your boat captain, and your..."

"Date," she said softly, slipping her lip under her front teeth to keep from giggling like a girl at how she felt right then.

"Oh? Okay, then, my night is complete."

She gave in to the laugh. "It doesn't take much to please you, does it, Miles?"

His green eyes glinted as he looked at her, his smile growing. "I'm just hoping for that moment when you're ready."

Her heart tripped. "Ready for..."

"The kiss I'm patiently waiting for." He looked skyward. "How pathetic, huh?"

"Not pathetic at all," she said, putting her hand on his chest, because it felt good and strong and, whoa. His heart was beating fast. For her? "I think you're..."

"Amazing? Intriguing? Slightly desperate but still amusing?" he prompted when she didn't finish fast enough.

"A chick magnet," she teased. "And I'm attracted."

His whole face lit up. "Really?" He inched a teeny bit closer. "Then maybe we should—"

"They're here!" Teddy called from the deck.

And Eliza realized she still had her hand on Miles's chest. "Hold that thought."

"For how long?"

"As long as it takes."

"Go do you, E. I'll be here."

She beamed up at him, sorely tempted to inch up on her toes and plant the first one—the first of many, she suspected—on his lips. But she resisted, and pivoted, heading out to float down the stairs to greet Nick and Savannah.

They met halfway through the gardens, and Eliza had to stop and press her hands to her mouth at the sight of the wee little Dylan wobbling along on his own two feet.

"He walks!" she cried out, which might have been a mistake, as she startled him and he nearly tumbled. Nick instantly saved him, dropping the suitcase Eliza recognized as the one she'd left in Coconut Key for a "quick" trip to meet Teddy Blessing.

"Walking?" Savannah joked as she hustled closer, her

thick brown hair looking even more luxurious than Eliza remembered, her eyes sparking with that natural humor that she exuded in every situation. "More like a drunk leaving a bar after last call."

"But how did he get so big in just a few months?" Eliza exclaimed as she returned the hug Savannah wrapped her in.

"We just had a big one-year birthday party last month in Coconut Key." She added a squeeze and inched back. "We missed you."

"We sure did," Nick said, leaving the suitcase on the path and scooping up Dylan before he took another tumble. "You said two days when you left the Keys." He slid into that wide, gorgeous smile, his blue eyes pinned on her, his hair even more golden from the sun, and his face tanned and relaxed. Fatherhood and married life in Coconut Key was obviously the role of a lifetime for the talented actor, and he was thriving.

"It's been how many months since you left for an overnight visit?" he teased.

"I'd say too many, but every one has been lovely. I've missed you, though." She reached up to hug the broad shoulders of the man who'd been her friend for about fifteen years, when he walked into her Century City office on the cusp of teenaged superstardom, and admitted that his manager was a shark. He was looking for an agent who had her head on straight, he'd said, and heard that Eliza fit the bill.

They'd joined forces that day and shared a mutual

dislike of all things Hollywood, despite the fact that the machine made both of them a good living.

Nick had been her biggest "get" as an agent, and he'd kept her at All Artists Representatives long after she should have left that particular rat race. When he ditched the business to live in the Keys with Savannah and Dylan, Nick and Eliza remained friends. After Ben died and the agency unceremoniously fired her, she'd gone to his beach house in Coconut Key and enjoyed a brief and lovely respite from her mourning.

"Actually, it's been almost five months," she added. "What can I say? I found my place."

"I can see that," he said, studying her closely.

She shifted her attention from Nick to the baby in his arms—although Dylan sure wasn't a baby anymore. "Hello, French Frye! Do they still call you that down in Coconut Key?"

He gave her a drooly smile, showing off a few tiny teeth that had just been starting to make their appearance the last time she saw him.

"Look at that face!" She pressed her hand against his soft cheek and felt an unexpected sting behind her eyelids.

Olivia *had* to have a baby. She had to.

Shaking off the thought, she looked back up at Nick, who looked at her, then Savannah, exchanging silent communication with his wife.

"Eliza!" he finally said. "You look amazing!"

"Thank you!"

"You really do," Savannah chimed in, putting a hand on Eliza's shoulder and fluttering her long hair. "You've gone from stick-straight auburn to wavy strawberry blond. I love it."

"Beach hair," she said, then gestured toward the water. "Sun and sand and a lovely new family."

"You wear it all well," Nick said, scooting Dylan higher on his hip as he glanced around. "So this is the famous Shellseeker Beach you've mentioned."

"It's the most magical place," she said, unable to keep the joy out of her voice.

"It's gorgeous," Savannah said. "I've heard of Sanibel Island my whole life but have never been."

"Then I hope you'll stay for a while. We have a cottage I think you'll like, right on the water. I know that's no thrill for you, and it's much smaller and less grand than The Haven, but you'll be cozy."

"*We* have a cottage?" Nick raised his brows as he lowered little Dylan to the ground and stepped back to grab the suitcase he'd dropped. "So you're really working here?"

"More or less." She gestured them toward the house. "Like I've said in my emails and when we chatted on the phone, Teddy has embraced me as a partner and I'm living in her house, which is right there."

She pointed to the beach house and the now rather crowded deck.

"And we're having a party in your honor," she added on a laugh. "So, sorry if you wanted a quiet first night."

Savannah gazed up at the group and gave a quick wave. "Hello there, shellseekers! We've come for Eliza, and we may take her back."

"Not a chance!"

"Over my dead body!"

"We'll fight you for her!"

The peppering of comebacks made everyone laugh, and sent a warm rush to Eliza's cheeks. "It appears they like me," she joked.

Savannah walked ahead, holding Dylan's hand, moving at his slow pace and no doubt enjoying the oohs and awws over her little boy.

"I'm so happy for you, Eliza," Nick said, slowing his step to look down at her with genuine affection. "I can't believe how good you look. Vibrant and alive and like..." He sighed. "Don't take this the wrong way, but you don't look like you're grieving anymore."

"Not like I was," she told him. "I miss him every day, but my daughter's here, and, I don't know, that makes it easier. And I have these wonderful people..." She swept her hand toward the deck. "And a purpose, and a place, and I even have a..." She stopped herself before she said something insane like "a man" or "a boyfriend" or "a guy I'm dying to kiss."

"You have a...?" He lifted both brows in interest, dragging out the question with a mix of disbelief and teasing.

"Hush." She tapped his arm. "It's nothing. But apparently I've still got it at fifty-three, whatever *it* is." She winked at him, making him chuckle, and they walked up the stairs to the main living level of the beach house.

On the way, she heard her suitcase clunk, sounding like the symbolic ending of her brief interlude in Coconut Key. She'd needed that time, though, she thought as she reached the top of the steps. But she needed this place more. And she was very excited to show her friends this wonderful new world she'd discovered.

"I LOVE THAT WOMAN," Olivia said when she sidled up to Eliza while they cleaned up after dinner and prepared desserts.

"Savannah? I knew you would."

"She's hilarious and smart and you didn't tell me they met when she was working at Starbucks on Christmas Eve. And by met, I mean—"

Eliza held up her hand. "I know the story, Liv. It's got a happy, happy ending, but please don't have a one-night stand with a stranger."

"It might be the only way I get..." She inched around Eliza and looked out to the group talking around the table. "A little munchkin like they have. He's so cute! No, I don't mean his heartthrob daddy. Also, how is that kid so good, but Bash behaves like an actual maniac?"

Eliza laughed. "Don't compare them. Dylan has two parents and an absolutely devoted village of family around him. Savannah's mother, Beck? She's a natural nurturer, so I guess Sav has picked up some tips."

As if she sensed she was being talked about, Savannah worked her way into the kitchen, arms free of her baby for the moment.

Olivia motioned her over to join them. "We're just cooing about your adorable baby," Olivia told her.

"He just went down for a nap in the room decorated baseboard to baseboard in *Frozen*. Talk about adorable. Squeaky-voiced Elsa was right there with me when I put him down and helped me get him to sleep."

"Harper?" Eliza laughed. "She's so cute."

"I gotta have a girl next."

"Wait. He's napping?" Olivia asked, sounding a little shocked. "How do you get a kid so well-behaved?" She glanced at Eliza, her look saying it all—Bash would never nap in this situation.

"Sheer luck," Savannah said. "And I hope it holds out." She put one hand on her stomach and her eyes danced. "'Cause the oven has a fingernail-sized resident."

Eliza gasped and felt her jaw drop. "Really?"

"We haven't told the free world yet," she whispered, "but Nick said I could tell you. And I assume, if you two are anything like my mom and I are, you'd tell your daughter."

"Congratulations!" Eliza gave her a hug, keeping her voice low so everyone didn't ask about it. As she pulled Savannah into her, she looked over her shoulder at Olivia's face and saw something rare: envy.

Poor kid. She and Savannah were just about the same age.

"How far along are you?" Olivia asked, also speaking softly out of respect for Savannah's privacy.

"Just passed two months, so it's early. I'm due in May, and my older sister, Peyton, is due with a baby girl in January."

"Your mother must be excited," Eliza said, remembering what a great, easygoing grandmother Beck Foster was.

"She's living her best life, that's for sure." She wiggled her brows. "Cupid has shot his arrow."

"Still with Oliver?" Eliza asked.

Olivia's eyes widened. "Your mother is in a new relationship?"

"Not brand new, but since my own wedding," Savannah told her. "Oliver, the thunder from down under, who also happens to be my father-in-law, has swept her off her feet. She only comes up for air long enough to steal Dylan for a day and buy more pink stuff for Peyton's yet-to-be-named little girl."

"That's so encouraging," Olivia said, adding a little elbow nudge to Eliza. "See? Love can happen at any age."

"Is it Miles?" Savannah guessed.

Once again, Eliza gasped. She'd worked so hard not to be flirtatious with Miles once their company arrived, but apparently not hard enough.

"Nick whispered to me that I should try and figure it out," she explained. "You must have dropped a hint without a name when we got here."

"I guess I did, but..." Eliza gave a self-conscious laugh. "I'm not even widowed a year."

Savannah playfully scowled at Olivia. "I'm sorry, is it 1822 or 2022?" she asked, making them laugh.

"She's a little hung up on the one-year thing," Olivia explained.

"I'm just getting used to the idea." Eliza leaned in. "Is it that obvious?"

"Not obvious at all," Savannah said. "But I was looking for it, and I knew your daughter had the hunky long-haired dude sewn up."

Olivia gave a dry laugh. "No one is sewing Deeley up, but yeah, we're together."

"Nick figured it out, too, just warning you, Eliza," Savannah said. "And Nick and Miles just took off together, ostensibly to take our bags to a cottage with a name that sounds like something you eat, not sleep in."

"Bay Scallop," Eliza said, glancing out the glass wall toward the beach and imagining that conversation. "All the cottages are named after seashells."

"And speaking of your husband," Olivia added. "He seemed pretty adamant about not doing any public appearances."

"He's done with those," Savannah said. "Although props to Catherine Deneuve in there who practically ooh-la-la'd him into helping out with your grand opening. I'm sorry he won't do it."

Olivia shrugged. "It was a long shot, but I understand he's a very private person."

"The store sounds wonderful, though. We're here for

a few days, so I'd love to come by and destroy a credit card."

"And I'd love to sweep up the pieces," Olivia joked.

"Done and done."

"And I'd love to know what Nick and Miles are talking about," Eliza admitted. "Plus, I really should be the one to take him to the cottage, so excuse me, you two, I'm just going to check on that situation."

She slipped away, leaving the girls to talk, and peeking around the party for any sign of Nick or Miles. She headed downstairs to the path, hoping to find them at Bay Scallop. Her heart felt light, which was probably a result of being surrounded by friends. Not to mention it was another glorious evening on Shellseeker Beach with a palette of turquoise and pink and air redolent with flowers and salt and peace.

Nick was right. She was so happy here. In fact, the only source of any stress in her life was these silly nerves about taking the next step with Miles. She mulled it over as she walked, approaching the cottage deep in thought.

Miles had made his feelings clear, but still she felt scared of the idea of being with him. Really being with him. Being with him in a way she hadn't been in a long, long time, and never with anyone but Ben.

Just as she reached Bay Scallop, she saw the sliding doors open and heard men's voices from inside, both very familiar.

Slowing her step, she listened, just for the sheer joy of knowing two people she truly cared about, two men who most likely would never have met but for her, were talking to each other.

She couldn't make out what they were saying, but the tone sounded serious, not like the laughter and easy banter she expected from Nick and Miles.

Very serious, she noticed as she took one step closer.

Without making a sound, she climbed onto the wooden deck and froze just to get the essence of the conversation, so as not to interrupt something personal.

"I don't mean to speak out of turn," Nick said. "But Eliza is very, very important to me. I've known her for a long, long time and I love her like a sister."

Sweet, Nick, especially since she had him by twenty years. But what was his point?

"I understand what you're saying," Miles replied, his voice somewhat taut.

"Do you, though?" Nick said. "I think it's great that you and Eliza are..."

"Seeing each other," Miles finished for him, the words giving Eliza a kick.

"That's fine. That's great, actually," Nick said. "But she's a truly good person, Miles. Not your run-of-the-mill woman you can mess around with."

Miles chuckled softly. "No one is messing, I assure you."

"I don't want to see her get hurt, that's all."

She was touched by the sentiment, and mature enough not to let it bother her. Nick loved her, and she appreciated the concern.

"Then let me make sure you understand something," Miles said.

She stood a little straighter, leaning in, anxious to hear what he'd say.

"I'm not, oh, I don't know the word in today's vernacular, but I'm not *dallying* with Eliza," Miles said. "I think she's the most amazing woman I've met in years, maybe ever."

He did? She smiled and knew it was time to make her presence known, but she wanted to hear this. She needed to hear this.

"And as far as my intentions?"

Eliza bit her lip, waiting.

"I'm crazy about her, and willing to give her all the time and space she needs, because when she's ready, I'd like to marry her."

What?

Eliza had to put her hand over her mouth to keep from audibly reacting. Did he say—

"Whoa," Nick replied, echoing her own feelings. "That's...fast."

"Oh, I'll bide my time. But Eliza is a gem, and I don't intend to lose her."

"I couldn't agree more, Miles," Nick said. "And if this is the direction things are going, then I guess we better get to know each other even more. We'll definitely stick around for a few days."

"Then let's plan a cruise on my fishing boat," Miles suggested. "Tomorrow night? We'll make another party of it."

"Sounds great. And Savannah's going to love this cottage."

As they talked, Eliza leaned against the wall, closed her eyes, and tried to process what she'd just heard. She was scared to *sleep* with the guy?

Whoa. Sure, she might sleep with another man— someday, in the distant future, maybe—but she would *never* be married to anyone but Ben Whitney. Period. Full stop. *Never.*

But maybe Miles didn't realize that.

Chapter Fourteen

Deeley

As he usually did when Miles hosted a group on his boat, Deeley arrived at his friend's house early to give him a hand with getting ready for a cruise. With the guests visiting from the Keys, plus Claire, DJ, Noah, Olivia, and Eliza, the deck of *Miles Away* would be crowded.

And Miles liked to treat his guests well, so Deeley knew he'd find the man in the kitchen, preparing a small feast of food and drinks.

Sure enough, Miles was up to his elbows making seafood salad when Deeley arrived, opening the door and hustling back to the kitchen while Tinkerbell barked, circled, and licked Deeley's bare calves.

They talked for a minute, then Deeley headed out to remove the canvas covers and fill the onboard coolers with ice. The minute he was on the deck, he felt at home, always as comfortable at sea as he was on land. He stood for a moment at the helm, knowing that at some point in the late afternoon/early evening cruise, Miles would have him drive the boat.

He'd like his own cruiser like this someday, he thought as he stared down the deep-water canal. A boat like this cost...more than he'd have as long as he was supporting Marcie and Bash. Yes, the government helped, but that woman went through money like nobody's business.

Pushing the thought from his mind, he finished storing the covers and wiped down the already pristine banquettes, walked through the standard safety steps, and returned to the house to help Miles bring the food and drinks.

They'd barely finished and popped a cold one when Tinkerbell's endless and excited barks told them the guests had arrived.

Deeley took a deep breath in anticipation of seeing Olivia. Man, he missed her when they were apart for mere hours. He was in deep—deeper than he expected to be with his current responsibilities weighing him down—but she was so willing to help. How could he not love her?

He stumbled a little as he hoisted himself to the dock, and not because the water made his footing unsteady. A *word* made his footing unsteady.

Love?

Not after the way her whole body registered disappointment when he told her he didn't want kids. He'd sensed that a person as loving and giving as Livvie would want her own family. They didn't need to have that conversation to confirm that, but it had to take place. If they were headed toward that L word, and it sure felt like they were, then they had to be on the same page.

The same page? Based on the look in her eyes, they were in different books entirely.

He couldn't give it any more thought, because Miles ushered the whole group down the dock, all of them laughing, talking, and ready for boating fun. Eliza, a regular on this boat, led the way, with Tinkerbell, of course, as close as she could get to her favorite woman.

They were flanked by the movie star, Nick, and his pretty, witty wife, Savannah. No kid, he noticed, but then he seemed to recall when they cooked up this plan last night, Camille and Teddy looked like they might actually fistfight over who got to babysit.

"Welcome aboard," he called to them.

"You know my first mate," Miles said to them.

Nick extended his hand in greeting to Deeley. "Nice work if you can get it," he said.

"The best," Deeley agreed, stepping back so the tall, athletic man could easily step on board. Deeley gave an assist to Eliza and Savannah, who leaped on board right into her husband's arms.

"Do you hear that sound?" she asked.

"Water splashing?" Nick guessed.

"The sound of a child with babysitters."

"Who won the arm wrestling match?" Deeley asked. "Teddy or Camille?"

"They all won," Eliza said. "Plus Jadyn and Harper. They're having their own party and Dylan is in heaven."

"Of course he is," Savannah said, looking around the boat. "His first full sentence is going to be, 'Women love me.' That child is in his happy place surrounded by as many of his adoring fans as possible." She gave an elbow nudge to Nick. "Like father, like son."

Nick snorted. "No more adoring fans for me, as you know. Just one." He gave a kiss to his wife, who grinned.

"One and two-ninths," she whispered, touching her stomach.

Deeley drew back, not having heard *that* news the night before, but Eliza swooped in and started showing them around as Claire and DJ greeted him with a hand-shake and a hug.

"Isn't Noah joining us?" Deeley asked. Ever since DJ had his near-miss with a lightning bolt, the three of them did everything together. It was like they were making up for all the years they weren't a family by being attached at the hip.

Claire gave a sly smile. "Our son has a date tonight."

"With Katie?" Deeley guessed. Then he laughed as he realized how that sounded. "Livvie keeps me updated on all the Shellseeker Beach gossip."

Laughing, they boarded the boat and Deeley turned to see Livvie strolling toward him, her dark hair loose tonight and spilling over tanned shoulders bared by a tank top. She carried a white sweater and wore soft faded jeans that accentuated her long legs and sassy stride.

"Hey, gorgeous," he murmured, reaching to wrap her in a hug.

"Look who's talking," she teased, letting him pull her close, then lifting her face for a light kiss.

"How were things at Sanibel Sisters today?" he asked,

searching her eyes for clues as to how her latest venture—the store and Marcie—was treating her.

"Good," she said. "I closed early since we don't have official hours until the grand opening, but we had a decent sales day."

"No chance you got Nick to change his mind?" he asked under his breath while their guests were touring below deck.

She shook her head. "Nope. He is very private, and quite separated from his former life as a TV star. But it's fine; we'll have a great grand opening and the press will come. I'm spoon-feeding them the Marcie empowerment story."

"And she's okay with that?"

"Absolutely. Unlike Nick, she has no qualms about speaking to the press."

His heart kicked with a sudden realization. "Is she going to talk about Tommy? She's not allowed to—"

"She knows she can't discuss how he died or what kind of assignment he was on. Believe me, that woman wouldn't do anything to rock her government-check boat, not that they pay her much."

"I know. It's paltry considering..."

"Hey." She put her fingers over his lips. "It's working out just fine. A few bumps in the road, but—"

"Like what? I can talk to her. Is she coming in on time? Being nice to the customers?'"

"She's on time. *Nice* isn't exactly her strong suit, but I'm teaching her to curb her tongue. And..." She gave her head a quick shake. "Nothing I can't handle. And let's not talk about her tonight." She looked around, smiling at the small gathering, the gorgeous late-afternoon light off the water, and the gleaming boat where they'd had some of their most fun times together. "I hope you'll get a chance to talk to Nick," she added. "He's a great guy, nothing like you'd expect from someone who had his own hit show on Netflix."

"I'm sure I'll talk to him," he said. "We're going to be out a few hours."

"But...alone. I mean, you two probably have a lot in common."

He lifted a brow. "He was a movie and TV star. I own a paddleboard rental business."

"But you're the same age and he's a...a guy."

Deeley smiled, wondering if she knew just how transparent she was. Of course she wanted him to hang with the guy and hear all about how nothing in the world beat the thrill of being called "Daddy."

He'd been called that enough by Bash the other day. It didn't feel thrilling—it felt terrifying.

"I'll definitely talk to him tonight," he assured her. "Like I said, Miles has the long route planned all the way up and around Captiva."

She inched up on her tiptoes and gave him another quick kiss, then climbed on the boat and joined the party. He took one second to watch her move, the familiar ache of affection only growing with each passing day.

He finally got his chance to hang with Nick Frye much later, after the cocktails and food were enjoyed and put away, the conversation and laughter had finally died down, and the sun had dropped below the horizon.

The temperature went down with the sun and the ladies grabbed light blankets and sweaters, all curled on the banquette together, heads close as they chatted and laughed. Miles was at the helm, starting the ride back to the island, and DJ took the co-captain's chair, fascinated by everything about the boat, asking a million questions of its owner.

"We fish off the stern," Deeley told Nick as he ushered him to the back of the boat. "If you're here for a while, Miles will take you way out for some fantastic catches. Do you fish?"

"A little. My brother-in-law, Val, is an avid fisherman and we go out a lot together. His wife, Savannah's sister, is having a baby in a few months, so she hasn't been going out much on his boat. He hits me up, even though I'm not much of a fisherman."

"So you have a one-year-old and..." Deeley raised his brows as the two of them settled into the swivel seats facing the wake.

"And one on the way," Nick admitted with a laugh and roll of his eyes. "Savannah is the worst at keeping a secret."

"Why keep it a secret? And congrats, man."

"Thank you." His whole face lit up, and Deeley could see why the camera, and a good segment of the female population, loved him. "I'm stoked, I'll tell you. But it's pretty early in the process, and I think you're supposed to wait three months to make it official. I think at this point, as many people know as don't."

"And you have a niece or nephew on the way," Deeley mused.

"Niece. Peyton's having a girl."

"So...lotsa kids."

"It's great."

Deeley eyed him, knowing that this man, who was close to his own age, must have gone through some of the same issues he had. Livvie told him how Nick and Savannah had met, and that a literal one-night stand turned into fatherhood and, now, a new life.

"Is it great, really?" Deeley asked, hoping that Nick Frye would say all the things Deeley needed to hear. Or at least what he suspected Livvie wanted him to hear.

It's the best thing ever, easy as can be, and the kids are no worry at all.

Yeah, right.

Nick looked straight ahead as he considered his response, which only gave whatever he was going to say more weight.

"It's freaking terrifying, man."

Oh, boy. Not what he wanted to hear. "Yeah?"

"It's a *life.*" Nick gave a soft laugh, unaware of what those three words had done to Deeley. That was it, his whole issue, in one stinking sentence. *It's a life.* And Deeley didn't trust himself to be responsible for that. He had a bad track record.

"I mean, the weight of it can be monumental," Nick continued. "Every time I pick that kid up, I think about how much he depends on me. And Savannah, too. We both feel it. He needs us for survival, not to mention to form him into an awesome, productive, amazing person who loves his life and leaves the world a better place. Of course, I want to be there for every single minute and give him everything he needs, from breakfast to college. That's a weight like nothing I've ever felt before."

Nope, this was definitely *not* what he—or Livvie—wanted to hear.

"But that's just the crap that keeps you awake at night," Nick said with another laugh. "The rest of the time it's, you know, diapers and toys under your bare feet in the dark when that kid is screaming bloody murder in the middle of the night. Fun and games, day and night."

Deeley stared at him. Nick stared right back, waiting a few beats, then he threw his head back with a hearty laugh and gave Deeley's arm a punch.

"Just kiddin', bro. It's the single greatest thing that ever happened to me, with the possible exception of..."

"What?" Deeley asked when he hesitated. "Winning some award? Being named *People Magazine*'s whatever they named you?"

"Are you kidding? I was trying to think of a way to describe Savannah. She's the best thing that ever happened to me. A woman with a good heart, a quick wit, a beautiful smile, and a great family who loves you for you are and not what you do? You find that? You don't care about a few sleepless nights, trust me." He inched over. "Your Livvie meets all those qualifications, am I right?"

So right.

"Hey, what's all the boy chatter about?" Savannah joined them, putting two hands on Nick's shoulders and leaning over to kiss his cheek. He took her hand and spun in the chair, easing her onto his lap.

"Nick, did you know that Fabio here used to be a Navy SEAL?"

Deeley laughed at the nickname, but Nick sat up straight, as impressed as most people, which was a reaction Deeley loathed. He always wanted to add, "A Navy SEAL who lost a man," but didn't.

"Dude. And I'm sitting here talking about diapers and...crap to a flipping Navy SEAL?"

"Hey, love me for who I am not what I did," Deeley joked.

But Nick regarded Deeley with unabashed respect, which only cut him a little deeper. "Seriously, man. Thanks so much. For your service and sacrifice. Thank you."

Deeley simply nodded, and looked out at the water. Let them think he was musing about his glory days in the service.

The truth was, he was trying to figure out how he could tell Olivia that her plans had failed. He'd talked to Nick, who felt the same way he did about the magnitude of that responsibility. The conversation only confirmed that the last thing Deeley could ever be was a father.

Chapter Fifteen

Katie

Well, she wanted an official date, and Noah had obliged in every possible way. From picking Katie up—with flowers for her, a teddy bear for Harper, and a bottle of wine for Jadyn to thank her for babysitting —he drove them across the causeway to a beautiful waterfront restaurant in one of the big hotels facing Sanibel.

Not only was it fun to get "off island" and see her home from a different perspective, it was even better to get dressed up, wear makeup, and look across the table at a very handsome man who treated her like a princess.

Conversation was easier than with any guy she'd ever talked to, as they both exchanged more stories about their lives—which couldn't have been more different. But their views on life and people and food and movies and music and everything seemed to align.

Katie wasn't the least bit surprised when he insisted on picking up the check, which she thanked him for with a hug when they stood up to leave.

"How about we take a walk down there?" he asked, pointing to a long wooden dock that jutted out into the still waters of the bay between the mainland and Sanibel Island. "It's a perfect night."

"It sure is," she agreed, but meaning so much more than the divine late October weather.

Taking her hand, they meandered through the upscale hotel and found their way outside to the dock, quiet while they breathed in the salty, warm air and enjoyed the last pink lights of sunset.

"I guess you missed the big boat ride for this," she said as they reached the dock.

"This is better." He gave her hand a squeeze. "And I would have been a fifth—er, ninth—wheel on that one with all those couples. And you missed the impromptu gathering at Teddy's house with a kid they actually do call French Frye."

She laughed. "Jadyn's taking Harper there, so I'll hear all about it," she told him. "And she is absolutely loving this new daycare gig. I honestly think she's serious about being a preschool teacher."

"Why would she lie?" he asked.

"I don't know, Noah. I've simply never seen anyone change so much."

"Claire says DJ is a different man than the one she knew in college, and not just since his near miss with a lightning bolt. People do change, Katie."

She smiled up at him. "People change so much they can call their parents 'my mother' and 'my father.' Think you'll ever call Claire and DJ 'Mom' and 'Dad?'"

"I have started calling her Mom.' Started as kind of as a tease, but..." He lifted a shoulder. "It feels natural. And DJ? Maybe, if they get married."

She gasped. "You think they might?"

"Who knows? They like each other a lot. I've caught them smooching." He winked as he used the word. "But my father isn't a long-term planner, as you know. And Claire's job might be letting her work remotely now, but can that last forever?"

"And she'd go back to New York?"

"I hope not, but..." He gave her hand a squeeze. "Come on, we've talked my new and unexpected family to death. Have you made any decisions about yours?"

"You mean will I let Jadyn tell them where I am?" She let out a sigh. "Not yet. I'm still scared."

"Because you think they're going to swoop in, steal Harper, and whisk her off to Disney World for a personal session with Elsa and...that other *Frozen* chick."

She laughed, but then grew serious. "If I am not there for the moment she meets Elsa, someone's going to die. But it's more than that. I'm just so content here. I like my life, it's simple and reminds me of..." She swallowed, not wanting to continue, but he put his arm around her and led her to the railing by the water.

"Finish," he said. "Please."

"It reminds me of when I was Harper's age or younger, and my mother was alive."

He sighed with sympathy, reminding her again that they'd both lost parents when they were very, very young, which was another way they were similar.

"The memories fade into nothing," he finally said. "I don't really remember anything but scents and sounds, some words, some flashes of time that come and go like a breeze. I might even be imagining them."

She looked up at him, her heart completely softened by the fact that he might be the first person to truly understand.

"I guess you've noticed that I never talk about my mother," she said softly.

"I have," he said. "Would you like to?"

She smiled, getting a little lost in his dark, intense gaze. "Part of me would like to," she said. "The other part would prefer to stand out here in the twilight and be on a date with a boy I really like."

"A boy." That made him smile. "Why can't you do both?" he asked. "I'd like to know about that part of your life, or what you remember. Will it make you sad to talk about it?"

"No, it's been a long time. Everything was so different then. We weren't rich, not like my dad is now. We lived in a fairly ordinary house outside of Boston, and my mother was a stay-at-home mom. Her personality? Well, I guess you won't be surprised that she was very... sparkly. She liked pink and had light hair with curls and always laughed and sang to me."

"Ah, that's where Harper gets it. What was her name?" he asked gently.

"Rose. It's Harper's middle name." She closed her eyes and tried to picture her. Not the lady from the photographs she had, or the one in the snippets of videos that she once found in her dad's office on an old CD. But the real lady, the one in her memory. "Her name was Mary Rose McShay, but she went by Rose."

"An Irish lass."

"Yeah, her family was."

"Where are they?"

She shook her head. "My dad lost touch with them when he married Brianna. I don't think I've seen a cousin or one of my grandparents since I was maybe twelve."

"Estranged families really stink, don't they?"

She nodded, then made a face. "Except I'm doing the same thing, aren't I?"

"Yeah, I guess you are. I didn't think of it like that."

Turning, she leaned on the railing and looked out over the bay, her gaze slipping to the iconic lighthouse at the end of Sanibel. A humble brown structure that didn't look as dramatic or majestic as most lighthouses, it was symbolic of her home. Seeing the light flicker as evening fell gave her a sense of peace. And the courage to share the story of Mary Rose McShay Bettencourt.

"The last hundred or so days of her life were spent in the hospital, a place she was far too familiar with."

"Oh, she was sick. I wondered if it was an accident or...cancer?" he guessed.

"No, she developed a rare blood disease called aplastic anemia. It's essentially bone marrow failure."

"I'm so sorry, Katie." He reached for her, pulling her in.

She nodded her thanks, but her heart and mind had slipped back to the end, when she'd just turned eight years old, allowed to go into that ICU room only once or twice a day. It had been so cold. That was all she could remember, really. Mommy sleeping, machines beeping, and a nurse bringing Katie a warm blanket so her teeth didn't chatter.

She closed her eyes and pictured the room at Mass General, the view of the Longfellow Bridge over the Charles River from the window. She could see the pattern of her mother's nightgown and...and...

She could see Dad, bent over by the bed, sobbing silently.

"My dad cried." She blinked and drew back as this new memory revealed itself. "I'd totally forgotten that. I remember the room, the smell, the freezing temperature, but I'd forgotten that I turned around once and saw my father doubled over and sobbing."

Tears sprang to her eyes as the mental image became crystal clear, slicing her in sympathy for him.

"I've never seen him cry before or since."

"My dad cries at sappy commercials," Noah said, clearly trying to help her through this memory by holding her tight and keeping it light.

"Never," she whispered, still shocked by the memory she'd dredged up.

Noah put a hand on her cheek, tender and warm. "At the risk of sounding like a wanna-be shrink, Katie, how does this make you feel?"

She managed a weak smile, but it faltered as she realized the answer.

"Like I probably broke his heart, too." Tears spilled at the realization. "He was all tough exterior, like a money-making machine. After my mother died, I don't remember him doing anything but working. I don't even

know how he had time to meet Brianna, and get remarried, because he lived in his office. I missed him all the
time."

Without thinking about it, she wrapped her arms
around Noah, taking strength from him, and comfort.

"It's why I did it, you know." She leaned back and
looked up at him, hating that she had to make this confession. "It's why I messed with the worst possible guy—a
person who worked at one of our mansions. I knew he
wasn't the nicest guy, that he got a kick out of being with
his rich boss's daughter. I didn't care. I just...did it."

"To get your father's attention?" he guessed.

"Maybe. I had straight A's, went to Brown, was a
totally good girl, but it wasn't enough to get his attention..." She wiped a tear with the back of her hand on a
laugh. "So much for being on a fun date with a boy I like.
I'm sorry, Noah."

"Don't be. This is working on you," he said, holding
her tight. "Jadyn's showing up is making your subcon-
scious get all stirred up, and you know you have to make a
decision about seeing your dad, or talking to him. You
probably buried all this, right in the sand of Shellseeker
Beach. Now she's here, and you have to dig it up and face
the truth."

"You *should* be a shrink," she said on another mirth-
less laugh.

"Or a writer." He gave her a squeeze. "And if I were
writing this book, you know what I'd want to have
happen?"

"I'd see my dad, forgive him, and move back to

Boston where Harper can live rich and happily ever after."

He looked a little horrified. "I was just going to say that you should let Jadyn tell him she's with you, that you are happy and healthy, and maybe, sometime in the future, you'll see him at a neutral place. Like his friend's house in Captiva."

"That's not very dramatic for a novelist."

"It's realistic."

She nodded. "You don't think I should go back to Boston?"

He gave her a "get real" look. "I just found you, Katie Bettencourt. First real date, first insanely deep conversation, and first..." His breath hitched and he just looked at her.

"First kiss," she whispered. "On my tear-stained face."

"Best kind." He lowered his head and lightly pressed his lips to hers, the delicate, delicious kiss sealing what she knew she had to do.

"Harper was an absolute angel all night," Jadyn proclaimed as she snuggled on Katie's sofa much later that night.

She wrapped her hands around a to-go cup that Teddy must have filled with tea when she sent Jadyn and Harper home to Katie's apartment when their girls' night ended.

"She's such a nurturer, Kay. She was all over that little Dylan, just like she is with Bash. You know what they say in Early Childhood Development classes about super-nurturing little ones? That they have excellent mothers who've taught them well." She lifted the cup. "Kudos to you, Mommy."

Katie just stared at her, feeling her fingers dig into the throw pillow she'd picked up and wrapped her arms around as she prepared to have this conversation.

"Um, that was a compliment," Jadyn said. "Usually followed by 'thank you' or a humble laugh."

"Thank you." Katie barely said the words.

"Okay, then. You must have had quite the date with Noah." She leaned forward. "Do you want to tell me about it?"

She shook her head, trying to find the right words for what she had to say. She'd start with the easy stuff. "Yeah, it was great. We went to dinner and walked along the bay, and had a wonderful time."

"He's a doll, Katie. Great-looking, good heart, and when he calls Harper 'Doodlebug,' I'm just dead, you know?"

She nodded, knowing even more about the nickname than Jadyn did. His own mother, the one who'd adopted him and died on September 11th, called him Doodlebug. But that seemed far too personal to share.

"He's going to be a writer," she said. "A novelist."

She braced for the expected eyeroll, the comment about how he better have a backup plan, and maybe a little judgment for the fact that Noah barely had a high school diploma—let alone one more advanced.

"He'll be a good one," Jadyn said. "Teddy told me he loves to read."

"You talked about him with Teddy?"

"We talked about everyone. Teddy was chatty, and Camille was hilarious. They gave me the scoop on everyone, but I didn't stay to wait for the boating crew to come back. I wanted to, but I thought it was more important to have Harper here at home when you got back. She was sleepy, and I know you wanted her home with you tonight."

"Thank you for that. And for babysitting. She adores you."

Jadyn beamed, a smile that made her hazel eyes look as happy as Katie ever remembered. "Trust me, it's mutual. She's such a firecracker and..." She blew out a breath. "Yeah. I love her to pieces."

They didn't say anything for a few heartbeats, just sat in amicable silence while Jadyn sipped her tea and Katie tried to think of how to say what was really on her mind.

"Teddy told me my aura was a deep yellow," Jadyn said. "Do you know what that means?"

Katie smiled and shook her head. "That you're content? Teddy's aura readings can be a little vague, but she's usually close to the truth."

"She said my essence is...grounded. 'Like soil in the earth.' What do you think of that?"

"I think that's high praise from a gardener like Teddy. There are few things that woman likes as much as the ground and the things that grow out of it or in it. Flowers, herbs, crystals, stones—if it comes from the earth, she loves it. So, yeah." She smiled. "She must like you."

Jadyn propped her arm on the back of the sofa and let her head rest on her palm, staring at Katie. "Bet that's the last description you'd ever think someone would use on me, huh? Grounded."

"Well, people change," Katie said, hearing the echo of those same words in Noah's voice.

Jadyn let her eyes close. "Thank God, you finally believe me."

"I do." Katie squeezed the pillow and leaned forward. "You've changed, Jadyn. And I'm not going to be so small as to hold your old self and your old sins against you."

Jadyn lifted her head, sitting up straight, blinking back tears.

"Katie," she whispered. "I'm sorry I was such a wretched sister. God really made me see that when He dangled death by cancer in my face."

Katie shook her head, not even wanting to talk about that. "I'm sorry you went through that. I wish I'd been there."

Her sister reached her hand out and took Katie's. "You're here now."

"Actually, you're *here*," she corrected. "And I'm glad of it."

They looked at each other, hands clasped, for a long time. Long enough for Katie to take a step through a door that finally felt wide open.

"Jadyn, have you ever seen my...*our* dad...cry?"

Jadyn ran a hand through her waves, thinking. "Why?"

"I just want to know."

"Well, yeah, I've seen him cry. He threw a glass across the dining room once, and screamed at my mother, and bolted from the room. He was definitely fighting tears."

"I don't remember them arguing like that."

She just gave Katie a look, silent—and the guilt punched.

"Because of me? Of my leaving?" she guessed.

"It was hard," Jadyn said. "Hard for everyone."

She exhaled, leaning back. "Was that it? The only time?"

"When the doctor told me I had to have a hysterectomy," she said. "He got pretty choked up. Actually, just walking into Mass General made him a mess."

"It's where my mother died," Katie said.

"I know. He told me."

For some reason, that threw her. She could imagine a lot of things, but her father and Jadyn having a mournful heart-to-heart about Rose?

Jadyn reached for her hand again. "Why did you ask, Kay?"

"I had a memory tonight, of him crying. And it..." She exhaled softly. "Will you call him?"

Jadyn blinked, as if she couldn't follow. "Now?"

"No, I can't talk to him tonight. I don't..." She swallowed. "Let's take some baby steps. Start with a phone call. Tell him you're with me. That I'm happy, healthy, and Harper is, too. Tell him I'm a good mother."

"A *great* mother."

Katie smiled. "I'll let you know when I'm ready for the next step, here or there or somewhere."

"Oh, Katie!" She shot across the sofa and threw her arms around Katie's neck, squeezing. "I'm so happy!"

Katie laughed softly, then lifted both hands and returned the hug. "I'm glad you're here," she said, easing back to look into her sister's hazel eyes, only a little surprised to see tears. "You're a good sister, Jadyn Bettencourt. And a great aunt."

"Kay." She squeezed again. "I love you."

She let the words settle over her like that heated blanket from the hospital she'd remembered earlier that night. No one in her family had ever said those words to her, not since her mother died.

She knew what she should say. She felt the words form in her head, tasted them before they came out.

She should say, "I love you, too, Jadyn." But she couldn't quite do it. Instead, she patted Jadyn's back and squeezed again.

Baby steps. They were all she could take for now.

Chapter Sixteen

Olivia

When Olivia walked into Sanibel Sisters, she heard something rare for the boutique—a man's voice coming through the open door to the back office. She knew Nick and Savannah were stopping by today, but that wasn't Nick. This man's baritone was deep, with a distinct southern drawl, and whatever he'd just said made Camille gasp noisily.

Was she okay?

As she rushed toward the back, Camille strode out of the office, followed by a tall, white-haired man dressed in a plaid shirt and ancient jeans.

"Oh, Livvie, I didn't hear you come in," Camille exclaimed. "This is Abner Underwood, our next-door neighbor who owns the bait shop. Abner, this is my partner, Olivia Whitney. You will never know what Abner just showed me. A secret door!"

She wasn't sure what threw her more—a secret door or the name *Abner*. Olivia assessed the man, taking in a network of lines on his face that said he lived in the sun and never met an SPF he would use. He was at least six feet, at least seventy-five years old, but strong and stable looking, with a spark of warmth and humor in his eyes.

"Hello, Abner."

"Please, call me Buck, ma'am. Everyone does."

Because Buck was less of an eyebrow-raiser than Abner? She smiled at him and shook his hand. "Hello, Buck. I take it you own Angler's Paradise? The bait-and-tackle shop?"

"Oh, that name. It's just known as Buck's 'round here, but my nephew went and changed the name coupl'a years ago." He looked skyward as every word he spoke slid out like buttermilk and honey, all slow and sweet and southern. "He thought it sounded more upscale for the Sanibel tourists. But I opened the place back in '68. Anyone who's anyone on Sanibel Island would call that place Buck's." He gave a big, slightly yellowed grin and glanced at Camille. "Hope you ladies will, too."

"You've been here since 1968?" Olivia's eyes widened. "That's some retail record."

He chuckled. "Well, I started sellin' bait out of the back of my truck and parked it right here on Periwinkle, right between some of the best fishin' holes. Then I put up a shack. Then that got knocked down in a storm, and some developers came in and put up this strip. I bought in early."

"That was smart," Olivia said, already liking this unassuming neighbor. "And what's this about a secret door?"

"It's quite amazing," Camille cooed. "If you push the shelving unit behind the desk, you walk right into the bait place."

"Sarah Beth's late husband was a good friend," he explained. "He worked part-time for me, and he sometimes had to keep an eye on things in here if Sarah Beth had to run out. I'm kind of handy, so I built that doorway to make it easy for him." He gave a smile that wavered with his next sentence. "After he passed, it was sad for Sarah Beth, so I built her the shelves and kept the door. As the new owners, you're more than welcome to seal that up now. I'll do it myself for you but I don't recommend you do."

"Why not?" Olivia asked.

""Cause the door gives you a way to get out quickly, should need be. You're women alone in a store and you should be safe."

"That's very thoughtful, Abner," Camille said. "Assuming no live bait is going to crawl through the opening."

He barked a laugh and looked at her, his gaze warm and amused. "Not to worry, ma'am. I'll make sure the nightcrawlers and grubs stay right where they're put."

"Nightcrawlers?" Camille gave a dramatic shiver, which just made Buck laugh some more.

"They're partial to French blood," he teased, lowering his voice and leaning closer. "Tastes like fancy wine."

Camille's eyes popped, but even she had to laugh while Olivia just watched with no small amount of pleasure. Was this big ol' country boy *flirting* with Camille?

After holding her gaze for a long moment, he nodded and stepped toward the door. "Anyway, you ladies holler if you need anything at all. I'm here all day, so's my nephew. Well, he's technically my great-nephew but no use makin' his head bigger than it already is. But we always send our customers' wives over here so they won't notice their husbands buyin' new poles."

Olivia smiled at that. "We'll do the same, Abner."

"Y'all take care now." With a tip of an invisible hat, he strode out of the store.

"Well, he was nice," Olivia said, heading around the sales counter to check the receipts and log in.

"He really was," Camille agreed. "I can't understand half of what he says, but he's friendly."

"And he makes a good point about an escape route. Take it from someone who was once trapped in the back office of her own store."

Before Camille could answer, they heard a woman's voice outside the glass display windows, and they both looked to see Marcie standing under the awning, on the phone.

"Oh, look who decided to show up on time," Camille said dryly. "And dressed to work here and not at the bait shop."

Olivia wanted to smile at the joke, but the friction between Camille and Marcie was getting old. It would only get worse if she told Camille about the missing necklace, so she hadn't. But one more infraction or the hint of something like that, and she was going to have to make a tough choice.

"I told her that Nick and Savannah would be here today," Olivia said.

"So all you need to get her to come in on time looking the part is to lure her with the possibility of meeting a movie star."

Olivia's eyes narrowed. "She's trying, Camille."

"Trying my last nerve." She gave a quick laugh. "And now I sound like our neighbor, Buck," she added in an exaggerated Southern accent. "I'll get my bag."

"You don't have to leave the minute she shows up," Olivia said. "I'd love for you to be here when Nick and Savannah come in. You liked them both so much."

"I want to, but..." She eyed Marcie, who was tapping her phone madly, then talking again. "Okay. I did promise to show Savannah that Elan collection that just came in. She'd look fabulous in that line."

"Thank you," Olivia said. "Remember that for the grand opening we have several media outlets lined up to talk about our empowerment program."

"Ah, yes," Camille said. "The goodwill gold."

Gold, like the missing necklace, Olivia thought.

Pushing the thought from her brain, Olivia started working on yesterday's inventory numbers while Camille handled a few customers who stopped in. All the while, Marcie chatted and laughed, the thick glass making it impossible to discern what she was talking about.

Whatever, it must have been important, because she was now officially late for work.

Tamping down her temper, Olivia marched to the door and pushed it open, glaring at Marcie, who was babbling high-pitched and fast—and instantly slammed her mouth closed when she saw Olivia.

"I gotta go, sweetie. See you soon!" She stuffed the phone in her bag and looked apologetic. "Am I late? I tried so hard to be early. I didn't miss him, did I?"

Worry crawled up Olivia's chest. "You didn't tell anyone that Nick Frye was coming in here today to shop, did you?"

The blood that faded from her cheeks and the dead silent stare was all Olivia needed.

"Marcie! I told you not to."

"It's just my friend, Kaylie. She's a major, over-the-top, insane Nick Frye fan. All she's going to do is pretend to be shopping so she can see him. I swear!"

"And how many people did she tell?" Olivia demanded.

"I...I...I don't know. Not many, er, any. I promise, she'll be cool. And so will I."

Holding the door open, Olivia searched the other woman's face, ignoring the screaming beast in her own gut telling her that this was *not* working. And what happened the last time she ignored her skeptical gut instinct? She was darn near conned by a liar trying to use her to get to the Shellseeker Beach property.

Hadn't she learned a lesson from trying to "help" the wrong people? Marcie couldn't work here if she couldn't follow the rules. She had to go, as much as that was going to ruin things for Deeley.

Not now, though. The last thing she wanted to do was fire her minutes before Nick and Savannah showed up, probably with Olivia's mother and Claire and Teddy in tow. She didn't need a scene like that, and something told her Marcie could have a temper tantrum as ugly as her son's if she wanted to.

As she stood glaring at Marcie, two more young women walked up to the store and gave quick smiles to Olivia, slipping into the store and nodding when Olivia welcomed them.

"Text your friend back and tell her not to come," Olivia said when the women stepped inside. "And tell her not to tell her friends. And give me your phone, because you are not taking a picture of him."

Marcie drew back, making a face. "You're taking my phone? Like I'm some kind of teenager in detention?"

Because you act like one, Olivia thought.

"Not one picture," she ground out instead. "And text your friend and tell her not to come. I mean it."

Marcie looked past Olivia and her eyes flashed. "Um...kinda too late. Unless you want to tell them not to come in your store."

Turning, Olivia saw two women in shorts and T-shirts practically jogging to the store.

"Marcie! Is he—" The one woman shut up when Marcie gave her throat an imaginary slice with her finger.

"You guys," Marcie said, hustling toward them. "Be cool. Be very cool or my boss will kick you out."

One of them slid a dirty look to Olivia, and flipped her hair over her shoulder. "Free country. She can't kick me out of this store." With that, she powered right in, followed by her friend.

Olivia blocked Marcie from the door. "You keep them in line and quiet, or this is your last day on the job."

"Oh, really? Who'll do all your PR during the grand opening? Who's going to be your poor little single mom that you saved from a life of misery?" She pushed right past Olivia into the store, her voice raised as she addressed her friends.

For a moment, all Olivia could do was stand there and grip the door as fury, frustration, and disbelief rocked her. Was that really how sh—

"Is he here?"

At the high-pitched question from the parking lot, Olivia spotted three more women in their twenties and thirties, all running toward the store. And a few more behind them.

Biting back an angry curse, she spun to go back into the store and get her phone so her mother could warn Nick. But then she saw the very guest of honor himself step out of the coffee shop at the end of the strip center, followed by Savannah carrying the baby, and Mom.

Letting go of the door, she darted toward them, vaguely aware that three more women were coming from the other direction. Any second they'd have an actual Nick Frye mob on their hands.

"Hey, you guys," she called as she got closer, getting the attention of all three adults. "We gotta reschedule. Word got out."

Nick grimaced, making her wonder just how often this kind of thing happened to the man who'd given up the world of superstardom for a quiet married life in the Keys.

"My one and only employee couldn't keep her mouth

shut," Olivia told them as she reached them. "I don't think you want to go in there, Nick."

"Was it the woman you're mentoring?" Savannah asked. "Eliza just told us about that program, and it sounded so promising."

Olivia nodded. "It's great in concept, but I'm afraid the execution hasn't quite panned out. Sadly, I'm going to have to let her go."

"Oh, that's a shame," Savannah said. "As a former Starbucks barista, I just loved that idea. Not to mention that I really wanted to shop. Camille has me jonesing for that Elan line made just for 'summer in the winter.'"

"Also known as cruisewear," Olivia said on a sad sigh. "You'd look amazing in those clothes, Savannah."

"I can handle it," Nick said. "Honestly, once those rabid fans see you, Savannah, they back off. And Dylan is a distraction."

"No." Olivia shook her head. "I can't put you through that. If you want to come back later or..." She lifted a brow. "Or hide out in the bait-and-tackle shop while I get rid of them, we can whisk you in through the secret door in the back."

"You had me at bait-and-tackle," Nick joked. "We need to get something for Val's birthday next week."

"Did you say a secret door?" Olivia's mother asked. "That's intriguing."

She laughed and turned, not seeing any of the fans, who must all be in the store. "Let's hop into Buck's, who is also known as Abner, and just to make things interesting..." She ushered them toward Angler's Paradise. "I think the guy's got a crush on Camille."

Reacting to that with surprise, they slipped into Buck's bait shop and, after explaining the situation, Buck escorted them to a door in the storage room. When it popped open, she was standing in front of her own desk in the back of Sanibel Sisters.

"Thanks, Buck! I'll text you when the coast is clear, Savannah!"

She stood for a moment, listening to what sounded like a throng of women in her store. How could Marcie ignore a request like that?

It didn't matter, she had. And she wasn't sure how Deeley would take it when he found out she'd let Marcie go, but Olivia had to have a spine. Straightening it, she marched to the sales floor to get rid of them all. Including Marcie.

NOT ONE OF them bought a thing. A few of them gave Marcie a hard time, two claimed Olivia was lying about Nick not showing up and said they'd be watching the parking lot, and one had to be escorted out when she tried to tuck a tank top into her purse.

"Nice friends, Marcie," Olivia muttered when they were finally alone, glancing at her phone to see a text from her mother.

Can we come in yet?

"They're not my friends," Marcie said. "I only even

know Kaylie from the bar and that Lilly chick works in the trailer at Eddie's construction site. Whatever, it's over. Sorry."

"But you're not sorry," Olivia said, eyeing her and winding up for the final blow. She'd done more than her fair share of firings, and knew that some went smoothly and others went sideways.

She'd put her money on sideways.

"Livvie?" Her mother's voice came from the back. "Is it clear yet? Dylan is in need of a changing table, and they don't have one in the bait shop."

"Imagine that," Savannah added, poking her head through the door. "Oh, it is clear."

"They were hiding back there the whole time?" Marcie demanded.

Olivia pointed at her, making a quick decision to postpone the conversation until Savannah and Nick had gone. "Behave," she said in her most withering tone.

"Please. I'm not Bash."

Olivia just shot her a look, then went back to greet Savannah and show her where she could change Dylan.

While she did, Nick strolled into the store, and all Marcie could do was stare.

A little resentful that this traitor even got to meet Nick, Olivia seethed and exchanged a look with her mother, who of course stepped forward to show all her class.

"Nick, this is Sanibel Sisters' salesperson, Marcella Royce. Marcie, meet Nick Frye."

"Hi," she said breathlessly, wiping her hand on her

skirt before taking his to shake. "Huge fan, Mr. Frye. When are you going to do another season of *Magic Man*?"

He gave her his classic heartbreaker Nick Frye smile. "When hell freezes over," he deadpanned. "Or my kid is a teenager and I have to escape."

"You and Marcie have toddlers in common," Mom said, coming closer. "Marcie's little boy, Bash, is two. She's a single mom, too. Very admirable."

"Yes, it is," Nick agreed. "I couldn't imagine raising Dylan without the posse we have in Coconut Key." He leaned closer and Olivia could have sworn Marcie swooned. "I hope you're on commission, Marcie."

"I...am. I haven't made much, though."

"Then your luck is about to change." He pulled out his wallet, withdrew a card that was no doubt titanium, and handed it to her. "My wife never shops. She talks about it, loves it, but there aren't a lot of high-end stores in Coconut Key, and she deserves a splurge. Talk her into everything that looks good on her today, okay? And trust me, that'll be everything in the store."

"No limit?" Marcie asked, waving the card.

"Just the sky," he joked, just as Savannah and Dylan emerged from the back. "Knock her socks off, Marcie."

"That's all done." Savannah held her toddler's hand, but he broke free and tore toward Nick.

"Da! Da! Da!" Arms up, he threw his head back in abandon, letting out peals of laughter when Nick scooped him up and buried his face in Dylan's neck. "Come here, Big D! I love you!"

Olivia's heart slipped all over her chest and thudded to her belly as she watched the exchange, gripped by emotions she guessed to be a cocktail of envy and longing and wonder and raw maternal instinct.

Didn't Deeley want that? Didn't he want to know that kind of love? Because she did, desperately.

Her gaze shifted Marcie, who stared with her own barely hidden emotions. Her fangirl gaze had morphed into something else, something sad and lonely. Something that reminded Olivia of why this young woman, despite her rough edges, was standing here. Because her little boy's father was gone, and regardless of how that happened, she was stuck in this role alone.

Pressing her hands to her chest as a wave of sympathy swamped her, Olivia barely heard Nick announce that he and Dylan were headed back to Buck's for some "boy" shopping, and then they would be hitting the beach.

After he kissed Savannah, he reached out a fist to tap Marcie's knuckles. "Remember. No limit. When my wife is happy, so am I."

Her eyes glistening, she just nodded, speechless.

"Now, who is going to send me in the direction of the Elan collection?" Savannah asked.

"Marcie will," Olivia said quickly, before anyone else spoke.

Marcie's eyes flickered in surprise, as if she knew she'd done nothing to earn the honor or the commission.

Olivia got close to her and whispered, "You heard the man: no limit."

"But...don't you want to..." She couldn't finish as she glanced at Olivia.

"Consider this probation," Olivia said. "Show me what you can do."

"Thanks." With that, she squared her shoulders and walked toward Savannah. "Let's start with some basics and add some color, accessories, and a whole lot of gorgeous," she announced to what could be her last customer. Or her best.

Olivia and her mother shared a look, and Camille sighed.

"I hope you know what you're doing," Camille said under her breath.

"I hope I do, too."

Mom put her hand on Olivia's arm and smiled. "You have a good heart."

"Hush," she whispered, hating that she was choked up. "No one should know that. Especially my employees."

Chapter Seventeen

Eliza

It had been a week since their last date, and that was just about all the time Eliza could wait. When Miles asked if she wanted to take another late-night cruise under the stars, she didn't hesitate to say yes.

She'd missed him the last few days while he'd been away on an assignment—once again tracking a cheating spouse—and Eliza had spent more than a few hours wondering what Miles had really meant that night she'd overheard him talking to Nick. In fact, enough time had passed that she'd half convinced herself she'd heard wrong. It was time to find out.

She pulled a light blanket over her legs and stroked Tinkerbell's snoozing head on her lap, loving this moment of rocking in the boat as the sun disappeared after its long day's work and twilight fell over the water.

While Miles dropped the anchor and opened wine, she gazed at the three-quarters moon that hung over the Gulf and the pale-yellow glow of Sanibel's lighthouse.

"I'm sorry I didn't get to say a proper goodbye to Nick and Savannah," Miles said after they'd caught each other up on all that had happened while they were apart. "They're a terrific couple."

"They'll be back. Nick was enchanted by Sanibel, and I saw him scoop up quite a few real estate magazines from Teddy's table of local literature for guests."

He lifted his brows. "He'd buy a place here?"

"You never know. They both loved the vibe, which is similar to the Keys, but really unique, too."

"Definitely," Miles agreed. "But they seem so settled in down there."

"They are, but they have money, time, and freedom, and I think they might like a little getaway for the kid. *Kids*," she corrected. "Another on the way."

"Yes, I heard that wretchedly-kept secret." Pouring them each a glass of wine, he nestled close to her on the long banquette, then tapped his feet on the deck. "There's a better way to use this thing, you know."

"This bench? How so?"

"It's also a tanning bed, not that I do much sunbathing." He looked skyward. "Or it can be a watch-the-stars bed, depending on the time of day."

She took in a slow breath and let the word "bed" play over in her mind.

"It doesn't have to be a sleeping-together bed." He tapped her nose. "Will you relax?"

"Am I that transparent?" she asked on a laugh.

"Like glass, E. And I do sense a tiny bit of stress emanating from you tonight. Step aside and I'll get us more comfortable." He handed her his glass and gestured for her to stand. "Down, Tink," he ordered.

The dog instantly obeyed and moseyed over to the other side of the deck to flop down to finish her nap.

Miles flipped a few latches, reached under the banquette, and pulled out an extension that looked much like a sofa bed.

"Of course, I can stay in the Captain's chair if you'd prefer that."

She searched his face, taking in the angles, the laugh lines, the spark in his green eyes, and the curl of his very handsome lips.

"I'd prefer you right next to me," she said softly, gesturing toward the sunbed. "Let's see some...stars."

He chuckled and produced a few throw pillows for their heads, another light blanket, and set up a table next to them for their drinks.

"I can't tell you how many times I imagined this with you, Eliza," he confessed as they got situated and comfortable.

"You have? Is this your big go-to move with women?"

"I said with *you*, Eliza. I haven't had a woman out here. Deeley a few times, but he doesn't count. He slept up here and I crashed below the times we've gone way out. He's not nearly as alluring as you are."

She laughed at that, sitting up to take a sip of her wine and check out the flickering lights of Sanibel, then letting herself lean back and get even closer to him. "My daughter thinks he's alluring," she said.

"I've noticed. I barely see the guy anymore, he's so smitten."

"Not smitten enough," Eliza murmured, getting a look of interest from Miles. "Has he ever told you that he doesn't want kids?" she asked.

"Not in so many words. He never even told me about Bash, though; he doesn't talk about personal stuff too much."

"What *do* men talk about?" she wondered on a laugh. "It can't be fishing, sports, and work all the time."

"Yeah, it can be." He turned to his side, propping himself up as though he were quite interested in the personal stuff. "So Deeley doesn't want kids and that's a problem for Olivia, huh? Are they that serious?"

"I think they could be. I guess it depends on your definition of serious." She held his gaze, wondering if this was the opening she needed to address what she'd heard. "They really care for each other. I'm pretty sure the L word has been used, or will be. Does that make them serious?"

"Do you think they'll get married?"

There it was—the perfect opening. Now she needed to step through it.

Taking a breath, she asked, "Do you think that's the only place a relationship can go? Marriage or...break-up?"

Awkward, but she wasn't exactly sure how to tell him what she'd heard and ask what he meant. Maybe she could figure it out by his response.

"At their age, yeah. I think so."

She swallowed. "What about at our age?"

His looked a little surprised at the question, but he didn't give anything else away. "I guess it doesn't really change, although kids aren't a question, so..."

"So..." she echoed his tone.

He inched up, ostensibly to get his wine glass but

maybe because he wasn't comfortable with this conversation. Then why did he tell Nick his intentions were to marry her?

As he sipped, he studied her, quiet for a long time even after he put his drink down. She wouldn't be surprised if he announced he could hear her heart, it was pounding so hard.

"Are you asking me what's the end game here?" he finally asked.

"I'm..." She pushed up. "Confused," she finished.

"By me?"

"By something I heard you say."

Both brows shot up. "Really. Could you share?"

She nodded, pulling her knees up to wrap her arms around them, maybe as protection. "I heard you say something to Nick when you were showing him around his cottage. Do you remember?"

It was too dark to see if any color left his face, or even if his eyes showed a reaction. All she could see was a totally expressionless, but handsome, face that gave away nothing.

"Yes," he finally said. "I know exactly what you heard."

"And..." She let her voice raise in question.

He looked down, his broad shoulders moving with a sigh as if he needed a lifeline.

"Were you trying to make him feel better about us dating?" she asked, offering him that lifeline.

"No."

Oh, okay. "Were you just shootin' the breeze, and

being a guy, and—"

"No," he said, drawing the word out and maybe letting a little laugh into his voice.

"Then you should explain what you meant when you said—"

"I intend to marry you."

She inhaled at the words, letting them fall like a thud on the deck, punctuated by the soft splash of water against the hull. For what had to be ten heartbeats, neither one of them said a word, only stared at each other.

She broke the silence. "So you weren't kidding."

"Not something I'd kid about, E."

Very slowly, still holding his gaze, she eased back on the pillow, the weight of his admission almost too much to bear.

"But I certainly didn't want you to know that," he added.

"You didn't? I kind of think I'm the first person who should know."

"Fair enough," he said with a tip of his head, lowering himself next to her, propping his head on his hand again. "I didn't want you to know *yet*."

"When was I going to find this out?"

A smile broke. "When...it happens."

When it happens? She let the words play over her mind. "That sounds like you're pretty certain this is going to take place."

"Eliza," he said on a soft sigh, very lightly touching her cheek. "I don't want to sound like some confident, cocky SOB who expects you to fall into my arms. But this is who I am, a man who is all in or all out. I don't dip my toes and test the waters. I don't dabble and fool around or...or...date strictly to have needs met. Sorry if that sounds crass."

It would be crass if he said he *did* date for that reason, so she just shook her head, not wanting to interrupt this explanation.

"The very first day I met you, I felt something." He looked across the deck to the sleeping Tinkerbell. "We both did, and I know I joke about that, but Tink knew and I...hoped."

She managed a tight breath. "What did you feel?" she asked, trying to put herself in his shoes that day when she came in with a picture of a young Camille and Claire—a sister whose name she didn't even know yet—and asked for help.

"I felt..." He closed his eyes, searching for a word. "Connected. I felt like you had...a heart that I...I wanted to know." He spoke the words haltingly, which only made them more convincing, adding pressure to that heart he wanted to know. "I never met anyone who made me feel like that."

"Wow," she whispered. "I had no idea. I mean, I knew you were attracted to me, and I to you, but—"

"But you were—you *are*—recently widowed, Eliza. And you loved your husband. I was—I *am*—willing to wait for however long it takes for you to be ready to love again. I think I've explained that to you, right?"

He had, but not in the context of...marriage.

"You might have to wait forever," she said softly, hoping the words didn't hurt. "Because, Miles, I don't want to marry anyone else. I married Ben, once and forever."

He looked at her, silent, letting her continue.

"I could maybe have a relationship, whatever that means. I could kiss you. I might spend the night with you. Maybe we'd take a trip together or...or...I don't know. None of those things are off the table, depending on how this goes. But..." She sat up completely to make her point, and he rose, too, never taking his eyes from her. "I won't ever, ever marry another man. I just won't," she said, hearing the vehemence in her voice. "So you should know that, if you're looking for marriage."

"I wasn't *looking* for marriage," he said, taking her hand. "I apparently was looking for you, and didn't even know it."

"But did you hear me? Am I clear enough? I won't, Miles. You have to know that."

"Shhh." He quieted her by cupping her cheek in his hand. "I hear you. I believe you. I do not question you."

"Does it change anything? Do you want to stop seeing me?"

"Do you?" he asked.

"No," she replied without hesitation. "I like you."

"Good, because I like you, too." He drew her an inch closer, but only held her gaze. A kiss felt inevitable, but he merely eased them both back down to the sunbed and pulled the blanket over them.

They heard Tink's feet on the deck, and, no surprise,

she popped up next to Eliza, curling into a ball next to her, making them both laugh.

"But Tink?" Miles said on a soft laugh. "She *loves* you."

THE NEXT MORNING, after falling dead asleep on Miles's boat until the early rays of sun rose over Sanibel, Eliza met Claire for their sunrise walk, only a little late and still dressed in the white jeans and T-shirt she'd worn on her date, carrying her sneakers to their designated meeting place near the tea hut.

That got a double take from Claire.

"Are we doing the walk of shame?" she teased, gesturing at Eliza's outfit. "Either that or you're dressed up today."

"No shame, not technically," she said. "Although this is what I wore last night. Don't judge."

"Not judging a thing, but, dear sister of mine, you better be prepared to spill the details."

Eliza laughed, feeling surprisingly giddy and alert for having spent the night nestled on a sunbed between a strong man and a snoring dog. "There's not that much to spill. I mean, unless Miles wanting to marry me is a detail I should drop."

Claire froze mid-step, spread both arms out as if stopping traffic, and tried to pick her jaw up from the sand. "*Excuse me?*"

Still laughing at the reaction and feeling freakishly

light after the conversation she'd had with Miles last night, Eliza hooked her arm in her sister's and told her all about what he said.

After considering all the facts, like the lawyer she was, Claire pronounced Miles "dear, honest, and a national treasure."

"He's all that, and I can't deny that I love spending time with him," Eliza said. "As long as he knows where I stand on marriage, then there's nothing to break us apart. I actually think it was a super productive conversation."

"But you spent the night."

"I slept on the deck of his boat with him and Tink," Eliza corrected. "The man still hasn't kissed me."

Claire gave her a dubious look. "There's taking things slow and there's glacial. Why not?"

"I don't know, but I'm very comfortable with this pace. I actually think he's going to wait until I've been widowed a year, and then we'll have one big fat makeout session that will leave me with beard burn and aching loins." Eliza snorted. "I know, I sound like a romance novel."

"You sound happy," Claire said, throwing an arm around Eliza's shoulders. "And I'm happy for you."

"And what's happening on your home front these days, Claire? Are you still sleeping in your own room in that three-bedroom house?"

Claire bit her lip.

"What?" It was Eliza's turn to come to a screeching halt. "Are you sharing a room with DJ now?"

"And sneaking out at dawn before Noah wakes up."

She looked skyward. "We're like teenagers."

"First of all, yay. I'm happy for you, too."

"Thanks." She let out a musical laugh. "It's fun."

The understatement cracked up Eliza. "I bet it is."

"And it's not...casual," she added, sighing. "At least it isn't for me."

"Is it for him?"

Claire didn't answer right away. "I don't know. The thing about DJ is he believes only in the here and now, the joy of the moment, the gift of the present. He's not into planning or futures or..." She laughed. "*Anything* like you two talked about last night. Those two men couldn't be more opposite."

"But he's staying on Sanibel, right? He's not talking about going back to California?"

"I think so. He's even mentioned buying Papa Luigi's restaurant when Sanibel's current pizza king retires next spring, but I don't know if that's serious." She pressed both hands to her mouth, her golden-brown eyes glistening with tears of joy. "I do know we feel like a family, and I have never experienced anything like this."

"That is amazing." Eliza slid an arm around her and squeezed. "But what about your job?"

"I'm hanging in there, handling a few cases, billing hours and doing meetings by video. I probably should get back to New York and show my face for real, maybe check on my apartment."

"Or quit your job and sell your place and make things permanent here," Eliza suggested.

All Claire did was moan like she'd seen something

fabulous and coveted it.

"What are you waiting for?" Eliza asked.

"I guess for DJ to feel...secure." She gave a wistful look. "Which might never happen with a man like him."

"If he lives in the moment, you have to make the moment what you want it to be," Eliza said. "Maybe if you sell the apartment, set up a long-distance situation with your job? Maybe that's the support he needs to make the restaurant happen. Maybe then you will be the moment he wants to live in."

She took a deep breath and let it out slowly. "That's very scary with a guy like DJ. But..." She reached over and gave Eliza an impulsive hug. "I like the way you think, sister."

As they parted, Eliza felt the phone in her pocket vibrate, making her frown. "It's kind of early for a call, isn't it?" she said as she reached for it.

"Probably Miles saying he misses you," Claire teased.

She tapped the screen and angled it away from the rising sun to read the text. "Actually, it's from Nick." She frowned and felt her whole heart drop as she read what he'd written, almost able to hear his deep and familiar voice deliver this bad news. "Oh, dear."

"What's wrong?" Claire asked.

Eliza just sighed and closed her eyes. "I have to talk to Olivia," she said, showing Claire the text.

"Oof." She slapped her chest. "Yeah, you better tell her in person." Claire pulled her in and gave her a kiss on the cheek. "You got this, sis."

"It's not me I'm worried about. It's my daughter."

Chapter Eighteen

Deeley

"You are *kidding* me." Deeley dragged his hand through his hair, staring at a breathless Olivia. She'd come marching across the sand to the cabana a minute ago, vibrating while he checked out some customers renting kayaks, then dragged him into the back to deliver her news.

"I wish I were kidding."

"She stole Nick's credit card number and racked up *how* much?"

"Ten grand! She charged ten thousand dollars to the card he happened to mention had no limit." She snorted derisively. "And I handed Savannah over to her. I encouraged the whole thing and let Marcie handle her huge purchase and get commission for it."

With a grunt, he pressed his palms to his forehead, not quite able to even comprehend this. "Why would she do that? After all you've done for her? Why would she bite the hand that feeds her?"

"Because she thought she could get away with it. I guess it was too tempting for her. And now she could go to prison."

Deeley looked up. "Is he going to press charges?"

"The credit card company could," she said. "He got it all taken off his bill and had his accountant do the digging, and they finally found one of the stores she shopped in online—she'd had things shipped to her address in Fort Myers."

"Could this hurt Sanibel Sisters?" he asked, suddenly realizing the ripple effect Marcie's horrible act could cause.

"Well, I certainly can't use her for PR purposes at the grand opening now, can I?"

"Did you talk to Nick?" he asked.

"My mom and I called him together and, Deeley, he was so nice. Savannah, too. I mean, they weren't happy, but they reacted with such class. They've been dealing with this for a few days and even debated telling us."

"Why?"

"Savannah felt bad for her, and they were both worried about screwing up our grand opening, with all the publicity I had planned." Olivia dropped her head back with a moan. "Savannah *encouraged* Marcie that day, Deeley. She told her about how she was a barista and thought she was going to be a single mom. I mean, they connected and then Marcie *stole her credit card.*"

He closed his eyes, tamping down another wave of fury as he rooted for hope where there was none. "Is it possible it wasn't her? Is there any remote chance someone else got hold of that card? This Eddie dude she's mentioned a few times?"

Olivia shook her head. "She used the number to shop online, not the physical card. But she had all the information needed, including the authorization number on the back and his billing address, which she got when Savannah bought all those clothes at Sanibel Sisters."

"Man, I'm sorry, Liv."

"It's not your fault, Deeley. I have to let go of my need to fix things and help people even when I get walked all over in the process."

The pain in her voice cut him in half as he reached for her. "No, Livvie. You are not going to change because a couple of people took advantage of you. You have a good and altruistic heart and I love that about you."

"When did I get altruistic? I used to be a skeptical corporate shark. Now I'm soft in my old age."

He just shook his head. "Don't expect her to come in to work today, Liv. She might get wind that she's been busted, and she won't even show."

Olivia cringed. "You're right."

"I'm going out there right now."

"To her house? Why?"

"To talk to her. To let her know how much trouble she's in. To..." He blew out a breath. "I don't know. I don't know how to undo all this."

"Neither do I," Olivia said. "But I'm coming with you. Can you close up shop for a few hours?"

"Yeah." He wrapped his arms around her again, kissing her forehead. "I'm so sorry I put you in this position, Liv."

"I put myself in it, and she is the culprit, not you."

For a long time, he just stared at her, putting his hands on her cheeks and letting emotions he didn't know he was capable of feeling rock him to the bone. She was so perfect. She was truly the best woman he'd ever known, and he...he...

"I love you, Livvie."

Her eyes flickered in surprise, then she gave a soft laugh. "Now, Connor?"

"When better? I mean it. You're...everything. I love you."

She looked up at him, seconds ticking by as he waited for the usual response. The one he wanted to hear. The expected reply.

But she just bit her lip. "This is probably not the best moment for these, uh, admissions."

"I don't agree. You're proving what you're made of, and I love it. Sorry, but—"

"Don't apologize. I'm just...surprised. And distracted. Let's handle one mess before we tackle anything else."

Mess? The word kicked him. That's what she thought of his confession of love? A mess?

Closing his eyes and swallowing a response, he stepped away, locking up the cabana, still wrecked by the Marcie news and...and that underwhelming response. He stewed about it the whole time they drove through traffic to get off the island, and over the causeway.

While he did, he listened to Olivia call Camille and gently break the news, easily able to hear the high-pitched reaction from the always dramatic Frenchwoman.

But Livvie remained calm, and reasoned, and kind.

She also contacted Miles to get some legal and investigative advice, asking all the right questions and staying clear-headed the whole time. Meanwhile, Deeley had to catch himself from letting the speedometer go up as high as his blood pressure.

Was that because he was furious with Marcie for blowing everything, or because the woman he loved had essentially called their relationship a mess? Why did she feel that way? What could have caused her...*oh*.

Suddenly, he had complete clarity.

"It's the kid thing, isn't it?" he asked as she finished another conversation with her mother, mostly discussing the best way to handle the media she'd lined up for the Sanibel Sisters grand opening in four days.

"Excuse me?"

"The reason you don't want to say...*it*. My stance on kids. Or is it just that you've been burned so bad in the trust department that—"

"Yes," she interjected. "It's the kid thing."

He winced, letting this new information settle over him. He knew it was an issue—he'd seen the disappointment in her eyes when they'd had the conversation.

"I guess I hoped it wasn't that big a deal," he said softly.

"Well, it is."

"Big enough to keep us apart?" he asked, half terrified to hear her answer.

For a long time, she didn't talk, but shifted on her seat and looked out the window. He let her formulate her answer, knowing Livvie didn't just shoot things out without giving them careful consideration.

"Yes," she finally said, the single syllable like a shot to his heart. "So I need to know why, because...well, I need to know. And don't tell me garbage like the world is a bad place or it's crowded or *whatever*."

He could feel her turn to him, but he stared straight ahead, really—*really*—not wanting to have this conversation right now. But she'd demanded it, so now he'd have to come up with some plausible reason other than the truth.

"I don't think I'd be a good father," he said, knowing it sounded weak, but praying she'd buy it.

"Oh, please, Deeley. Do better."

"I don't," he insisted.

"Didn't you have a good father?" she countered.

"I had a great father. I *have* a great father," he corrected. "It's not anything like that."

"Then why?" she asked, reaching over to underscore the question with a touch of her hand. "Why make a sweeping decision that you can't or won't have kids? You're thirty-three. How can you make a decision like that?"

He zipped by a car going too slow. "I just know."

"Well, then *I just know* we're not right for each other," she shot back. "I won't let myself fall in love with someone who isn't right for me. I'm not in this for the short-term good time, Deeley. I didn't uproot my life in

Seattle and move here because you're cute and fun and give me all kinds of hormonal feels. I want more than that, and I won't settle for less."

No, she wouldn't. That much he knew.

He glanced at her, getting a good look. "God, you're beautiful," he muttered.

She threw him an "are you serious" look. "You think that's going to shut me up?"

"I was just thinking that for all the packaging that first attracted me to you, Liv, it's the inside of you that really gets me."

"Deeley—"

"You're so patient and calm, and always willing to go to the ends of the Earth to help someone you love. You're so smart and creative and funny and you know just what to do with Bash and—"

"Deeley! That's not going to work. I need the truth. I need to understand you."

He tapped the brakes as he realized he was kissing eighty. "I'm getting there," he admitted. "I just want you to know that I value everything about you, enough so that I'm going to tell you. It all goes back to Tommy Royce."

"Marcie's husband," she said. "You don't talk about him much, only that one time, right here in this truck, when you told me how he died and that you felt responsible for it. Is there more to his story than that?"

"How can there be any more?" he asked, his voice tight with emotion. "I let a man die under my watch."

"The Navy said differently."

"The Navy wasn't there."

"You said you don't know what happened when that underwater explosion went off."

Of course she was trying to defend him. Trying to make him feel better about his terrible mistakes. That was why he loved her, and why he didn't deserve her...or kids.

He didn't respond as he slowed down near Marcie's house. He stopped before he reached the turn, knowing this whole conversation would either be forgotten or blown to bits once he turned onto the dirt road to her house and the next wave of hell broke loose.

He owed this to Livvie.

Facing her, he looked her right in the eyes. "Until you feel that your decisions, or your hands, or your head are the reason another person isn't alive, you can't understand what's going on here." He tapped his chest with his fist. "Losing Tommy made me realize the unfathomable value of a life, and how fragile it is. You think you know, you give it lip service, but you don't really know until a decision that you've made, a split-second decision that seems like it should be the right one, takes another person's life."

He waited a beat, closing his eyes, wanting desperately to effectively communicate this soul-crushing fear.

"I'm terrified to be responsible for a child's life, Livvie. I'm paralyzed by the fear that I will make one wrong turn—literally or figuratively—and that child will be dead."

When he opened his eyes, she was staring at him in horror. Or disbelief. Or maybe disappointment. Nothing good.

"I know what that feels like," he added. "I can't ever go through it again. Tommy's death nearly killed me. No, dying myself would have been the easy way out."

"I can't imagine," she said softly.

No, she couldn't. "Those months after it happened, I was in the darkest place I've ever been. I relived every second of that mission, over and over and *over*. I never even figured out what went wrong, it all happened so fast. But I set the fuse and it killed my buddy, my SEAL teammate, and the father of that child." He pointed in the general direction of Marcie's house. "It's taken years to get to somewhere you might consider normal. But I still wake up sometimes and see his face, or I look at Bash and know I robbed him of his father, or I think about my own kid...vulnerable and dependent and so, so fragile. I don't trust myself, and that's the God's honest truth. I do not deserve that gift, and I won't take it."

She looked at him, her expression unreadable. Was that disappointment in her eyes? Frustration? Relief? Confusion? He didn't know, but it sure wasn't love.

"Anyhow," he faced forward and shoved the gear into Drive. "You thought I was a bad bet when you believed I was just a beach bum with no money or ambition."

"I know you're not, Dee—"

"I'm way worse than that, Liv. I'm a coward. I live in fear that I'll make one wrong move someday, and it will cost another life. And if that life is my kid's? My very own kid..." He hated that his voice grew thick and nearly cracked, but honestly, falling apart in front of her was the least of his worries. "It's my problem, Liv. Not yours.

Now you've seen my real weakness, and you know why I don't want..." He frowned, looking past her as something on the property moving toward the street caught his eye. Something small and fast and...what the hell?

Deeley squinted into the blinding sun, seeing a tiny body, naked but for a diaper, toddling full force out of the yard to the street.

He threw the door open and started to tear after the kid. "Bash!"

He was vaguely aware that Livvie was right with him, matching him step for step as they ran toward the child, her voice even louder as she screamed for Bash. There wasn't a car in sight, but that didn't make the moment any less horrific.

Deeley reached him first, snagging the crying, screaming, kicking little body and squeezing him into his chest.

"Where Mommy?" Bash hollered through his snot-covered mouth, saliva and tears mixed on a filthy face. "Where Mommy go?"

She was *gone*? Seriously?

Fighting the urge to howl, he forced himself to stay calm and hold Bash with a death grip as he walked back to the house. Livvie was running ahead, no doubt ready to clobber Marcie. But he knew they weren't going to find her.

He couldn't lose it now. He had to stay calm for Bash. He had to hold this kid and love this kid...for Tommy—who deserved so much better than Marcie, a truly pathetic excuse for a mother.

The front door was open and he walked in, nearly retching at the odor of last night's takeout and...cigarettes? She smoked in front of Bash? The playpen was literally broken, and he could just imagine it had finally collapsed under Bash's relentless and destructive attempts to break out.

No more *attempts*. He'd obviously sprung himself.

Livvie stood in the kitchen, dead silent, staring at him. Only then did he realize she held a piece of paper, her face bloodless.

"What?" he asked, coming closer as he lowered Bash to the floor.

"Wibbie! Wibbie!" Bash launched himself toward her, both arms out.

"Hey, baby," she cooed as she lifted him, stroking his wild blond hair. "Are you all right? You hungry, little man?"

He seemed momentarily overwhelmed, then found his thumb and stuck it in his mouth, dropping his head on her shoulder like he'd just let go of the stress of the world.

Holding him close, she slipped Deeley the paper and stepped away while he read what Marcie had written.

Eddie wants to marry me and we're going to Vegas. Please take care of Bash. M.

Deeley searched her face, barely able to process it all. "If we hadn't shown up at that very moment—"

She placed her free hand on his lips. "We did."

All he could do was stare and fight the urge to spiral into a what-if nightmare. Then he shifted his gaze to

Bash, who looked like he'd never leave his Wibbie's strong and secure shoulder.

Livvie just continued to stroke the little boy's head, calm and strong and steady when he needed it most. Deeley had never loved anyone as much as he loved her in that moment.

Chapter Nineteen

Olivia

Who just left a kid like that? It was beyond the pale, and so unthinkable, Livvie had to work to keep her whole body from vibrating while she bathed, fed, and dressed Bash.

Deeley called Miles for legal advice, making sure he shouldn't report Marcie missing to the authorities and verifying that they wouldn't be complicit or in trouble for taking Bash out of his home.

Miles assured them they were simply acting as babysitters, and that the best thing to do was get Bash to safety and give it a few days until they heard from Marcie.

If they heard from her.

The stress had hit the little boy even harder, and he fell asleep in Olivia's arms while Deeley cleaned the place and worked to keep his temper in check.

"I'll pack some clothes for him," Olivia said, standing and shifting the dead weight of a sleeping child. "Then we can take him back to Shellseeker for...however long we have to."

He turned from the sink, looking ravaged from the

experience. "I don't know how to thank you, Liv. You have the grand opening this weekend."

"You don't have to thank me," she told him, leaning over to put Bash in the broken playpen with his favorite blanket. "Anyway, you already told me you loved me."

Finally, a smile. "My timing did stink. You were right."

She took a few steps toward the kitchen and he immediately came closer, meeting her halfway. "No, Marcie's timing stunk," she said, folding into his arms. "Yours was perfect."

He squeezed her a little and kissed her head. "A mess, huh?"

She inched back, frowning. "This?"

"Us. You called us a mess."

"I did?" She shook her head. "I didn't mean it that way, I just..."

"Don't love me back."

"Not true," she replied, barely letting him finish.

He lifted a brow. "Huh? Well, usually in that situation, when one person says—"

She put her fingertips on his lips, quieting him. "The minute I go there, the very second I give in and confess how I feel, I'm finished, Deeley. I'm yours. I'm in it for the long haul. I have never said those words to a man, not ever."

His blinked in surprise, then he sunk a little in her arms. "You were waiting for perfection."

"I'm holding perfection."

"Hardly," he said with an eyeroll. "You're holding...a compromise."

"No, no," she said, shaking her head. "I feel everything for you, Deeley. Every possible feeling. But I have to be sure, and you know I want a family. Are you intractable on that subject? Like, it can't even be discussed?"

"I told you my problem, and ten minutes later, Bash darn near ran into traffic, making my point."

"You can't make decisions based on fear."

He searched her face, thinking. "Like I said, until you know the feeling of having caused a person to lose his life, you cannot understand the weight of it on me."

She just sighed and pulled him closer, resting her head on his shoulder. She did love him, but if she said it—

"*Wibbieeeeeeeee!*" The screech broke them apart.

"Everybody's timing stinks today," Deeley whispered, giving her one more kiss on the head before they went to get Bash.

IT SEEMED natural that everyone gathered at Teddy's that night. When change rolled into Shellseeker Beach like the next high tide, this found family seemed to make their way to their matriarch, Theodora Blessing. And Olivia was eternally grateful for that.

There would be food, tea, love, and laughter, some answers, more questions, advice, and comfort.

Teddy did not disappoint and had all of that in abundance, mostly because she'd been planning a party for the next night to celebrate a successful grand opening of Sanibel Sisters.

There'd be a grand opening the next day, but there certainly wouldn't be much of a "story" for the local papers and television stations Olivia had invited to meet the first trainee in the program she'd so cleverly named Sisters Helping Sisters.

Now what would she tell them?

She had no idea, because all that mattered was this little guy, currently sucking his thumb, nestled in Harper's lap while she showed him a *Frozen* story that she'd memorized so well, it was like she was actually reading it in her very best, most solemn voice.

At five, Harper was twice the mother Marcie was.

Olivia leaned against the doorjamb of the tiny spare room, watching the exchange, smiling every time Bash popped out his thumb and pointed to the page to exclaim, "Elsa!" with joy in his voice.

"He seems content." Her mother sidled up next to her, offering a cup of lemon balm tea that Olivia remembered saying she wanted but forgot to drink. "Are you?"

Olivia nodded her thanks and finally took a sip. "I'm hanging somewhere between furious, overwhelmed, and relieved. Content seems a long way off."

She put her arm around Olivia and gave her a light hug. "I'm so proud of you, honey."

"Proud?" She choked softly. "Ever since I got on this island, I've turned into such a pushover. I used to be the queen of the cynics."

"You're discerning, Liv, not cynical. You were distrustful of Camille, and now you're partners."

"I gave some stranger a chance to date me and found out all he wanted was access to my business and this property," she shot back. "And I dragged Marcie into Sanibel Sisters, and she robbed my customer and one of your best friends."

"With Scott, you were trying to broaden your horizons."

She answered with an eye roll.

"And you never trusted Marcie," her mother continued. "But you were trying to improve her life and give her a chance. You knew she had issues."

"Issues? She left a toddler alone in a house and took off!" She grunted. "My character judgment has gone down the tubes. And what's going to happen to him, Mom? When she comes back from Vegas, she'll have this guy who we don't know trying to be Bash's father. Or worse, someone who'd agree to walk out of that house and leave a two-year-old alone? She shouldn't even be allowed to keep him!"

"Does she have any relatives that you know of?"

She shrugged. "Deeley's talking to Miles about trying to find them, but I don't want to hand him over to just anyone. Neither does Deeley."

"It's a mess," her mother agreed.

At the use of the word, she gave a sad smile, thinking of her conversation with Deeley earlier. "Deeley told me he loved me," she whispered, getting wide eyes and a smile from her mother.

"I could have told you Deeley loves you," she said. "But it's nice to hear it from the source."

"Is it?"

Mom drew back. "What did you say?"

Olivia just stared straight ahead, as silent now as she'd been then.

"You don't?" her mother asked.

"Of course I do, but if I admit it, if I fall for him, if I give up on the idea of children, then...I feel like I lose what I want."

"He might change his mind," she said.

"He might not, and honestly? Is it fair to go into a relationship hoping to change something so fundamental? That feels wrong." Olivia crossed her arms. "I miss Dad so much."

Her mother startled a little at the unexpected admission, then smiled. "He'd know what to do, and he'd know what to say to you right now."

"Dad?" Olivia laughed and imitated his deep voice. "No guts, no glory, Livvie girl."

"And he'd be right."

"There are no guts or glory involved in love, Mom."

"That, my dear, is where you're wrong. It takes guts to give your heart to someone and when you do, the glory is indescribable."

"There you are." Two strong hands landed on Olivia's shoulders, gently turning her around. "How's my girl?"

She looked up at Deeley and nearly melted at the

sight of his lion-gold eyes and the mane to match. Yep, *indescribable*.

She was vaguely aware her mother slipped away with an excuse to check on food in the kitchen, leaving room for Deeley to replace her next to Olivia.

"You mean how's your boy." She notched her head toward the bedroom. "Learning how to 'let it go' with the team from *Frozen*."

He didn't even look. Instead, he stared into her eyes. "Nope. I meant my girl. My woman. My Livvie, my love."

Her eyes closed as she let him pull her into an embrace, and she could practically hear Ben Whitney's voice whispering to her.

No guts, no glory.

Very slowly, she eased back and looked up at Deeley, knowing this was the biggest risk she might ever take.

"Connor Deeley..."

One brow flicked north.

She put both hands on his cheeks, his whiskers rough on her palms, but the look in his eyes so soothing on her heart.

"I love you," she said softly. "*Too*."

Chapter Twenty

Katie

Before she started cleaning the day of Sanibel Sisters' grand opening, Katie rushed to Slipper Snail to be there when Olivia and Deeley brought Bash in. Livvie would be at the store from morning to evening, and business was popping at Deeley's cabana, so they'd agreed to leave Bash with Jadyn for the whole day.

And since it was a Saturday, Harper could be there, too, instead of cleaning with Katie. She and Jadyn—and Harper—had made the plan yesterday, when they spent the whole afternoon poolside at a mansion on Captiva. They'd been waited on by the Carlsons' staff, and had honestly loved every minute of the pampering.

Olivia and Deeley were already in the cottage when Katie arrived, giving Jadyn changes of clothes, phone numbers, special snacks, and a list of instructions that made them sound like, well, like brand-new parents.

"I'm at the cabana all day," Deeley said, and by the way Jadyn bit back a smile, Katie suspected he'd told her that quite a few times. "Just come and get me if he's out of control or has a tantrum or tries to run off."

"He doesn't look like he wants to go anywhere," Jadyn assured him, pointing to the other side of the living area where Harper already had him involved in a game of Hungry Hungry Hippos.

Olivia hovered over him while Harper attempted to explain the game, but Bash just kept

smacking the lever and screaming, "Hippo come out!" followed by gales of laughter.

"No, Bashie," Harper said with the patience of a saint. "We take turns doing this. Watch."

Jadyn gave Deeley a reassuring smile. "Honestly, he's so used to it here, we never have any problems."

Once again, Katie marveled at how Jadyn never wavered from her "preschool teacher" persona in this atmosphere.

"The two of them are a tag team," Katie whispered to Olivia. "You have nothing to worry about."

Olivia sighed and straightened, her hand still on Bash's shoulder, as if she might need to grab him and keep him from taking off at any second. "Thanks, Katie. I sure wish you could come to the opening today. I shouldn't be nervous, but I am."

"I'm sure it will be a huge success."

"And I'm worried no one is going to show or else some media person will come and demand to meet the Sisters Helping Sisters candidate who is currently...in Vegas? Who knows?"

Katie closed her eyes, pained by the thought. "Hey, if your media folks want 'sisters helping sisters,' just send them here. That's what Jadyn and I are doing."

Olivia inched back, clearly considering the idea. "Not a bad plan, Katie. Not for today, but if this whole daycare thing works out for Jadyn? Then we'll have another 'sisters helping sisters' story." She gave Katie a squeeze. "I'm so happy to see you and Jadyn getting along so well."

She looked past Olivia to where Jadyn was letting Deeley give her more instructions. "We really are."

"And your parents?" she ventured, brows lifted. "Do they know?"

"She told them she's with me and I'm fine. That's it for now."

Olivia nodded. "That's good, Katie, really. Now, I better go before Camille has a complete breakdown." She bent over and kissed Bash's little head. "Be good." Another kiss. "Be kind." Another one. "Be calm."

Deeley came over and joined the goodbye, crouching down into Bash's face to tap his chest lightly.

"You get an A-plus in behavior today, Basho, and I'll take you out on the paddleboard again. Remember the water?"

"Water! Water!" He leaped up and started to move, but Deeley caught his shoulders in an easy grip.

"*After* Miss Jadyn tells me you were perfect all day. No tears, no temper, and lots of nappy time."

Katie bit her lip at the big former SEAL calling it "nappy time" and glanced at Olivia, who wore the same expression of tender disbelief.

Deeley gave Bash a few high-fives and a quick kiss, then he stood with a deep exhale, turning to Jadyn. "Remember, I'm—"

"We *know*." She gave him a light push to the door. "Go to work, both of you."

When they finally left, Jadyn shook her head and smiled. "Those two will make amazing parents someday."

"And you are an amazing preschool teacher...*today*."

"Aww. Thank you, Kay." She pressed her hands together and looked down at the kids, who were in a rare moment of complete peace at the game table. "Doing this has made me absolutely certain of my path. I'm so grateful to you and everyone here who's helped so much." She reached out for what would have been a shockingly rare hug a few weeks ago, but they were frequent and heartfelt now. "You have no idea what this time has meant to me."

Katie hugged her back, unexpected tears welling. "Same, sister." She added a squeeze. "And I meant it that time."

"I know you did. And you better get to work, too! Those cottages aren't going to clean themselves."

"You sure? I know it's a long day for Bash, so I'll pop in and out all morning. I can help this afternoon."

"We're good. Right, Harpdawg? On Saturdays we go shellseeking, don't we?"

"Wear your sunscreen and stay close to Aunt Jay-jay, okay?" Katie gave kisses to both kids and grabbed her bag. Outside, she came to a complete halt before she stepped off the deck of Slipper Snail and stared down the path.

Roz and Asia were coming toward her, pushing baby Zane in a baby carriage, with Roz clucking and shaking her head.

"We need a favor, Katie," Asia called. "Can your sister's little babysitting business take one more child for an hour?"

"Absolutely!" Jadyn popped out to the deck before Katie could answer. "We're always open to new students."

Roz gave Jadyn an incredulous look. "He's an *infant*, not a student."

"Hush." Asia waved her off. "I'm dying to go to the grand opening of Sanibel Sisters, and I'm not dragging this baby boy to that."

"Of course not!" Roz said. "Too many germs."

"Germs will make him strong, but I can't shop and truly enjoy the experience." Asia stopped the stroller at the deck, easily lifting the wheels up to the wood.

"I'll watch him!" Roz whined.

"Mother, please," Asia countered, clearly sick of Roz's arguments. "I want some time with you. I want to thank you for all you've done for him, and buy you something special at Sanibel Sisters. And he needs to learn that sometimes mommies shop."

"He's three months old!"

"Never too soon." Asia beamed at Jadyn and Katie, her eyes glinting with sass. "Right, ladies?"

"Absolutely," Jadyn agreed, her fingers wiggling over the baby carrier as if she couldn't wait to pick him up.

"Don't lift him!" Roz said. "Never wake a sleeping baby. He can stay right there until it's time to eat. You'll know the eating cry because it's very high-pitched. If it sounds like, say, you're twisting a balloon, kind of like *wah-wah*, then ignore him and let him cry because he'll go right back to sleep. Don't let him try to get that paci—"

Asia elbowed her mother to the side and got in Jadyn's face, handing her a large bag. "If he cries, loud, soft, or ballooney, change him, feed him, and feel free to pacify him any way you like."

"But he just ate!" Roz cried—which was answered with a look from her daughter.

"I got this," Jadyn assured her. "Clean diaper, a bottle if he wants it, and lots of love."

"That's it." Asia planted a quick kiss on Jadyn's cheek and blew one to the sleeping baby. "We'll be an hour, tops. He may sleep the whole time we're gone."

"But if he does wake—"

"Stop, Mother." Asia tossed some long braids over her shoulders as she put two hands on Roz's back to move her along and end the discussion. "I have no doubt he's in good hands."

And off they went, leaving Katie and Jadyn laughing at them until Bash screamed bloody murder.

"Whoa!" Jadyn spun around and darted inside, then Katie heard Harper cry out. She pushed the little carriage into the house to find Harper with two hands on her cheek.

"He hit me!"

"I'm sure it was an accident," Jadyn said.

"Hippos!" Bash flipped the board, scraping Harper on the arm. That was it. Her patience evaporated as her whole face crumpled into tears and Jadyn scooped Bash up to take him aside and distract him.

"He's so bad, Mommy!" Harper cried out. "Why is he so bad?"

Before Katie could calm her, the baby started to wail. And that was no sweet, twisty balloon cry.

"I'll clean later when they get back from Sanibel Sisters," Katie announced. "You need another set of hands."

"I'm afraid I do," Jadyn said, easing Bash onto the sofa. "Harper, go get that diaper bag on the deck."

"But he hit me twice!"

Bash leaped up and started to jump. "Hippos!"

For a flash, Jadyn and Katie shared a look of total union and sisterhood. It lasted less than a fraction of a second, but in that instant, Katie had no doubt they were sisters. For real and for certain, their minds and hearts aligned.

"Down you go, big boy," Katie said, snagging the bouncing maniac and holding him with stiff arms so he didn't smack her with his wild hands. "Harper, you're not hurt. Get the bucket and the sunscreen. We're going shellseeking while Aunt Jay-jay feeds the baby and puts him back to sleep."

"You're a godsend," Jadyn said. "Thank you."

THE TRIP to the sand was exactly what the daycare doctor ordered.

Katie held tight to Bash's hand and Harper carried the bucket, and everyone was calm and excited. Katie relaxed into the sheer joy of watching a child discover the fun of shellseeking, coupled with the bliss of the moment she just shared with her sister. They'd come so far, so fast, and it was nothing short of a miracle.

"Noah!" Harper called out, and Katie looked up from the collection of shells in Bash's hand, catching sight of Noah jogging down the beach, waving at her.

And then she felt even warmer in the October sunshine.

She straightened slowly, frowning as she simply sensed something was wrong. He looked concerned...and why would he leave the tea hut during this, his busiest hour?

"Hey, Noah," she called. "Everything okay up there?"

He seemed a little breathless, as though he'd run fast to get to them, a sheen of sweat on his brow. "Yeah. No..."

"Look what I found, Noah!" Harper called, holding out a shell. "Not even broken!"

"That's awesome, Doodlebug." He gave her hair a little ruffle. "Can you find one to match it? I need to talk to your mommy."

"'kay!"

"Stay in my sight," Katie called to her, but her attention was riveted on Noah. "Is something wrong?"

He glanced at Bash, who'd dropped to the sand between them to dig a hole with two hands, full concentration on the project.

"Katie," he said, catching his breath as he reached out

his hands and put them on her shoulders. "Someone's come here."

She blinked at him, a tendril of worry wrapping around her heart.

"He stopped at the tea hut and asked for...Jadyn."

Oh. She knew. She already knew. "My father," she tried to whisper but the word caught in her throat.

He nodded, squeezing her tighter, as though he expected her to bolt. Which was exactly what she wanted to do.

"Jadyn told him." Her heart cracked at the betrayal. "I asked her not to. I said tell them I'm okay, but..." A sob welled up, the punch of pain worse because they'd just shared that moment, when all the while—

"No, that's not it at all. One of the staff from that house where you went to yesterday told him. Did you tell someone you worked in Shellseeker Beach?"

She grimaced, remembering the conversation she'd had with the sweet cook who'd made them lunch. She knew Shellseeker and it had seemed innocent...

She sighed. It didn't matter. He'd found her, and at least Jadyn had kept her promise.

She dropped her head back and tried to control her response to the fact that her father was *here*. "This isn't what I want. I don't want to leave here, Noah."

"You don't have to!" He eased her closer. "Listen to me. You're an adult. You don't have to fall back into old patterns because he shows up. He seemed really nice and—"

"He's not."

"People change, Katie. Jadyn has."

"Yes, she had cancer. She changed. But my dad? He hasn't said a kind word to me since my mother died and—"

"Stop it," he insisted, bringing her to complete silence. "I spent my entire life wanting what you had. A *family*. I carried around hatred for people I didn't know and when I met Claire, I wanted to ruin her life the way I thought she'd ruined mine. I was drowning in unforgiveness, Katie, and it didn't do anything good for me."

She stared at him, feeling her whole world slip and slide and disappear. "Harper...isn't going to understand."

"Then you're going to tell her," he said softly. "You're going to show Harper what it means to give someone a second chance and forgive them. He's her family, Katie. Like it or not, your dad and his wife are her family."

"She's here, too?"

"I didn't see her, but listen to me—family is the best gift you can give your daughter, no matter who or what that family is."

The sob strangled her again as she glanced over her shoulder to see her baby twirling in the sand, holding up a seashell and singing, "Let it go!" before tossing it away.

"She's giving you the same advice," Noah whispered. "Let it go, Katie. I won't let anyone hurt you or take you away from me. Let go of the past, babe. You will be happier. You'll be a better mother. You'll be a better person."

"Seashell!" Bash popped up between them and threw a handful of shells in the air, a few of them hitting Katie.

As she stepped back, she glanced over Noah's shoulder and saw a familiar man walking toward Slipper Snail with purpose in his step.

"Ohhh." She pressed her hands to her lips as she squinted at him, a powerful wave of emotion washing over her.

Her father looked a little older, maybe not as fit as he'd been. But it was him, the man who'd raised her—for better or worse. The man who'd provided for her—even though he didn't give her the love she needed. The man who sobbed at his wife's deathbed.

"Come!" Bash yanked her hand. "More shells!"

"Imagine how this kid's going to feel someday," Noah added. He didn't have to finish the thought for her to know what he meant. Bash's own mother didn't want him.

And her father, for all his faults, wanted her, or some piece of her. It was up to Katie to decide how much she gave.

She inhaled slowly and turned once again to Harper.

"Let it go!" she sang again, and Katie couldn't help but smile at the perfect timing.

She squeezed her eyes shut and reached for his hands. "I know you're busy at the tea hut, but can you walk Bash down to the cabana and ask Deeley to keep him for a few minutes? This conversation is too important."

"Of course."

"And I'll bring Harper."

He leaned down to kiss her cheek. "I'm proud of you, Katie."

"Thanks, Noah. For that, and for the advice." She smiled through tears, the weight of the moment pressing down harder than the sun. She took a deep breath, then called to Harper. "Hey, Doodlebug!"

She giggled and waved her shell. "That's what Noah calls me!"

"How'd you like to get the biggest surprise of your life?"

"A surprise?" She gasped like the world had just stopped revolving. Little did she know, it might. "What is it, Mommy?"

"Well..." She reached down and gave Bash's hand to Noah with a smile, then strode toward Harper. "Bash and Noah are going for a walk, and you are about to meet that man right there." She crouched down to get closer to her, but pointed toward her father, who was standing at the end far end of the boardwalk, staring at her.

Very slowly, her father held up a tentative hand in greeting.

"Who is that, Mommy?"

"That, Harper Rose Bettencourt, is your grandfather."

For a moment, Harper looked like she would sway and fall right over on the sand. "I have one of those?"

"You do."

"Oh, Mommy! Everyone has a grandma and grandpa but me! Is there a grandma, too?"

Somewhere, she thought. "There is, but right now, you can meet your grandpa. Do you want to?"

Harper squeaked out a cry, turned, and broke free, running toward him, arms outstretched with trust and love and anticipation. "Grandpa! Grandpa!"

It was as though she'd been waiting for him. And maybe, deep inside, Katie had been, too.

She followed Harper, not running, but drinking in the vignette like she was watching a movie in slow motion. Dad scooped Harper up and lifted her in the air, twirling her around while she let out musical giggles that rang out over the sand.

When she reached him, they just stared at each other for a moment, silent.

She had to do this. She had to be the one. She had to let it go.

"Hey," she whispered, closing the space with her arms outstretched.

He pulled her in for a hug and all she could feel was his heart, hammering like it might come right out of his chest.

"Don't be mad, Kay," he murmured. "I've missed you so much."

Her whole body felt like it melted in the sun, and all the hate and anger and fear spread around her and disappeared.

"I've missed you, too, Daddy."

Chapter Twenty-one

Eliza

Sanibel Sisters hummed with a party atmosphere as the grand opening celebration got underway. Groups of women came and went, shopped and sipped mimosas and nibbled at the festive charcuterie boards Camille had prepared, laughing as they waited in line for the next dressing room.

Olivia rang up sales while Camille worked the room like it was her very own coming out party, clearly in her element. Eliza and Teddy greeted guests at the door and Claire had outdoor duty, encouraging other shoppers at the strip mall to stop by the party.

"Welcome to Sanibel Sisters," Eliza said, handing out a discount flyer to the next lady who came in.

"What happened to Sarah Beth?" the woman asked, a question they'd gotten frequently.

"She's reconnected with her high school sweetheart and moved to Amelia Island," Eliza said. "My daughter owns this store now, along with..." She never knew how to reference Camille, since "the woman who stole my father from my mother" certainly wouldn't fly. Nor would "my sister's mother."

So she just tipped her head and said, "Camille Durant, who is right there, waiting to charm you."

The customer grinned. "I'm happy to be charmed, and so pleased for Sarah Beth. Thank you!"

"Be sure to get a mimosa," Eliza called after her, sharing a quick smile with Olivia.

Of course, her daughter was on her retail game today. This was a big day for the little girl who ran Eliza's Closet when she was ten. Her dream of owning her own boutique officially came true today, and most of the time, Livvie was beaming with pride and joy.

But every once in a while, Eliza caught her checking her phone or the door, and that smile faded a bit.

With Teddy handling the door and a break in the customers checking out, Eliza slipped over to give her girl encouragement and love.

"I say we take a drink every time someone asks for Sarah Beth," Eliza teased.

She made a face, not amused. "I just got a message from the TV crew from that local station. The producer didn't care that our empowerment program is currently on hold. He's sending a reporter anyway. Very slow news day in Lee County."

"That's good!" Eliza said. "You can talk about the growth in retail and how awesome Sanibel Island is and get great PR."

"They want a story, not a store. I don't have anything except leaving Promenade to come here, which wouldn't make my former employer happy, and I don't want to do that."

"The French former flight attendant brings *haute couture* to Sanibel?"

She nodded. "I'll go that route if I have to." She picked up her phone, eyes wide. "Holy heck."

"What is it? More media?"

"No. Katie's father showed up and she had to take Bash to the cabana. Deeley said Noah's giving him a hand and they have it under control, but..." She looked up as the door opened again. "Oh! Look who's here! Savannah! And she brought friends!"

Eliza turned and did a double take at the women walking in, sucking in a soft breath.

"Beck! And Lovely!" she exclaimed, gasping again when she saw a very pregnant Peyton behind them, looking radiant and ready to pop.

Eliza rushed ahead to open the door and throw her arms around the women who'd become friends during her extended stay in Nick and Savannah's guest house on the beach.

"We come to shop!" Savannah announced, hugging Eliza first then turning to gesture to the others. "And I brought friends."

"Oh my goodness! Beck!" Eliza gave a squeeze to Savannah's mother, a beautiful, warm woman who had given Eliza so much hope about the possibilities of change in the middle of life. "How wonderful to see you! And you, little Dylan." She added a kiss to the baby Beck held.

Turning to Olivia, she launched into introductions, hugging each woman as she did. "This is Lovely, Beck's mother." She patted the older woman's cheek, warmed by her constant smile. "Oh, we have a tie-dye top you're going to love."

"You know me so well, dear girl." Lovely gave her a kiss and went to hug Olivia. "This must be your Livvie we've heard so much about."

"You probably don't have much for me here, Eliza," Peyton said. "But I had to come and see you." She rubbed her belly. "I'm growin' a girl."

"I heard! Congratulations. Come in and, oh, meet Olivia!"

As they streamed in, Savannah leaned into Eliza, her eyes twinkling. "We came by private plane," she announced in a hushed whisper. "The perks of being married to Nick Frye."

"How sweet of him to send you here."

She lifted a brow. "He didn't send us, he came along, ready to do whatever media junket you have planned."

"What?" Next to her, Olivia gasped softly. "He's here?"

"He's in the bait shop next door with his father, Oliver, and my brother-in-law, Val." At Eliza's look of disbelief, she added, "He feels completely responsible for what happened."

"How?" Olivia and Eliza asked in unison.

"He thinks if he hadn't told Marcie over and over that there was no limit on his card, she wouldn't have done... what she did."

Olivia rolled her eyes. "I doubt that's true. And anyway, it gets worse. She skipped town."

Savannah gasped. "She's gone?"

"And left her child," Eliza added, trying to keep the disgust from her voice.

"No!"

"He's fine," Olivia assured her. "He's staying with Deeley and me until she comes back. But...Nick. Really? He'll talk to a local TV station?"

"He will, my prince among men. In fact..." She looked to the back. "When he walks through that door from the secret entrance, he'll be a prince among women."

"I can't believe this," Olivia said, then looked over her shoulder. "And here's the TV crew!"

From that moment on, happy chaos reigned. Nick Frye sent a gasp through the crowd and worked his magic for the camera. The local paper came in for part of the interview and snapped pictures while Nick—and Savannah, who stood by his side—chatted about what a great store Sanibel Sisters would be, and that Savannah planned to visit frequently to shop here.

"Will you move to Sanibel, Nick?" the reporter asked.

"It's tempting," he said as a barrage of questions came from the crowd.

Eliza stood with Beck, who was holding Dylan in her arms with the ease and comfort of a seasoned grandmother.

"So you left for an overnight visit and never came back," Beck teased, leaning into her. "Were we that awful?"

Eliza laughed. "You were wonderful. Coconut Key gave me exactly what I needed, when I needed it."

"And how about now?" Beck asked, her green eyes locked on Eliza, curious and warm. "You're doing well?"

"So well," she said on a sigh. "Teddy is like a mother to me, Livvie's moved here, and I have Claire. Oh, did you meet my sister, Claire?"

"I did. She's awesome. And Nick said you've met someone." Beck lifted her brows. "How wonderful, Eliza."

"I met..." She closed her eyes and smiled. "A really good guy who is a dear friend and could be more when the time is right." She elbowed Beck. "Speaking of, how's Oliver?"

"Definitely more than a friend," she said on a laugh.

"Please tell me you're all staying for a little while. Teddy and I have been talking about a little beach blowout tonight to celebrate the new store's grand opening."

"We're on a charter plane," Beck said with a shrug. "We can come and go whenever we like."

Just then, the front door opened and Miles walked in. "Oh, look who's here." Eliza threw a look at Beck. "My, uh, friend."

Beck glanced over her shoulder and gave a secret nod. "I approve."

"Excuse me for one second." Eliza slipped away and went to join him, greeting him with a hug. "Look who showed up to surprise us all."

"Not a surprise to me. Nick texted me when the

plane landed to see if we could go out on the boat this afternoon."

"Look at you, hobnobbing with the rich and famous."

He laughed, the noise and laughter around them disappearing as she looked into his eyes. "I think they're trying to steal you back and get you to Coconut Key."

"And how would you feel about that?" she teased flirtatiously.

"That it would break my poor heart into a thousand pieces and I'll fight them to the death."

"Aww." She nestled closer, looking up at him, a little lost, a tiny bit dizzy. "Never fear, Miles. I'm not leaving Shellseeker Beach."

"Well, Tinkerbell will be happy to hear that."

She smiled at him. "Just Tinkerbell?"

"And her poor, smitten owner." He gave her a hug just as two more men from Coconut Key, Oliver and Val, stepped into the store, in time to razz Nick during his interview.

Eliza chatted with them, then went back to her grand opening duties, unable to wipe the smile from her face.

Chapter Twenty-two

Deeley

By late afternoon, when the last of the board rentals had been returned, Deeley turned to the sleeping kid in the corner, grateful he'd kept the portable playpen at the cabana and even more grateful that Bash had been downright angelic that day.

"Talk about rising to the occasion, you little beast," he whispered, walking over to find Bash snoozing as he had been for almost two hours. Before that, he and Noah had tag-teamed the kid, and wore him out. Except for one little meltdown, handled with lunch, Bash had mostly charmed customers and stayed in his own lane.

Exhausted, but satisfied with his day's work, Deeley dropped onto the bench and grabbed his phone, smiling at the pictures Olivia had sent him.

"What a class act that Nick Frye is," he mused, stunned by the news that the celebrity had flown to Sanibel to help Livvie and Camille get the publicity they so needed to kick off the store's grand opening. "He didn't need to do that," he said, half to himself, half to the little dude in the playpen. "It wasn't his fault your mother..."

He let his words trail off, not even wanting to plant

them in a sleeping kid's brain. *Nothing Bash's mother did was his fault,* Deeley thought with an ache in his chest.

Leaning forward, he pressed his hands on the side of the portable playpen, staring at that tiny chest as it rose and fell peacefully. So innocent and helpless. So utterly dependent on people who let him down.

"Don't worry, bruiser. Your mom's coming back, eventually. Maybe she and Eddie will figure you out." But there was no guarantee of that. In fact, the very thought of some guy he'd never met getting his hands on Bash made Deeley a little sick.

Deeley had always known the future didn't look too bright with Marcella Royce as this kid's mother, but he hoped so hard that she'd come around and get her act together.

Instead, she stole money and took off to elope in Vegas and left a toddler *alone in the house.*

As he sat and stared for a moment, Bash let out a little whimper, then rolled over, his eyes popping open as he woke. Deeley braced for the howl or a leap into the air— Bash always crashed into consciousness, going zero to sixty in a second.

But like everything else today, he was different. Subdued, even. Was he sick? Deeley stood and looked down at him, waiting for whatever would come next.

"Water?" Bash murmured, the first word sounding so deceptively sweet.

"It's out there."

He rubbed his eyes and pushed up, lifting his arms. "Water, Deeley?"

"I don't know, Basho. It's getting late and I'm tired and..." Who the heck was going to take this kid anywhere to have fun again in his life? Who knew what Eddie would ever do for him?

A slow smile pulled at Bash's lips as if he knew what Deeley was thinking. And in that moment, he looked exactly like Tommy. Exactly. Tommy when he wasn't battling demons and hating the world. Happy Tommy, which was about fifty percent of the time. Maybe if he'd lived, those demons would have disappeared and Thomas Royce would have been the world's greatest dad.

But he didn't live, so Deeley owed this kid a ride.

"All right, you monster. You win." Deeley scooped him up and swung him in the air.

"Water!" His eyes got big. "And peepee."

"You gotta go? In the pot?" He heard his voice rise in excitement. "Livvie'll be so proud of you. C'mon. You do what you gotta do in the bathroom there, and we'll suit up and take a fun little ride on the board again."

He put Bash on the ground and walked him into the toilet, crossing his arms and leaning against the doorjamb, looking away, 'cause everyone deserved privacy.

"All done!" he cried. "Shake, shake, shake!"

He snorted a laugh and found the smallest life vest. "I gotta say, Bash-man, you have had the best day I can ever remember. What's different?"

"Water!" he insisted as he slid his chunky little arms into the vest.

Before Deeley snapped the front latch, he placed his hand on Bash's forehead, not entirely sure what he expected to feel, but his skin was cool enough. A little damp from a nap in the cabana, but he wasn't flushed and his eyes looked normal. And he'd remembered to use the bathroom, so, nah. He couldn't be sick.

Fact was, under all that tempest of a human was a very sweet little boy. Again, just like his father, who ran fire hot and ice cold. Some might call that bipolar, but that would have gotten Tommy kicked out of the Navy. So he was just...hot and cold.

"Off we go, kiddo." He took his little hand and guided him out to the sand, which was nearly deserted this late in the day. "After this, we gotta help set up a party for Teddy," he said, as if the kid could actually follow this chatter.

Except Bash wasn't paying attention. Instead, he was stumbling after a white ibis and her babies, giggling when the bird squawked and flew away.

"Nice beach, right?" He took Bash's hand and guided him toward the boards. "Ready to ride?"

Bash let out a squeal of joy when he saw the board— Deeley's widest and safest—and the paddle.

"You know, instead of walking, I'm going to sit with you today." The Gulf was ridiculously calm, already turning a deep, deep blue as the sun dipped toward the horizon. Paddling would be more fun than dragging the board over the water, so he hoisted Bash on the board, hooked him in for safety, and climbed on behind him.

"No standing today, Bash-face," he said, bracing the little boy with his legs and the paddle, getting a giggle for the latest iteration of his name. "But we can paddle."

He easily guided them over the barely-there surf where the waves broke, taking tiny baby strokes with the paddle so they didn't go too fast.

"Water!" Bash flapped his arms in joy, but after a minute, he calmed down and actually leaned back into Deeley's chest with a sigh of complete contentedness.

"This is pretty great, huh?" Deeley said, turning them in a fairly large circle and staying close to the shore. "I could get used to this," he admitted softly to himself, his whole being feeling as relaxed as the child in front of him. Water definitely had a calming effect on both of them. "I can't wait to teach you how to stand and..."

What was he talking about? Eddie would teach Bash things...he hoped. How would this new guy change Deeley's relationship with Bash? Guess he'd find out soon enough.

Bash turned his head and looked up at Deeley, sucking hard on his thumb.

"You should probably take that out of your mouth, but, you know what? You've followed enough rules for one day. Enjoy chomping your digit, Basho."

He smiled from behind his thumb, giving Deeley's heart that kick again.

"Man, you look like your daddy," he muttered.

"Daddy!"

Deeley squeezed his eyes. He had to stop saying that. He had to not use the D-word in front of Bash, because he was about to get a new daddy.

"Where Daddy?"

"He's...in heaven." He stabbed the paddle into the

water with just a little too much force. "He can see you every day, I promise."

Probably a big fat lie, but what else could he say?

"Daddy." Bash slapped Deeley's legs. "You Daddy."

"No, not your daddy," he said. "Your father was... much bigger and stronger and smarter and...more complicated." His voice got thick, but he had to say this. Was there any other legacy he could give Sebastian Thomas Royce than some great insights into his dad? "And he'd have loved the living daylights out of you."

"Daddy!" he insisted with another slap.

Everything in his heart just melted as he looked down at the kid.. Bad to the bone, maybe. But with love and discipline and...parents...this kid could be amazing. But not if his parents *left him alone in a house.*

Had that been Eddie's idea?

He stilled the paddle and brought it in front of Bash, out of the water. "You have my word I won't lose touch with you, kiddo. No matter what. I won't, because I have to tell you about your daddy, and how—"

"Daddy! Fish!" He pointed past Deeley, definitely not interested in listening to his heartfelt vows.

Deeley started to laugh at himself, turning at the sound of a splash, then a hefty wave rocked the paddleboard.

"Big fish," he said, staring at the water for a shadow of a tarpon or whatever had passed them. "And we better head back in now, Ba—"

Twenty feet away, the surface broke and all Deeley could do was stare in shock. It was a tarpon, all right, trapped in the mouth of a tiger shark that had just snagged it for dinner.

Swearing softly, Deeley stabbed the paddle in the water and whipped them around to the shore, which wasn't far but felt like a world away.

"Fishie!" Bash hollered gleefully, and all Deeley could do was lock his legs and squeeze the little body with every instinct screaming: *protect!*

Get to shore. Get to shore. Get to shore.

He stroked to the rhythm of the mantra, his years of training kicking in without thought. *Move with speed. Don't think. Trust your instincts. Don't make a mistake.*

And what the hell was a tiger shark doing out here?

Of course, they roamed this water, looking for the junk they liked to eat, much of it not the least bit organic. They were the garbage disposals of the ocean and could be...deadly. Not always, not often, but they certainly could feast on a toddler.

"Want to pet the fishie!"

With a rush of adrenaline that nearly blinded him, he squeezed his legs tighter to lock Bash into place and used every fiber of muscle to stab the paddle through the water. A tiger shark would circle if it was on a hunt, but it had already found dinner and was no doubt chomping that tarpon right now.

Would that be enough?

As much as he wanted to turn and look, he didn't dare break his concentration. Fifteen more strokes and they were safe. Twelve. Ten.

"Fishie!"

And there was the fin, black and menacing and swimming right between the board and where he wanted to go.

How did this happen? Why? And how was he going to get Bash to safety?

Another jolt of adrenaline shot hot through his body, with a flash of déjà vu from that night on the boat with Tommy. It all happened so fast. One minute he was setting the explosive and Tommy was far away and the next...

Tommy was gone.

"Fishie!"

The shark rolled right up and poked its ugly face out of the water, serrated teeth bared, blood from the tarpon still splattered on the gray of his body.

"Look him in the eye!" Deeley yelled, pulling up everything he'd ever learned about surviving a shark attack. Not that it was going to help Bash, who was wiggling now, trying to get free.

Nothing was going to help Bash. No one but Connor Deeley could save this kid and he would die trying.

"In the eye!" As the shark circled once again, it came up, not three feet away. Staring right into its ugly eyeballs, Deeley shoved the paddle in its nose, making Bash scream.

It disappeared for a second, long enough for Deeley to give the water three more strokes—but then the shark rocked the board from underneath and almost flipped them.

"Deeley! Oh my God, Deeley!" He heard Livvie calling from the sand, but he didn't even spare a second to look. Swearing, he twisted and turned to right the board with the paddle. The shark shot up again, closer still, and this was it.

One of them was going to win and it was not going to be Moby freaking Dick.

He lifted the oar and let it come smashing down on the shark's head, shoving it back into the water, then jammed the paddle into the shallows, hopping off, and unclipping Bash with one hand, scooping him under his arm, and running out of the water. He half expected that monster to take a bite of his leg, but somehow he reached the blessed sand of Shellseeker Beach and nearly collapsed on it.

But he didn't stop until he reached Livvie, who threw both arms around him and Bash.

"Fishie!" Bash announced. "Saw fishie, Wibbie!"

All Deeley could do was fall to the sand as the adrenaline dumped through him like Niagara Falls.

"Oh, my God, Deeley. You could have..."

Died. He could have died. The reality of that echoed in his head.

Livvie took Bash in her arms and dropped to the sand with him. "Are you okay? Are you hurt? Is Bash?"

He tried to talk, but couldn't possibly form a word.

"Daddy hit the fish," Bash said. "Fish wif big teef."

"He's...confused again," Deeley managed. So stinking confused. To think he almost...*No.*

Catching his breath, Deeley pushed up and turned to the water, scowling at the home of his nemesis, the beast that almost killed them both. His board bobbed in the surf and twisted, making him blink in shock.

A section of the back had a clear, visible bite mark.

He almost fell back to the sand, but Livvie was next to him in a minute, still holding Bash. She wrapped her free arm around him.

"Don't look at that."

He just closed his eyes. "Never, Livvie. It's never happening."

From the look on her face, she knew exactly what he meant.

Chapter Twenty-three

Katie

"I have a grandpa!" Harper announced to Teddy as she and Katie walked in, early for the party, prepared to help.

"I heard that news," Teddy said, her blue gaze moving to Katie with curiosity. "And how did that go?"

"Pretty well," Katie said.

"He brought me prezzies!" Harper held up one hand to show a furry pink purse with a kitty face, and bright matching sunglasses in the other. "See? And he's coming tonight, Aunt Teddy!"

Teddy's eyes widened. "Really?"

"I'm going to put these in my room." Harper zipped off to the back of Teddy's to the spare room.

"Katie," Teddy whispered, pulling her in for a hug. "How are you?"

"You tell me, oh great one."

Teddy rubbed her back and took a deep, deep inhale.

"Do you smell fear?" Katie joked.

"I smell that pretty body spray you started to wear ever since Noah showed up."

Katie laughed lightly and Teddy gave her one more

squeeze. "We have a few minutes before Bailey's delivers the food," Teddy said, easing her onto the sofa. "Please tell me everything. I don't want to guess or read your aura. I want to hear it from you."

She nodded and sat down. "Well, it was a little awkward at times, but Jadyn—who was as shocked as I was—kind of kept things comfortable. And Harper enchanted my dad. Brianna didn't come but he said, if things went well, then she might come to meet Harper, too. They didn't want to freak me out, which was very kind."

"Does he want you to go back to Massachusetts?" Teddy's voice was just tight enough for Katie to know how her dear friend felt about that.

"No. He joked about buying a house here, which might not have been a joke because he already had one of his people contact a real estate agent."

"Seriously? How do you feel about him living here?"

She smiled. "I doubt he would, and Harper would love it. Actually, he wants the agent for Jadyn. He wants to buy property or a building on Sanibel so she can open a daycare center and eventually a private preschool."

"Wow! Here?"

"Well, it's pretty obvious we need another and..." Katie pressed her hand to her chest. "I'm really happy to have a sister here."

"Oh!" Teddy practically whimpered as she hugged Katie. "I'm so thrilled to hear this! I've been so worried since Noah told me they were here."

"Noah." She just closed her eyes and shook her head. "He's amazing, isn't he? He was the one who kind of spurred me on. He's a big proponent of, you know, forgiveness and family."

Teddy's lips curled up in a smile. "Yes, he is. And..." She reached for Katie's hands. "Are you going to forgive this family of yours?"

"I guess I am. I haven't talked to my father about anything like that, but..."

"Have you asked for *his* forgiveness?"

She frowned, not quite getting the question, but she didn't have a chance to ask, because a delivery man from Bailey's appeared at the sliding glass door with bags of food.

Before they'd finished helping bring it all in, Eliza, Claire, and Camille arrived bearing the shocking news that Deeley had a run-in with a shark. He and Bash were safe, but Olivia was with them now and wouldn't be coming until later, if at all.

"A shark?" Teddy gasped. "We haven't had a shark sighting in years."

"Oh my gosh, that must have been horrifying!" Katie exclaimed, barely able to think about how frequently Harper was in that water.

The tenor of the room changed, along with the discussion, and Katie tabled her talk with Teddy. While they peppered Eliza with questions and she read Olivia's short text over and over, Katie kept glancing outside, waiting for Jadyn and Dad.

The whole time, Teddy's question tugged at her heart

and tapped at her head, which were definitely at war with each other on the subject

Have you asked for his forgiveness?

Katie didn't think she owed her father an apology...or did she?

She didn't get a whole lot of time to decide, because Jadyn texted her that they were pulling into the Shellseeker Cottages parking lot right now, and asked if Katie was absolutely sure she wanted him to come.

The question touched her, as had everything Jadyn had done that day. Her sister truly cared about this relationship, and about Katie's feelings, and that was...well, that was kind of eye-opening.

I'll meet you down there, Katie texted back. She slipped away from Teddy's house and hustled down the steps. Her heart hammered as she walked through the gardens, looking down as she tried to get her thoughts together.

"Someone looks serious."

She glanced up and nearly collided with Noah. "Oh, hey. I'm sorry I haven't texted you much today, but it's been crazy. Did you hear about Deeley?"

"Yeah. I'm on my way to the cabana to talk to him." He put his hand on her shoulder and searched her face. "Are you running away?"

She let a slow smile grow. "No," she said. "This time, I'm not running away. My dad's here for the party tonight. I'm going to meet him and ask if he'd talk privately to me."

"About?"

"Forgiveness," she said softly. "Mine and his."

She heard him take in a breath as he pulled her into his chest and held her, his silence saying everything.

She swallowed a lump in her throat and looked up at him. "When you're done with Deeley, come and find me. I want to formally introduce you to him, Noah. I want him to know how...important you are to me."

He hugged her once more, leaning down so that his forehead touched hers. "Katie." He just whispered her name, but she felt all the emotion and affection he put into it.

Without another word, she stepped away and hustled to the parking lot, her heart lighter than it had felt in many years. Five and a half, to be precise.

She knew exactly what she wanted to say.

"You're offering me a walk on the beach at sunset with my daughter?" Katie's father lifted his brows, drawing her attention to the lines in his forehead, so much deeper than she remembered. "I'd love that, Kay."

Had she put those lines there?

Her heart dropped down to her feet at the thought, because she knew the answer. And she was ashamed of it.

They walked in silence past the tea hut, reaching one of the boardwalks that led over the sea grass to the sand. Dad slowed his step and glanced down at the khaki shorts and Docksiders he wore.

"Take 'em off, I guess?" He pointed to his shoes.

"You'll want to." Katie slid out of her sandals and waited while he did the same, his body not quite as nimble as she remembered.

Her father was in his late fifties, probably the same age as Miles Anderson. But he had none of Miles's athleticism, or the healthy glow of a man who lived life on his own terms...and on his own boat.

"Sorry, I'm an ox," he said, making her heart slip as she feared she'd given her thoughts away. "Money doesn't slow down relentless old Father Time, I'm afraid, or I'd buy me a better body."

"You're fine, Dad," she assured him. "And we won't go far."

"We can go as far as you want, Kay. I'm..." He chuckled. "I'm so happy to be with you."

Some more shame and guilt rose up in her. She'd looked at this situation from the eyes of a child for so long, it was kind of stunning. And yet, she was a parent now, so she should have at least considered what her running away had done to her father.

But she hadn't, not until Teddy had asked one simple question: *Have you asked for his forgiveness?*

"Dad, I asked you to come out here because..."

"We need to talk," he finished when she struggled with the words. "I know I owe you an apology for—"

"No." She stopped on the sand and looked up at him. "I owe you one."

He stared at her, silent.

"I don't know how I'd handle it if, in fifteen years, Harper...left me."

She saw his eyes grow misty and knew hers were probably doing the same, just at the thought of years without seeing her. "I can't stand to be away from her for five hours, let alone..."

"Katie, you don't have to—"

"Yes." She held her hand up to stop him. "Yes, I do." Taking a slow breath she reached for his hand, which felt thick and foreign in hers. But she wouldn't let it go. "Walk with me, Dad."

He did, looking a little stunned as they started toward the setting sun.

They didn't say a word, but listened to a few squawking birds and the soft splash of the water. They passed a couple taking pictures of the sunset, and threaded their way through three sandcastles that had been the day's labor of love for some vacationing family but would be gone with the next tide.

"You certainly picked a good place to hide," he finally said. "Your mother would have loved it here."

She missed her next breath as his words hit. He never talked about Rose Bettencourt, not from the day she'd died. It was one of the things she despised about her father, one of the reasons she believed him to be heartless.

"She loved the beach," he continued, as if discussing his late wife was normal. "Of course, I didn't have the money I have now, or I'd have bought her a place near the water. But the times we went, she loved..." He reached down and picked up a random shell. "Seashells and sunshine and..."

He stopped talking and looked out to the horizon, his gaze a million miles—and probably quite a few years—away. Then his eyes focused as he looked at her. "She loved you," he finished. "More than anything in the world."

"I know," Katie whispered. "I remember that about her."

"And she would have..." He grunted as if every word hurt. "She would have known what to do when you..."

"Got pregnant," she finished for him.

"Come on, Kay, it wouldn't have happened," he muttered. "You'd have had a *good* parent and not..."

She put her hands on his shoulders, squeezing. "I probably did have a good parent, but I was too blinded by the loss of her to realize it."

"We were both blind." His voice cracked. "When she died, we...I...she..."

"Dad, don't," she whispered. "We've grieved her for darn near twenty years, but now? Today? I don't want to look back at what her death did to us. I don't want to wallow around in why I left or why you..." She shook her head. "I just want you to forgive me."

"Baby girl." He hugged her again. "I do, with all my heart, and I'm so sorry, too."

They stood for a long time like that, silent as they both fought tears. When they finally separated, she smiled up at him.

"This is my home now," Katie said. "And I found a family here. I hope you love them all as much as I do."

He nodded, his expression tight, as if he was holding himself back from saying anything.

"But I love you," she added. "And I think I forgot that somewhere along the way."

"I love you, too, Katie."

For a long moment, she couldn't speak. Mostly because that had been so easy, she couldn't believe it had taken all these years.

"Now, tell me about this new family of yours," he said, taking her hand again and turning them around to walk back to Shellseeker.

"Well, I'll start with Teddy. I mentioned her today."

"Many times."

"Because she's so special." Wow, was that an understatement. "She's a healer and an empath. And she..." How could she tell him that with one question, Teddy had changed Katie's whole perspective on this situation? "She's great," she said instead.

"And what about this Noah that Harper keeps telling me about?"

"You met him at the tea hut this morning. And..." She squinted at the boardwalk and the familiar figure of a young man sitting at the end of it, so he must be done talking to Deeley. "You're about to meet him again. Officially, this time."

"Officially, huh?" Dad gave her the slightest jab with his elbow. "So, he's more than...a friend?"

She smiled as they got closer and Noah stood, his

broad shoulders square, his chin lifted. She didn't answer the question, but not because she wasn't sure. She knew. She just wanted Noah to know at the same minute she told her father.

Noah took a step onto the sand as they approached, dragging his long dark hair back from the breeze that blew it around.

"Noah," Katie said, coming close enough to take his hand with her free one. "This is my father, Clive Betten-court. And Dad, this is Noah Hutchins, my, um, my boyfriend."

Noah's eyes flickered just enough to let her know he was thrown by the term but not the least bit unhappy.

"Mr. Bettencourt, pleasure to meet you, sir." Noah shook his hand, formal and serious.

"Noah. The pleasure is mine, young man."

For a moment, Katie looked from one to the other, her worlds colliding and...nothing was ruined. On the contrary, right then, everything was as right as it could be.

As they walked up to Teddy's house, they all made small talk about the beach and the weather, the shells and tourists, but when they reached the end of the boardwalk, Noah held Katie back a few feet.

"Did you just call me your boyfriend?"

She looked up at him, fighting a little laugh of pure joy. "How else would I describe you?"

"Right now? About the happiest guy that ever walked on this Earth."

She let the laugh out and caught up with her father.

"Come on now, Dad. There are lots more people I love that I want you to meet."

As she reached his side, she turned around to see Noah's reaction, knowing he'd heard that.

He stared for a second, then smacked his chest with one hand over the other and looked up at the sky like he simply couldn't contain his joy.

She knew the feeling.

Chapter Twenty-four

Olivia

They'd made it to the party, but dinner had already been served and dessert was out when Olivia and Deeley arrived. Bash had been subdued for most of the early evening, probably because he sensed something had upset them. He had no idea he'd been in danger, and that's the way Deeley wanted to keep it.

Of course, they were surrounded by family and friends, and bombarded with questions. When Harper took Bash off to play, Deeley relayed the incident with sparse details, but that didn't make anyone less upset by the incident.

There were a few "pro" fishermen in the group from Coconut Key who shared their own shark stories, with everyone repeating all the usual statistics, like "It's more dangerous to drive down Periwinkle than swim in the Gulf."

Exhaustion and a low-grade misery pressed down on Olivia, who finally escaped the circle of conversation and slipped into the kitchen in search of a sizeable glass of wine. She found it, but her mother held the bottle, with enough sympathy in her eyes that Olivia nearly broke down and cried.

"Was it awful, honey?" she asked, putting the wine down to hug Olivia.

"Beyond awful." She flinched as she remembered Deeley whacking that shark with the paddle. "And I'm worried it was a setback for Deeley, who's already convinced he can't keep someone alive if he has to."

Mom nodded, not questioning that as she poured the glass of wine for Olivia.

"A brush with death can do that. Look what it did for DJ. And Jadyn, for that matter." She lifted her own glass. "The change can be for the better."

"This isn't better," Olivia said. "This is validation of his every fear. That man is never having kids and I..." She shrugged. "I have to decide what matters to me."

"I'm sorry it put a damper on an otherwise tremendous day," Mom said. "You know the stories are going to be glowing. One will be on the news tonight."

But she could barely muster the enthusiasm to celebrate what was an unbelievable grand opening. "I need to go find Nick and Savannah and thank them again," she said, turning back to the main room—but then leaned against the counter. "But I'm so dang tired and...sad."

"Don't be sad." Mom put her arm around Olivia's shoulders. "You don't know what's going to happen."

"What I do know is Deeley and I have a hurdle to cross. I don't know what we can do to get over it, but—"

"Livvie!" Teddy popped into the kitchen, her eyes wide. "There's a police officer downstairs. He's asking for Deeley, who's looking for you."

"He probably has to report the shark sighting," she said. "Do I need to be there? I didn't even see the whole thing. I got there at the very last moment."

"He needs you."

She closed her eyes and let the words sink in, then glanced at her mother.

"I know," Mom said. "'He needs you' is like your catnip, Liv."

"So true," Teddy agreed. "You love by helping people, Livvie."

"And I do love him," she said, not bothering to argue with them. "But do I have to give up my dreams because he can't let go of his fears?"

Her mother sighed and looked physically pained at the thought, but Teddy's eyes narrowed on Olivia.

"No, you do not," Teddy said. "You trust the process and your heart. You love with all you have, and all that love will come back to you. I know this is true."

Just like she knew her crystals were magic.

Livvie resisted the urge to roll her eyes, but handed Teddy the glass of wine. "I'll be back for that," she said softly. "And you're right. I can't let him do this alone."

As she walked out of the kitchen, she saw Deeley standing by the door, waiting for her. Because he knew she'd come. He'd counted on her, and here she was.

Oh, if only Teddy were right about how the universe worked.

"I have to do this report," he said, reaching for her hand.

She nodded and took his hand, then stopped as she caught sight of Bash and Harper at the kitchen table, while Noah and Katie cut cupcakes for them.

"You don't think we need Bash, do you?" she asked. "They might want to ask him a question."

"He thinks he saw a big fishie. And I'd rather he eat that cupcake and have fun," he added with a smile. "We'll get him if we need him. Come on, Liv."

She held his hand while they walked down the stairs to where three police officers stood together. Well, one Sanibel police officer in a blue uniform. With him were two Lee County sheriff's deputies, a man and a woman.

"How many LEs does it take to handle a shark sighting?" Deeley muttered.

"A shark *attack*," she corrected.

"He didn't attack," Deeley said, giving her a look. "I was kind of the attacker in that case."

"Self-defense, Deeley. You think they're here on the shark's behalf?"

He smiled and put his arm around her. "This is why I need you." They approached the cops and introduced themselves, although Deeley seemed to know the police officer.

"Sorry I didn't get pictures, Pete," Deeley said to Officer Jackson of the Sanibel Police Department. "But he was big."

All three of them exchanged a look, utterly confused, then Officer Jackson stepped forward. "I don't know what you're talking about, Deeley."

"The shark I had a run-in with today."

The other man shook his head. "I hadn't heard. Deputy Montgomery contacted our office looking for your home address. When I didn't find you there, I brought them out here, thinking you'd be at the cabana."

Next to her, Deeley stiffened as he looked at the tall, dark-haired deputy. "You're looking for me?"

"We're looking for Connor Deeley, a friend of Marcella Royce."

And his shoulders sank. "Oh, you're here because of the credit card stuff."

Deputy Montgomery looked even more confused. "Mr. Deeley, I'm afraid I have some bad news. Mrs. Royce and a man named Edward Hodge were in a fatal car accident two days ago just outside of Albuquerque on I-40."

"*What?*" Deeley and Olivia both breathed the word in utter shock.

"I'm sorry for the loss," the officer said, the words sounding like he'd been trained to say them.

"What happened?" Deeley asked.

"They hit a semi head on. Both passed at the scene."

Olivia pressed her hands to her chest, literally swaying at the news that she simply couldn't compute. Marcie was *dead*?

"I have her son," Deeley said softly, his hand on Olivia's shoulder like he needed support, too. "I guess you know that?"

But how, Olivia wondered, looking from one officer to the other.

"No, we didn't, but it makes sense," the woman,

Deputy Rodriguez, said. "The New Mexico State Police couldn't locate adult next-of-kin for Mrs. Royce, just the name of Sebastian, a child. But they were able to access her phone and found a contact for her husband."

"Who died a few years ago," Deeley said, dragging the words out like he was as confused as Olivia.

The deputy nodded. "They surmised as much. However, they were able to locate his last text exchange with the deceased, and that's how they found you, put out a national alert, and..." She turned to the local police officer. "Sanibel Police responded that you were a resident."

"Why me?" Deeley asked, his voice tentative.

"Thomas Royce named you as the guardian of their child, should anything happen to Marcella Royce."

"What?" Deeley barely whispered the word. "Why would he do that?"

"It's not unusual for a man in the military to name a guardian," Deputy Montgomery said.

"But I'd never met her when he was alive, and he..."

"I think you should read the texts, Deeley," Officer Jackson said, stepping closer. "It might shed some light on everything for you."

Deputy Rodriguez reached into a plastic bag and pulled out a cell phone in a bright red case that Olivia immediately recognized as Marcie's. "Here it is, along with some other personal belongings of Mrs. Royce."

Deeley took the phone as the deputy handed the bag to Olivia.

"You can take these," she said. "And I'll show him the texts."

As they talked, Olivia opened the bag and glanced inside, spying a wallet and something gold at the bottom. She reached in and her fingers closed over a heavy filigree necklace that she didn't even have to pull out to recognize.

Her heart dropped and her eyes filled with tears for Marcie, who'd squandered her son, her opportunities, and her life.

Olivia looked up at Deeley, who was staring at the phone, still visibly shocked.

"Livvie," he whispered. "Sit with me while I read this."

She nodded, sliding her hand into the crook of his arm. "Let's go over here." She guided him away from the officers, to a stone bench in the garden where she'd sipped so many iced teas and chatted with her mother and Teddy.

Now, it felt like a refuge from whatever he was about to find out.

He tapped the screen and heaved a sigh. "I can't even think straight right now."

"I know." She put a loving hand on his back. "What does it say?"

He scrolled through a lengthy text exchange, getting to the top. "This was the day he died."

"Really?" she sat up straight, a buzzing in her head. "That was the day he texted her about...you? Why?"

He didn't answer, his gaze locked on the phone as he read silently. She leaned in, trying to see the screen in the sun, getting words and phrases, but none of them made sense.

I can't take it anymore.

Pressure on my chest.

Not taking the meds.

"Was he taking meds or her?" she asked.

"He was, according to this. For depression. I had no..." Suddenly he sucked in a breath and looked at her. "Oh my God."

"What?"

"Look at this." He angled the phone for her to read.

I can't be a father to our child, M. I'm not capable. Some days I can't even bear to be alive. I'm not doing this anymore. I have to find a way out. Tonight. On the mission.

"Deeley, no! He killed himself?"

All the blood left his face as he stared at her, his eyes clouding with pain and disbelief. "That son of a... Why did he *do* that? Why?"

"Mental illness," she said without a second's hesitation. "Did you know? Could you see the signs?"

He stabbed his hand in his hair and pulled it back. "Maybe. I knew he struggled, sometimes he drank. But we were SEALs, for God's sake. No one had any *weaknesses.*"

"Well, Tommy did. And probably had to work like hell to hide them."

His face crumpled as he leaned over, fighting a sob.

"Deeley." Putting both arms around him, she squeezed. "I know this hurts. I know. But now you know that you're not responsible for his death."

His whole body stilled as the realization hit him. Very slowly, he sat up and turned to her, his expression ravaged. "But apparently, I am responsible for his son."

"Is that what it says?"

He lifted the phone and skimmed through the texts, stopping at one. "He said, 'Whatever happens to me, and it isn't gonna be good, I want my kid taken care of.' Marcie wrote, 'I can take care of him.' And then..."

He handed her the phone.

Tommy: *Well, if anything happens to you, please make Connor Deeley, my friend from North Carolina, the guardian of the baby. I don't have a brother, but he's the closest thing I got. He'd be a great dad.*

"Oh, Deeley. He did want you to take care of Bash."

"Read the rest."

Marcie: *I don't know that guy.*

Tommy: *You will. After tonight, you'll know him. Cause if I know Deeley, he'll come and find you. And he'll help you. And he'll help our kid. Do whatever paperwork you have to, Marcie. If something happens to you, Deeley will adopt our kid.*

Marcie: *Stop talking like this, Tommy. You're scaring me!*

Tommy: *Gotta go, M. Love you.*

And that was the end of the exchange.

For a long moment, they both sat in shocked silence, neither one really able to process all of this.

"He knew it all along," Deeley said on a gruff whisper. "That night. When we went out...he knew what he was doing."

The note of betrayal in his voice broke her heart, but she didn't say a word, just rubbed his back while he leaned over and fought the tears she knew he'd cry later.

"Hey, Deeley."

They both looked up to see the Sanibel police officer standing a few feet away.

"Oh, yeah, Pete." Deeley stood and dug deep for composure, taking Olivia's hand and offering Officer Jackson the phone. "Do I give this back to you?"

"There's a process for—"

"Deeley! Wibbie!" From the top of the stairs, Bash hollered his name, cupcake on his face, holding Jadyn's hand. "I want more cupcake! Can I?"

Deeley glanced at Livvie, color gone from his cheeks but his bourbon-brown eyes bright with something she'd never seen before. Determination? Hope? Love?

The last one felt right as he looked down at her. "I can't do it without you," he said softly. "I just...can't...do it without you, Liv."

She took his hand. "You don't have to." Together, they walked to the house, right to the stairs.

"No seconds on cupcakes," Livvie called to Bash. Her heart shattered as she thought about how they would have to tell this child that his mommy was gone forever. Thank goodness he was so young, and these days would fade in his memory. "But can you come here, big boy?"

Jadyn started to guide him down, but Deeley launched forward, arms out, to snag him like he weighed next to nothing. "Hey you, little fish-fighter."

He threw his arms around Deeley's neck, who pulled him in for a silent hug so long and deep, Olivia could see the pain of what he had to tell Bash etched on every one of Deeley's features.

For his part, Bash just smooshed his icing-covered cheek onto Deeley's, transferring some from one face to another.

"Let's go meet some really important people," Deeley said, carrying him back down.

The three of them walked over to the officers and stood for a second, then Deeley lifted Bash higher in one arm and draped the other over Livvie.

"Whatever I need to do, or sign, or accept," he said. "I will accept guardianship of this child."

The words nearly melted Livvie, but Bash just smashed his hand into the icing and smeared it on Deeley's cheek.

"We'll just have you sign a few papers, sir," Deputy Rodriguez said with a smile. "And the proper authorities will be in touch for the guardianship hearings and explain the whole process. We're going to leave Sebastian here with you."

As they walked away to get what they needed, Deeley turned to Olivia and looked down at her. "Guess what, Liv?"

"We have a baby?" she replied with a shaky smile.

"What's that going to do to us?"

Bash dropped his head on Deeley's shoulder and found his thumb. Olivia smiled from one beautiful face to the other.

"I don't know, Connor Deeley. But I guess we're about to find out."

Don't miss the next adventure in Shellseeker Beach! **Sanibel Tides** *continues the stories of this "found family" that stays together through every crisis, supports each other through every moment, and always has the humor and heart to face what life throws at them.*

The Coconut Key Series

Would you like to know more about Nick, Savannah, Beck, and the gang from Coconut Key that you met in **Sanibel Sisters**? Their story, along with many others, is told on the pages of Hope Holloway's first series. If you're enjoying Shellseeker Beach, you'll love Coconut Key. This completed series set on the sun-kissed sands of the Florida Keys!

The Shellseeker Beach Series

Come to Shellseeker Beach and fall in love with a cast of unforgettable characters who face life's challenges with humor, heart, and hope. For lovers of riveting and inspirational sagas about sisters, secrets, romance, mothers, and daughters...and the moments that make life worth living.

About the Author

Hope Holloway is the author of charming, heartwarming women's fiction featuring unforgettable families and friends, and the emotional challenges they conquer. After more than twenty years in marketing, she launched a new career as an author of beach reads and feel-good fiction. A mother of two adult children, Hope and her husband of thirty years live in Florida. When not writing, she can be found walking the beach with her two rescue dogs, who beg her to include animals in every book. Visit her site at www.hopeholloway.com.

Made in the USA
Monee, IL
10 June 2023

35572724R00187